MW00426033

The Chancer

Also by Patrick C. Walsh

The Mac Maguire detective mysteries

The Body in the Boot

The Dead Squirrel

The Weeping Women

The Blackness

23 Cold Cases

Two Dogs

The Match of the Day Murders

The Tiger's Back

The Eight Bench Walk

A Concrete Case of Murder

The Blood Moon Murders

Stories of the supernatural

13 Ghosts of Winter

The Black Vaults Experiment

All available in Amazon Books

Patrick C. Walsh

The Chancer

The eighth 'Mac' Maguire mystery

Garden City Ink

A Garden City Ink ebook
www.gardencityink.com

First published in Great Britain in 2018
All rights reserved
Copyright © 2018, 2020, 2021 Patrick C. Walsh

The right of Patrick C. Walsh to be identified as the author of
this work has been asserted in accordance with Section 77 of the
Copyright, Designs and Patents Act 1988.

No part of this publication may be reproduced, stored in a
retrieval system, or transmitted, in any form or means, electronic,
mechanical, photocopying, recording or otherwise, without the
prior permission of the copyright holder.

All characters in this publication are fictitious and any
resemblance to real persons, living or dead, is purely co-
incidental.

A CIP record for this title is available from the British Library

Cover art © Seamus Maguire 2018
Garden City Ink Design

'In gambling the many must lose in order that the few may win.'
George Bernard Shaw

For Mick and Maureen and for Ballydove and
better times

A meeting...

The man sat exactly where he'd been told to sit. It was too early in the morning and he was now regretting drinking so much the night before. He'd only meant to go out for an hour or so but it had turned into something of a session. To make it worse, he'd arranged to meet someone before he flew out which meant that he'd had to get up even earlier. When his alarm had gone off, he'd toyed with the idea of going back to sleep for another couple of hours and forgetting all about it. He knew that he'd still have plenty of time to catch his plane.

He'd lain there in the dark for a few minutes before realising that tired as he was, there was no way that he was going back to sleep. He got up and thought about the meeting while he showered. He found that he was excited. He'd been looking for an opportunity like this for years and it had been his life-long practice to never ignore any chance to do business.

Oh well, he thought, I can always sleep on the plane.

Airports are boring and, as he sat there waiting, he found himself nodding off. He rubbed his face with his hands and looked at his watch. Five minutes to go. A sound to his left made him turn. A door had been opened somewhere. A few seconds later a figure in a dark blue uniform and dark baseball cap appeared pushing a broom.

One of the airport cleaners, he thought dismissively just before his eyes closed and he went back to sleep.

That was the very last thought he ever had.

Chapter One

Mac hated travelling by air. He wasn't scared of flying as such, it was the getting to and from the plane that worried him. After the last time, he swore to himself that he'd never do it again. Yet, here he was once again in the departure lounge at his local airport waiting in the Special Assistance area for a lift to his departure gate. He looked at his watch again. At least another half an hour or so to go.

It had been a strange start to the day. He'd gotten used to being greeted by his dog Terry every morning and he found that he missed him. He'd taken Terry around to his neighbour Amanda the evening before as she'd be looking after him while Mac was away. He sighed and wondered once again why he always turned up so early when he was flying. A minute in an airport seemed as long as ten anywhere else.

It was very early in the morning and through the ceiling-high plate glass windows he could see that the first hints of dawn were breaking through the late September darkness. There was just him and another man waiting. The other man was grey-haired, in his sixties and fast asleep. Mac had seen him when he'd first walked into the area. As he was mostly obscured by a large pillar Mac had to lean to one side to get a look. He was still sitting there, unmoving and with his chin on his chest. Mac envied him. He could never sleep in an airport no matter how tired he felt.

Mac began wondering what getting to the plane might involve this time around. The last time he'd flown he'd had to stay behind on the plane for over an hour while he waited for someone to come and wheel him off. He'd found this extremely embarrassing as he was the only passenger needing assistance and the whole crew, including both pilots, had had to wait with him as well. They all did their best to keep a conversation going but it was strained and awkward to say the least.

When it came down to it, he just didn't like the idea of having to rely on someone else. He'd never had to do it until recently and he supposed that it was this loss of control that annoyed him the most. That plus the fact that, despite his very real pain issues, he always felt like a bit of a fraud being pushed around in a wheelchair anyway. Most people just stroll to the departure gate without giving it a thought but, for Mac with his history of back pain, it was now a major hurdle that had to somehow be negotiated.

He glanced at his watch again. Two minutes had passed. He sighed. He couldn't wait until it was over and he was in Ireland. He quickly edited that thought. As it was a funeral he was going to, he'd only be happy when he was once more safely back home in Hertfordshire.

The bored looking middle-aged man at the assistance desk went off duty and was replaced by another bored looking middle-aged man. This one wore glasses. He looked closely at his computer screen for some time before eventually glancing over at Mac. He wearily stood up and came over.

'Where are you going to, please?' the assistance man asked.

'Knock,' Mac replied as he fished out his boarding card and showed it to the man.

'So, there's only you then, sir?'

'There's him too,' Mac said as he leant over and pointed towards the sleeping grey-haired man.

The assistance man peeked around the column.

'Oh, I'm sorry but I couldn't see him from where I was sitting. This area's only temporary and I'm afraid that it's not been laid out very well. Would you like to wake your friend up for me?'

'Oh, he's not with me,' Mac protested.

'Oh, I see.'

The assistance man went back to the desk and looked at his screen again. He shook his head and looked puzzled. He wearily got up again and made his way over to where the elderly man was still slumped fast asleep.

'Excuse me, sir,' the assistance man said loudly. Then even louder, 'Excuse me, sir!'

The sleeping man didn't move. Out of curiosity Mac got up and went closer. The assistance man turned and looked at Mac and shook his head again.

'Probably had a heavy night last night,' he said with a shrug. 'People really shouldn't drink when they know that they're flying the next day.'

He noticed a piece of paper on the bench next to the man. He picked it up and had a look before putting it back again. Mac could see that it was a boarding pass.

'Well, it looks like he's going to Knock too but it doesn't look like he's ordered assistance,' he said to Mac. 'Still, I'd better check I suppose.'

He went back to his computer and scratched his head.

'It's definitely only you for assistance but I could try and squeeze him in if he's a bit the worse for drink. If you don't mind that is?'

Mac didn't have any objection at all.

The assistance man went back and tried gently shaking the grey-haired man again. This didn't work so he shook a bit harder. Finally, the sleeping man moved.

He slowly fell onto his side leaving a wide trail of blood smeared across the back of the seat.

'Oh dear!' the man said as he stepped back and gave Mac a desperate look.

4

Mac quickly went over and felt the man's wrist. There was no pulse although his hand still felt fairly warm. He felt the man's neck just in case. He still couldn't detect a pulse. The man had fallen onto his side at an angle and he could see that there were three penetrating wounds in the middle of the man's back more or less where his heart would be. The back of his jacket below the wounds was soaked in blood and there was a blood pool in the well at the back of the row of seats.

'Shall I call for a doctor?' the assistance man asked.

'If you want to but, as he's dead, I'd call the airport police first. Tell them that you're reporting a murder.'

Chapter Two

Two armed policemen turned up two minutes later and briefly examined the body. They quickly established that he was dead.

'Who is he?' the older policeman asked both Mac and the assistance man.

'I've no idea,' Mac said.

The assistance man said, 'There's a boarding pass in the name on Connerty on the seat next to him.'

The older policeman positioned himself so he could read it without having to touch it. He then walked away and got out his phone. While he was calling it in Mac noticed that the policeman's younger partner was about to put his hand into the dead man's inside jacket pocket.

'I wouldn't do that if I were you,' Mac said.

The policeman quickly withdrew his hand and then glared at Mac.

'Excuse me, sir,' the policeman said.

He went a little red faced as he said this and his 'sir' was anything but friendly. He obviously didn't like being told what to do by members of the public.

'I said, I wouldn't do that if I were you,' Mac repeated slightly louder as if the policeman might be somewhat hard of hearing.

He knew that it would probably annoy him even more but Mac found that he didn't care.

'And what's it got to do with you?' the policeman said as he came closer and stuck his now even redder face close to Mac's.

Mac found that he didn't like him.

'I'm just trying to help. If forensics find your prints all over the wallet then they'll assume that you're either stupid or that that you've just robbed a dead man. Go ahead if you want to though, it's your funeral, especially if the relatives report that cash has gone missing.'

The policeman stepped back and looked at Mac in mystification. His partner came back.

'I've just called the boss and he's told me that someone's already alerted the Major Crime Unit and they're on their way here, forensics too. They said it was a Mr. Maguire. Is that you sir?' the policeman asked.

Mac nodded.

'Oh, I thought that the name was familiar,' the older policeman said with a smile.

He offered Mac his hand. Mac took it.

'I saw you on TV when you did the press conference for the 'Match of the Day' murders. I must admit that I really liked what you said about how we should be managing our own forensics labs. You used to be a Detective Chief Superintendent with the Met, weren't you sir?'

'Yes, that's right,' Mac confirmed.

The red-faced policeman turned somewhat pale at this news. He made as if to come towards Mac, probably to apologise, but Mac's expression told him not to bother. He stood by the body glancing over at Mac from time to time in something like fear. Mac wasn't going to mention his incivility to anyone but he wasn't about to let him know that just yet.

Mac looked over at the assistance man who was sitting behind his desk with a somewhat dazed expression on his face. Mac had a thought and went over.

'What's the name of the man who you've just relieved?' he asked.

'Oh, that was Ken, Ken Barrington,' he replied.

Mac went over to the older policeman and had a word. He got straight onto his radio and put a call out to his colleagues to ensure that Mr. Barrington was intercepted before he left the airport grounds.

A clatter of footsteps in the distance announced the arrival of Dan Carter, head of the Major Crime Unit. He looked rumpled and as if he'd just got out of bed which, in this case, he probably had. However, Mac smiled as he always looked more or less like that anyway. DI Andy Reid and DS Adil Thakkar accompanied him.

'Mac!' Dan said with a smile. 'Calling a murder in yourself! Were you afraid that we didn't have enough to do or something?'

Mac shook hands with the three of them.

'I was waiting here to get a lift to my plane when a member of the airport staff tried to wake this gentleman here. As you can see there was very little chance of that happening.'

'What time's your flight?' Dan asked.

'An hour and fifteen minutes from now,' Mac said as he looked at his watch. 'I was waiting here to get a lift to the departure gate.'

'I'd appreciate it if you could hang about for half an hour or so until we see what we've got,' Dan asked.

'No problem. I take it that forensics are on their way?'

'They should be here any minute. We passed their van on the way here.'

Just as Dan finished speaking Mac saw Bob Yeardley and two other white suited figures walking towards him carrying their big black cases.

Dan turned around, 'Speak of the devil. While they're looking at the body there are a few things that we could be doing. Andy, can you see if there's any CCTV cameras covering this area? If there are, can you get us the footage as soon as possible and check to see if the victim appears elsewhere in the airport. He must have got here from somewhere. Adil, can you ask around the airport staff and see if anyone saw our victim. Find out as much as you can about who was on duty and take all their names and addresses. I'll send someone to help you when the rest of the team arrives.'

Andy and Adil walked off. Dan gestured for the older police officer to come over.

'Can you get a few more of your men to come over and ensure that no-one can access this area. I dare say that forensics will tape the area off and put a tent up but it's a bit too open for my liking at the moment.' The policeman nodded. 'By the way I take it that neither of you have touched the body?'

'No sir, of course not,' the older policeman said looking offended by the thought.

Mac and the younger policeman exchanged looks. He knew that he was off the hook and he nodded his thanks to Mac as he moved off to guard the area. Mac hoped that he had learnt a lesson.

He stood next to Dan and watched the forensics team tape the whole assistance area off and then start to erect a white tent that would ensure that rubber necking passers-by wouldn't be able to stop and gawk at the dead man.

'So, what do you think?' Dan asked.

'I've no idea really. I'd been here for nearly half an hour and he was there all that time. It looks like he was killed where he sat as there's no blood trail. There was a blood pool in the well of the seat and it had also formed a small pool on the floor at the far end of the seating. It wasn't visible from where I was sitting and so I just assumed that he was asleep. It looks like he had money, his suit is tailored and the shoes are good quality. There was no luggage so he probably had a case in the hold. Either that or it was stolen when he was killed. I also think that you'll be lucky to get any-thing on CCTV. This area's cut off from the rest of the departure lounge and the row of seats he was sitting on is right behind that big column there. I couldn't see

9

any cameras in here and I'd guess that you won't get a direct view from any of the cameras in the departure lounge either.'

Dan looked around the area and then frowned. He couldn't spot any cameras either.

'It does make you wonder if that seat was picked just for that reason, doesn't it?' Dan said. 'We'll just have to wait and see what forensics come up with then. It would be nice to know exactly who he was so we can at least get the ball rolling.'

'His surname's Connerty,' Mac said. 'His boarding pass was on the seat beside him. It didn't strike me at the time but that's a bit odd, isn't it? I mean most people keep their boarding passes somewhere safe as it's the last thing you'd want to lose before getting on a plane.'

'So, what are you thinking?' Dan asked.

'Well, perhaps whoever killed him put the pass beside him in the hope of gaining a little time. I dare say that the staff here wouldn't try to wake him until it was nearly his time to go. If that was the aim then it certainly seemed to have worked.'

A few seconds after he said this, Bob came out of the tent with a passport in his hand. Mac could see that it had a harp on the front. It was an Irish passport. Bob opened the passport so that Dan could photograph the page with the dead man's photo on.

'Want a photo of what's in his wallet too?' Bob asked as he placed the passport in an evidence bag.

Dan did.

A few seconds later Bob came back with a leather wallet and removed some credit cards and business cards so that Dan could photograph these too. Bob then replaced the cards and put the wallet into an evidence bag and sealed that too.

Dan immediately sent the photos by email to Martin Selby, the team's computer specialist, and then rang him to let him know.

After the short call Dan said, 'Martin was asleep but he's going to start work straight away.'

He then passed the phone to Mac who looked closely at a photo of the business card.

'Jack Connerty, Import and Export,' Mac said. 'It gives a mobile phone number but that's it. No email, no address.'

Dan went over towards the tent and had a quick discussion with Bob. While he did this Mac looked at the photo of the credit cards. They were from an Irish bank and they were all in the name of 'J. C. Connerty'.

He had a thought and got his phone out.

'They've found a phone on him, a cheap one by the look of it,' Dan said as he walked back towards Mac. 'I've asked them to send it to Martin right away for analysis. I might have to get him some help in on this one as he's going to have a lot to do.'

'I've just put his name into Google and nothing's coming up as far as I can see. It doesn't look like he's got a website for this import and export business which is strange,' Mac said.

'Hopefully, Martin might be able to come up with a little more. He usually does,' Dan said.

Like many wallets it had a clear plastic sleeve where a small photo could be inserted. Mr. Connerty had done just that. Mac looked closely at the photo. It featured a woman in her fifties who had her arm around the statue of a man playing an electric guitar.

'I know where that is,' Mac said as he pointed the photo out to Dan. 'It's in a place called Ballydove in Donegal. It's where I'm flying out to.'

'Really? Well, you might be able to help us out then if our dead man really does have some sort of link to this Ballydove.'

They both turned as they heard Andy walking back towards them.

'I've asked about the CCTV but I think that we're going to be out of luck. They've got some footage of our dead man walking towards the assistance area but it doesn't really tell us anything apart from the fact that he had no luggage. I've had a quick look at the live camera feed and that column blocks off the view from the cameras in the main departure lounge. I've asked them to send all the footage they've taken in the last twenty-four hours directly to Martin to have a look at anyway but I wouldn't hold out much hope.'

'My God, you'd think they'd have every corner of an airport covered, wouldn't you?' Dan said grumpily.

'According to the staff the assistance area is only here as a temporary measure so perhaps they didn't think that it was that important,' Mac said.

'Just our luck,' Dan said grumpily. 'Andy, can you liaise with someone about getting us an office or something that we can use as an incident room? I'm expecting the rest of the team to turn up before long.'

Andy went and had a quick chat with the older policeman before walking off.

'What about him?' Dan asked as he nodded towards the assistance man who was sitting behind his desk with a dazed look on his face.

'I'd doubt if he'll know anything,' Mac replied. 'There was change of shift about ten minutes before we discovered that Mr. Connerty was dead. He took over from a man called Ken Barrington. I've already asked the airport police to see if they could catch him before he leaves the airport.'

'Let's have a chat with him anyway,' Dan said as he walked over to the assistance desk.

Dan showed the assistance man his warrant card.

'What's your name?' he asked.

'Paul Parker.'

12

'So Mr. Parker, can you confirm whether or not you have a Mr. Connerty listed as requiring assistance?'

'I've checked several times and there's only the one passenger down in the system as requiring assistance. He's that gentleman standing there beside you,' he said pointing at Mac.

Dan gave the assistance man a puzzled look.

'So, why was he here then?' Dan asked.

The assistance man just shrugged by way of an answer.

Dan looked about him. At the end of the area there were three doors, two of which were double doors.

'Can you tell me where those doors lead out to?'

'The nearest two lead out into the main corridor where our assisted passengers can either pick up an electric buggy or a wheelchair to take them to their departure gate.'

'Where can you get to from there?'

Mr. Parker shrugged.

'Pretty much anywhere in the airport, I'd guess.'

'Are they always kept locked?' Dan asked.

'Of course, you need to know the code to be able to open them.'

'And what about that other door?'

'That leads into a small kitchen area that we use for our breaks and there are also some staff toilets beyond that.'

'Is that door always kept locked too?' Dan asked.

'I'd guess...' Mr. Parker replied hesitantly.

Dan walked down and opened the door.

'Well, I'd guess not then,' he added with a shrug when Dan returned.

'Where can you get to through there?'

'As I said the kitchen and toilets and that's it really,' he replied.

Dan wasn't convinced with his answer and gave him his best glare. Mr. Parker instantly got the message.

'Oh, there's also a fire exit at the end of the corridor. Some of the staff who smoke go outside when they want a cigarette.'

'Is that officially allowed?'

'I don't know, I don't smoke myself.'

'Once you're though the fire exit and you're outside would you be able to access other areas of the airport?'

'I'd guess,' he ventured.

'My colleague told me that you'd just come on shift. Who was on before you?'

'Ken Barrington,' he confirmed.

'If I need it, would you be able to supply me with Mr. Barrington's address and phone number?' Dan asked.

'I can give you his mobile but I don't know his address. I'd have to ask my supervisor but he won't be in for a while yet.'

Dan wrote down Mr. Barrington's number.

'Okay, please stay here for a moment until someone's taken your statement. Oh, I'd call your supervisor anyway as you'll need to find somewhere else for your assisted passengers to wait. This whole area will be out of bounds for a quite a while.'

This news didn't seem to cheer up Mr. Parker in the slightest.

Dan stopped and spoke to Bob on his way back.

'As there's a chance that his killer could have come in through one of those doors, I've asked Bob to check for prints and any other traces,' Dan said. 'As he hasn't shown up yet I'm wondering if we should ring this Mr. Barrington.'

'We won't need to,' Mac said pointing towards an ashen-faced man who was approaching them. He was being closely escorted by two armed policeman and he was obviously not enjoying the experience.

'How are you doing for your flight?' Dan asked.

'Forty minutes,' Mac replied.

'You might as well get going. Would you be able to help us out on the Irish side if we need it?' Dan asked.

'God, yes!' Mac immediately replied. 'I'm going over for a funeral but I'd be glad of any excuse at all to be doing something else.'

This made Dan smile.

'Okay, I'll get someone to let the Irish police know what's happened and that you'll be representing us for now. If you need any help let me know and I'll get someone straight over to you.'

Mac promised that he would.

'Okay then, I'll get Mr. Parker to arrange your lift to the departure gate,' Dan said. 'Have a good trip.'

An electric buggy took him to the gate and he was there with time to spare. Ironically this was one of the few times that Mac hadn't experienced any major problems with the assistance process itself. The flight was less than full and he had a window seat where he could watch the sun come up as they flew west towards the Irish Sea. Mac began thinking about the funeral and what lay ahead of him.

On the whole he'd have much preferred a trip to the dentist.

Chapter Three

It had all started a few days before when his sister Roisin had called him with the news that their Aunt Annie had died. It hadn't spoilt Mac's enjoyment of the drink he'd been having with his friend Tim as this particular aunt had been something of a stranger to him. His mother had two sisters and Annie was the youngest and the last of them to go. Roisin felt quite strongly that the family needed to be represented at the funeral.

Mac had agreed thinking that Roisin or one of his other sisters would be volunteering to go. However, Roisin was giving a keynote speech at a big nursing conference in London and his other sisters, Marie and Ellen, also had excellent reasons why they couldn't make it, so it was all down to him.

He knew that he couldn't grumble. His sisters had been doing all the heavy lifting when it came to family events for many years but that didn't mean that he had to look forward to it. However, he reminded himself that were some people that he could look forward to seeing while he was in Donegal. There were his cousins from Dublin, who he'd always got on with, and his Uncle Mick should also be at the funeral. He wasn't actually his uncle but a cousin who was quite a few years older than him. He'd always been Mac's favourite relative since he'd been a child.

Many years ago, when the farm hadn't been doing so well, Mick would regularly come over to Birmingham and get work in the one of the factories for six months at a time in order to send money home and, of course, he lived in Mac's house while he was there. This had started when Mac was around eight and he found that he always looked forward to his cousin's visits. He had to admit that this was also partly due to the supply of white pudding and Irish sausages that Mick brought with him every time he came over.

Even though he was a young man in his twenties Mick always had time for his younger cousins and he used to regularly take them out for walks and occasionally to the cinema when he had the money. It was a kindness that Mac had never forgotten.

With something of a shock, he realised that Mick must be well over seventy now. Mac's father had two brothers. The youngest, Rory, came to England with him but the eldest, Mick's father Owen, had stayed and worked on the family farm. The farm had then gone to Mick who still lived there although it was his son Seamus who now did most of the work. With some surprise he realised that Seamus himself must now be in his late thirties.

Inevitably his thoughts turned to his cousin Declan. He was Annie's only child and Mac had disliked him heartily since the first time they'd met when Mac was six or so.

Like most young boys Mac was a bit wild and he liked playing outdoors and pretending to be some-thing he wasn't. He and his friends in England would play at being pirates or cowboys or Roman soldiers, they'd climb trees, cut their knees and get into trouble every now and again. But not Declan.

When Mac had been young every summer the whole family, except for his father, would go 'back home' for the long school holidays. Although Mac loved his father, he always liked the part of the holiday when he wasn't there best. He and his sisters would be more or less left to their own devices as his mother sat with friends and relatives and caught up with a year's worth of gossip and news over endless cups of tea. Never ending days of running wild and playing games had been his idea of a real holiday.

His father would then come over and join them for the last two weeks. This was the more formal part of the holiday and would involve them dressing up and going around the numerous relations that existed on both sides of the family. Mac hadn't minded this too much as most of his family in Ireland were good fun but he always dreaded the visits to his Aunt Annie's house. She was the youngest of the sisters but she didn't look it.

He remembered his father saying to his mother when he thought that no one else was listening, 'Now are you sure that you two are really related? I mean look at you, you're gorgeous but her? She looks like a monkey who's just swallowed a lemon.'

He remembered that his mother had told his father off for saying this but she was laughing when she did so. Whenever Mac thought of his aunt that picture came into his mind. Her son Declan also looked as if he'd just swallowed a lemon. Even at the age of six Mac remembered him in his little suit and shirt and tie with a copy of the catechism clutched firmly in his hand. He wore that vague self-righteously smug smile that only the chosen are allowed to wear.

He thought back to the very first time he'd met Declan. They'd both been pushed out into the garden to play together and 'get on' as his mother had put it. Mac had looked longingly in at the window at his sisters who were playing a board game. He'd suggested to Declan that they could play at being cowboys and have a gunfight. He'd haughtily replied that such 'antics' were the work of the devil and he'd sooner read his catechism. Mac had spent the most boring couple of hours in his life kicking around the little garden and looking up at the sky as he prayed for it to rain so he could go inside. It had been pretty much the same every time they'd met since.

Declan had offered him a room at his house but Mac had quickly replied saying that the stairs might be a problem. While that might well have been true, he knew that it more of an excuse than anything else. He'd booked himself into a local hotel located conveniently just over three miles away from Declan's house. He'd be seeing him in the church that evening for the reception of his aunt's body. She'd then lie there in her coffin overnight before the funeral took place the next morning. Thankfully, the service that evening should be short. Mac was then going to plead back pain and disappear back to his hotel. He'd picked that particular hotel because it had a decent bar attached and also because his cousins Fiona and Thomas from Dublin had booked themselves in there as well. They too seemed to be happy to be situated a decent distance away from Declan.

The landing and his transfer to the car hire desk in the arrivals lounge were both smooth and uneventful. After the girl had given him his keys and explained where the car was parked Mac asked her if she had a car booked in the name of J. Connerty.

'Well, as you're not Mr. Connerty himself, I'm not sure that I can tell you that,' she quite reasonably replied. 'Are you a friend of his?'

'No, thank God, I'm not.'

The girl looked at him quizzically as he walked away. He'd have to get the local police to check it out later. He found his car easily enough and checked that it did indeed have an automatic gearbox before he did anything else. His left leg was becoming increasingly numb these days and a manual gear shift was not something that worked for him anymore. Before he drove off, he rang Dan to see if there had been any developments. There hadn't.

Fifteen minutes later he was driving serenely past the greenest fields in the world. He remembered the trek that he'd had to make to get to Donegal when he'd been a boy. First there was the long train ride from Birmingham to North West Wales and then the overnight boat trip from Holyhead to Dublin. Mac, living right in the centre of England, rarely got to see the sea and he'd be so excited that he'd never sleep a wink on the voyage over. Even if he couldn't see any further than the white tops of the waves in the darkness, the smell of salt and the sound of the water slapping against the hull of the ship were still quite thrilling. The most exciting moment of all would be when land was finally spied on the horizon in the early morning gloom.

People around him would awake as if from a magic spell and join him on deck as he watched the island of Ireland coming ever closer. Most would smile at seeing their homeland once again but Mac noticed that some didn't. They looked sad and he remembered wondering why that should be.

The ship would inch into the docks and tie up. Then there would be an interminable wait while nothing seemed to be happening. After a small eternity they were eventually allowed off the boat and they'd follow the crowd, all on their wobbly sea legs, to Busaras, the main Dublin bus station. The bus that would take them to Donegal would be there, waiting for them. After an interminable wait for the rest of the passengers to arrive the driver would start the engine and they'd be off! He'd drive them slowly through the quiet empty streets of the capital city just as the sun was rising.

Mac had always thought that this part of the trip was strange and enchanting, as though they were driving through a city upon which a sleeping spell had been cast. Once they'd left the city behind tiredness would finally overtake him and, when he opened his eyes again, he'd be magically back in Ballydove. Air travel was only for the rich in those days and the journey must have taken the better part of a day each way. Mac hadn't minded it though. It was an adventure.

You can really see the sky here, Mac thought as he drove along the road towards Tobercurry.

He realised that this was mostly due to the lack of trees. It was very different to leafy Hertfordshire where someone once told him that if you planted your walking stick in the ground it would sprout leaves in a matter of weeks. Here the trees looked a little scrawny and they all seemed to lean in the same direction.

Probably due to the wind, Mac thought.

He remembered his Uncle Owen once saying as they walked across one of the farm fields, 'In England they talk about there always being death and taxes but here we've got rocks and the wind too. The wind never stops and I'll swear that those shagging rocks must be breeding underground. To be honest, I'm not sure if I'm running a farm or a quarry at times.'

His father had told him more than once that he'd had to leave Ireland as the farm in those days couldn't support more than one family. Nowadays though, with all the modern machinery, farms were much more productive and the EU farm prices were vastly higher than the ones that Britain had been prepared to pay back then.

His thoughts circled back to the investigation and to his conversation with Dan. They'd learnt nothing at all from Mr. Barrington. Unlike Mr. Parker he was a smoker. He'd left his post about an hour or so before Mac had arrived to have a cigarette outside and when he'd returned Mr. Connerty was already seated and seemingly asleep. He'd glanced at his boarding card and decided to leave the job of waking him up to Mr. Parker. He hadn't noticed the blood. To be fair to him neither had Mac. They had also been able to locate Mr. Connerty's luggage and were able to get it off the plane before it left. Bob Yeardley and the forensics team were examining it as they spoke. That was it really.

He was already getting the feeling that Jack Connerty's killer must know the airport well. The murder had been carried out in the one spot not covered by cameras and also at a time when there had be no witnesses. Apparently, Mr. Barrington had called the area where Jackie Connerty was found the 'last goodbye'. It appeared to be a well-known spot where airport employees could meet up with relatives and friends before they flew out. The lack of CCTV cameras meant that no-one would know that they'd left their posts.

This again pointed at the killer as being someone who might have worked at the airport. Dan told him that he was going to look at everyone who was working there at the time of the murder. As the airport employed thousands of people this would be a big job and so he'd already started drafting in some local detectives and uniforms to help the team out.

After a pleasant drive Mac arrived at the hotel in plenty of time. He'd planned it so that he'd have time to have a lie down for a few hours in case his back was playing up. The pain wasn't that bad but he knew it would be better to be on the safe side and get some rest while he could. The girl at the hotel reception was friendly and chatted away about this and that as she booked him in. It was something he truly loved about Ireland and the Irish, the conversation.

The room was comfortable and had a lovely view over the fields to the sea in the distance. The sun was shining and it looked like a scene from a picture postcard.

'Scenery? What good is it? You can't eat the scenery.'

It was something he remembered his Aunt Annie once saying. She had lots of cheerful little sayings like that.

He set the alarm on his phone and then gratefully lay down and tried to relax. He felt as though he'd only just drifted off when the phone woke him up. He picked it up. It wasn't the alarm though, it was Dan.

'Mac, are you okay?'

'Yes, I'm fine. I'm at the hotel in Ballydove. What's happening?'

'It looks as if you were right and our man Mr. Connerty is from your neck of the woods after all. Martin has found out that he has a house in a place called Ardilaun just outside Ballydove.'

'Yes, I know where that is. It's quite close to where my cousin's farm is. Do you want me to go and do some digging around while I'm over here?'

'If you have the time. I know you're over there on family business but I'm not above asking as we have a lot on our plate at this end.'

'Oh, don't worry about that,' Mac assured him. 'It'll be nice to be actually doing something while I'm over here.'

'Thanks, I was hoping that you'd say that,' Dan said. 'Martin has contacted the Garda and told them that you'll be working on our behalf for a while. They said that one of their detectives will contact you and they'll act as liaison while you're over there. Take care Mac.'

Mac assured him he would. He then put the phone down and smiled. He hadn't been looking forward to all the family stuff anyway and this gave him the perfect excuse to keep contact with Declan to a minimum. He looked at the time on his phone. He'd slept for an hour which was good. He roused himself and got into the shower.

He'd just gotten dressed when the phone rang. Not his mobile this time but the internal phone. It was the nice girl from reception.

'Oh, I'm sorry Mr. Maguire but there's a Mr. Maguire down here who wants to see you...'

She stopped speaking and Mac could hear another voice in the background.

'I'm sorry but he says that it's actually Detective Sergeant Maguire who wants to see you.'

'Please tell him that I'll be down in a couple of minutes,' Mac said.

He looked at his watch. He had an hour and a half before he had to be at the church. He came down into the reception area and didn't have to be told who the policeman was. DS Maguire was sitting calmly in the corner. He was in his late twenties and he had jet black hair as yet untouched by any grey. He was dressed in a reasonable suit, white shirt and blue tie and his shoes shone brightly. He had that long rectangular face that seemed to be common in the West of Ireland.

A Gregory Peck face, he remembered his mother once calling it, and indeed he wasn't unlike the famous film star. Yet for all that Mac knew straight away that he was a policeman. He'd obviously recognised Mac too.

'DCS Maguire,' he stated as he held his hand out.

'DS Maguire, it's a pleasure. Shall we go into the bar?'

He nodded and followed Mac into the bar area. He was immediately intrigued by his new colleague. He'd spotted a look of deep sadness on the young policeman's face just before he'd looked up and noticed Mac walking towards him. He immediately began to wonder why.

Mac picked the table that was furthest away from the few people who were in the room. As soon as they sat down a young waitress approached them and looked expectantly at them. Mac had forgotten about there being waiter service in a lot of Irish bars.

'Er...I'll have a coffee, please,' Mac said.

'Yes, me too,' DS Maguire added.

When she'd gone the young detective opened the conversation.

'So DCS Maguire, I've been told that you're looking into Jackie Connerty's murder?' he asked.

'Oh, please call me Mac. I haven't been a DCS for a while now.'

'Thanks, as we're being informal you can call me Aiden. I believe that it was yourself that found Jackie at the airport, is that right?'

'Yes, I was waiting for my flight and Mr. Connerty looked like he was asleep. When someone tried to wake him, we discovered that he was dead. He had three stab wounds in his back so whoever did it really wanted him dead. We've only just kicked the investigation off and, as I was coming over here anyway, my boss asked me if I could find out what I could about Mr. Connerty's business dealings in this part of the world. I believe that he has a house over at Ardilaun.'

'Business dealings?' Aiden said with a half a smile. 'Now that would be quite a formal way of describing what Jackie got up to. Let's just say that he was an ardent supporter of the black economy and he'd pretty much do anything if it made him a profit.'

'What sort of things did he get up to?' Mac asked as he looked at his watch.

'Now don't you go worrying about missing Annie Sweeney's reception at the church. I'll give you a lift if you like and we can talk on the way.'

'Thanks,' Mac said with a smile.

'Well, getting back to the case a bit of history might enlighten you,' Aiden said. 'Jackie's family are well known hereabouts. During the war his grandfather made his money by smuggling butter and sugar to the North and then smuggling white bread and tea back to the South. His dad and uncle were in the smuggling trade too. His uncle became quite famous around here, they used to call him Rubber Ronnie because he was the man to go to if you wanted to buy a condom. Jackie carried on with the trade but he had to turn to other things after the UK and Ireland joined the EU. Suddenly there wasn't that much money in smuggling as it was mostly just agricultural diesel and cows.'

'Cows?' Mac asked.

'Oh yes, if you can sell a cow for a few euros more in the North then many people find it's worth their while.'

'What was Jackie like? Did you ever meet him yourself?' Mac asked.

'I've seen him in the pub a few times but I wouldn't say that I knew him. He wasn't popular with everyone but he a good talker and he'd put his hand in his pocket for a round every now and again. The best description I ever heard of him was what an old friend of my father called him, 'A chancer and romancer'. Yes, Jackie was that all right.'

'Did he have any enemies, anyone who might wish him harm?'

'Well, there've been more than a few people that Jackie's short-changed over the years who might like to rough him up a bit but murder? I can't see it really and, anyway, he's been spending a lot more time in your neck of the woods that he has around here lately.'

'Why is that? Do you know?'

Aiden shrugged.

'I've no idea but you could bet your life that wherever Jackie was there was bound to be some sort of scam going on as well.'

Mac gave this some thought as the young waitress came back with their coffees.

'Well, Jackie Connerty was coming here for a reason. How could we find out a bit more about him?' Mac asked as the waitress walked away.

'I'd start by going for a pint. Jackie used to do a lot of his wheeling and dealing in Magee's Bar on the Abbey Road,' Aiden said. 'If he was on his way over here it was probably because he had some sort of deal on the go. I'd guess that a few of the lads who drink there might know what Jackie's been up to but whether they'll tell us is anyone's guess.'

'It sounds like it's worth a shot to me,' Mac said with a smile.

Indeed, the idea of having a pint in a Donegal pub while still being able to progress the investigation seemed like the perfect next step to Mac.

'However, before we do that, I think we should go over to Ardilaun and have a word with Jackie's wife first,' Aiden suggested.

'His wife? Yes, that would be good. I'm sorry I didn't know he was married. I was just told that he had a house there.'

'Yes, and Maggie Connerty has been living in it for some years now. She used to be the district nurse around here and she's very well liked. In fact, I remember her looking after me when I was a kid. I'd doubt that she even knows that her husband's dead if it only happened this morning, so we may need to break the news to her.' Aiden looked at his watch and said, 'Come on then, it's time that you went and visited the Widow Sweeney. I'll bet that you're really looking forward to that.'

Mac's face told him that the absolute reverse was true.

'By the way are we related?' Mac asked as they drove towards the church.

'I believe that your grandfather and my great grand-father were cousins, so I guess we are,' Aiden replied.

'Have you always worked in the Ballydove area?'

'Well, I started off here but for the last year or so I've been working in Dublin,' Aiden replied.

There was a tone in his voice that told Mac that he didn't wish to discuss the subject further. They drove on in silence for a while. It was a taut, tense silence though and Mac started to wonder what had happened to his new colleague in Dublin to make him so defensive about it.

They drove through streets that were familiar to Mac and the memories came back thick and fast. However, the current Ballydove looked like a faded photograph of the colourful town that he had once known. He remembered it as being a busy place with lots of little shops. Some of these were now boarded up and the streets seemed to be deserted. They passed by a new shopping area. The two 'P's in the word 'shopping' had dropped off the sign on the outside and it was totally empty except for one shop that looked like Ballydove's version of a pound shop. The whole place looked run down and tired.

'Here we are,' Aiden said eventually breaking the silence.

Mac could see the outline of a grey stone building ahead topped with a sharp spire. It was typical of much of the religious architecture in Ireland in being large, drab and uninspiring. He remembered the endless hours of boredom he'd had to undergo as a child in such places when he was supposed to be on holiday and he wondered if that had influenced his feelings on the matter.

Aiden parked as close to the door as he could. Mac could see his cousin Declan standing outside the church entrance ready to greet the mourners as they arrived. Mac sat for a minute or so but didn't see anyone enter.

'I'll be waiting outside when you come out,' Aiden assured him.

Mac glanced over at Aiden. He could see that his young colleague's expression when looking at the church wasn't a friendly one. All in all, DS Aiden Maguire didn't seem to be a happy man and Mac found himself intrigued as to why that might be.

'I'll be as quick as I can,' Mac said. 'Wish me luck.'

He wasn't quite sure why he said that but at least it got a genuine smile out of his new colleague.

His cousin Declan smiled too as he saw Mac approach. Mac thought that it might have been a smile of relief at someone actually turning up.

'Ah Dennis, thanks for coming.'

His real first name was Dennis and, while he was known as Mac to everyone else, he was still called Denny by his sisters and oldest friends. Only Declan and Mac's mother had ever called him Dennis and she'd only done that after he'd broken something. He often wondered if that was why he didn't like his name.

'Declan, a sad day for you,' Mac said as he shook his hand. 'I'm sorry for your troubles.'

He'd decided to pick his words carefully. He didn't want to be a hypocrite and pretend that he felt any sadness himself because he didn't.

'A very sad day indeed,' Declan said with a mournful expression that didn't look all that different to his normal one. 'But we must comfort ourselves with the fact that my dear mother is now happy and is in heaven with Our Lord and all his Angels.'

Mac smiled and nodded but said nothing. He didn't believe in heaven and hell but he suspected that, if Declan's dear mother was anywhere at all, it would be somewhere nice and warm.

Mac made his way inside the church and was faced with a seemingly endless aisle that eventually led to three Romanesque arches in the far distance. The largest arch in the middle contained the altar before which stood a dark wooden coffin. The aisle was flanked by ranks of heavy wooden pews on both sides. Mac stopped halfway up the aisle and sat down. It was as near to his aunt as he wanted to get. If necessary, he'd claim that he had a bad back. He knew that he might be accused of being somewhat hypocritical in this but he found that he didn't care.

He looked up as Declan scurried past him. He turned and gestured at Mac to join him further up the church but Mac just shook his head and pointed at his back. The priest came out so Declan gave up trying to persuade him and joined the rest of the mourners. There were seven in all and Mac knew none of them. Unfortunately for him his cousins from Dublin weren't arriving until later that evening.

The priest started talking. Thankfully he was inaudible at the distance that Mac was sitting. The service took just over half an hour. He used the time to think. He knew that he might be making bricks without straw as he had so little to go on but he carried on anyway.

Jackie Connerty was a man in his sixties with so-called business interests in Ireland and possible the UK as he spent a lot of time there. He was killed in what was supposed to be a safe environment, an airport with refined security features and even armed police. So how had the killer smuggled a knife into such a secure area?

He felt that he might get a clue about that once the autopsy had been completed. If the knife that killed Jackie was asymmetrical and had ragged edges it could have been something that was made on site. In any large airport Mac guessed that there must be quite a few workshops used for repairing tools and vehicles and the like. To make a knife all you'd need is a strip of metal and a grinding wheel. That would certainly be safer than trying to smuggle a knife in.

He'd also heard about plastic and carbon fibre knives being used in the United States. While it was unlikely, it was still a possibility and again hopefully the autopsy should be able to identify if something unusual had been used to kill Jackie Connerty.

He ran the murder through his head as if it had been a movie. There was Jackie sitting in the seat he was found dead in. If he didn't need assistance then why was he sitting there? Mac could only guess that he'd arranged to meet someone there, a meeting in possibly one of the only areas in the airport that was not overlooked by cameras. His killer must have bided his time and waited somewhere until Ken Barrington had disappeared for a cigarette. As he didn't appear on the CCTV images, the killer must have come into the area through one of the three doors and left again by the same route.

Jackie must have noticed whoever came through the door, unless he'd been asleep of course, but if he was meeting someone then that might have been unlikely. The killer must have walked directly behind where Jackie was sitting and then grasped Jackie by the shoulder with one hand and pushed him down. Then three quick strikes with the knife in the back before pulling him upright and holding him in place until he was sure he was dead. The killer then only had to find Jackie's boarding pass and, as he was wearing a suit jacket, he would probably have only had to look in the inside pocket. He placed the pass on the seat and arranged the body to make it look like he was asleep to give himself as much time as possible to get away. It would have taken only a couple of minutes at the most. The killer would have had to touch Jackie several times so it would be interesting to see if any DNA evidence or fingerprints had been left behind.

Did that mean that Jackie might not have known his killer as he allowed him to get so close? There certainly didn't seem to have been signs of any struggle. Was the murder planned or opportunistic? The knife certainly made it looked like it was planned as it would hardly be something you might just have on you in an airport. Mac wondered who had access to the information about assisted passengers? Did the killer know that no-one would be requiring assistance at the time that the meeting had been arranged and so there would be no witnesses? Perhaps the meeting had been arranged for that particular time because of that fact.

Everything seemed to point towards the killer being an airport worker of some sort.

Of course, the elephant in the room when it came to this particular murder was whether Jackie had any connections with the IRA or any other paramilitary group. Mac was aware that Ballydove, being just a few miles from the border, must have a few such groups that were still around and, as Jackie was into smuggling, they might very well be involved in some way. He sincerely hoped not as it would really complicate the investigation. He'd have a word with Aiden about the likelihood of that.

Mac also decided that he'd need to have a word with Martin. He had lots of questions but virtually no answers. He needed more data. His thoughts were interrupted by the sound of echoing footsteps coming towards him. The priest had disappeared from the altar and Declan and the other mourners were slowly making their way down the aisle. Mac stood up as they passed by and then fell in at the back of the small procession.

Declan stood at the door and shook hands as the mourners filed out. Mac was last.

'A fine service, I thought,' Declan said.

'Yes, yes it was,' Mac replied not knowing what else to say.

'Will you not come to the house for a cup of tea?' Declan asked.

'Well, I'd love to Declan but I'm afraid I can't.'

'You can't come for a cup of tea?' Declan asked in surprise.

'I'm sorry but I'm on a case, a murder case.'

'Really? A murder in Ballydove?' Declan asked with an expression that showed his disbelief. 'Anyway, I thought you'd retired from the police. So, who's dead?'

'I'm sorry but I can't tell you that just yet,' Mac replied.

He knew that they needed to tell Jackie's wife first as news travelled at the speed of light in these small towns.

Declan's expression clearly showed his disdain at Mac's seemingly flimsy excuses.

'I'm really sorry but I have to go. Detective Sergeant Maguire is waiting for me,' Mac said as he waved towards the other side of the road.

He turned as he said this and only then noticed that he'd waved towards an empty street. There was no car and no DS Maguire.

Mac swore under his breath.

'Well, I hope you'll at least make it to the funeral tomorrow,' Declan said in a hurt voice.

'Of course,' Mac replied.

Declan slouched off down the street. Even from behind he looked lost and lonely. Mac felt guilty even though he knew he had nothing to feel guilty about. The sound of a car pulling up made him turn around. It was Aiden.

'Sorry but I had to get some petrol,' Aiden said as Mac climbed in. 'Ardilaun?'

'Yes, let's go and break the news to Maggie Connerty.'

The car passed by Declan just as he turned the corner. Mac waved but he didn't look around.

Chapter Four

As they made their way to Ardilaun, Mac thought that the Donegal countryside looked quite stunning in the evening sunshine. They drove down a winding country road flanked by vividly green fields that were dotted with some very large houses, most of which seemed new. Mac pointed these out to Aiden.

'Most of those houses were built just before the economy went down the tubes. They look nice but a lot of the people who built them are stuck here. It's cost them more to build those houses than they'd get back these days,' Aiden explained.

They passed by a massive house that was painted grey with a slick dark blue slate roof. It looked attractive and quite new, had a large garage on the side and quite a bit of land around it.

'See that house now,' Aiden said. 'I know the man who owns that and he's desperate to move. It's really well built and it has six bedrooms, all with en-suite bathrooms. He's only asking three hundred thousand euros for the house and he hasn't had a single enquiry yet.'

Mac was stunned.

'If you moved that house to Letchworth, where I live, you'd get at least a couple of million if not more,' Mac said. 'What's happened to Ballydove?'

'Well, my father says that it used to be a one-horse town but now the horse has unfortunately died. Of course, years ago we used to be a fishing port until they decided to do away with what should have been one of our main tourist attractions, St. Bridget's Falls, and put in the hydro-electric scheme. The harbour was already starting to silt up but that speeded the process

34

up dramatically. They certainly didn't see that one coming. So that was the end of the fishing then. However, we adapted and got by somehow. Then came the economic crash a few years back. We got hit quite badly by austerity and a lot of the local industries either shut down or moved out of the area. Although the rest of the country looks like it's recovering, I'm afraid that we've gotten a bit stuck around here. My father says that the town's like a boxer who's taken one punch too many. It's hit the floor and nobody knows if it will ever get up again. A lot of people want to get out but unfortunately they can't as no-one wants to buy their houses.'

Mac's heart sank as he heard this. He still had a lot of affection for the place and his family's roots there went back a long way on his father's side.

'But you came back?' Mac said.

Aiden shrugged his shoulders as an answer. It looked like that was the only answer he was going to get.

'You mention your father a lot,' Mac said eventually breaking an uncomfortable silence.

Aiden turned and smiled.

'I suppose I do. I must admit that he was the only thing I missed about the place when I was in Dublin.'

'What does he do?'

'Mostly the garden these days. He retired last year but, before that, he was a postman. He delivered letters all around this area for well over thirty years.' Aiden paused and thought for a moment. 'It might be an idea to have a word with him some time. He might know something about Jackie's background and what he got up to. Postmen usually get to know quite a lot about what's going on in small towns like this.'

'That's true. Yes, if it's okay, I'd love to have a word with your father.'

The car turned right at a crossroads and Mac found that the surrounding countryside had suddenly become very familiar. He realised that his cousin Mick's farm was only a mile or so further on down the road.

'Here we are,' Aiden said in a low voice as he pulled into a driveway.

Aiden pulled up in front of the house and turned off the engine. He sat quietly and made no move to get out. Mac knew that it was still considered good manners in parts of Ireland to give people a little time to prepare when you called by unexpectedly.

Mac looked at the house while they waited. It was a bungalow and rendered grey like many of the houses in the area. It wasn't as large as some though and Mac could see that some of the rendering had fallen off in places and needed repair. A grey-haired figure peeked out from the curtains before quickly closing them again. A few minutes later a woman appeared at the front door. She was in her sixties, slim and she had a nice smile.

'Is that you young Aiden Maguire that I see sitting out there in your car? Will you not come in for a cup of tea?' she asked brightly.

Aiden opened the door and got out.

'I thought that you'd never ask,' Aiden said. 'How are you keeping, Maggie?'

'Oh, I still get around, you know me, I can never sit still for long,' she said as she glanced over at Mac as he too got out of the car.

She gave him a puzzled look before leading them into a spotlessly clean and well-ordered living room. She gestured towards a sofa and they sat down.

'Now, how do you like your tea?' she asked.

'Maggie, can we forget about the tea for a moment?' Aiden said. 'Please sit down. We've got something to tell you.'

She sat on the very edge of the chair and gave them a worried look.

'It's not about Jackie, is it? Oh, please God say it isn't. He should have arrived this morning and I...'

'Have you got a picture of Jackie handy?' Aiden interrupted.

She returned with a framed photo and passed it to Aiden without a word. The photo was of herself and a man. It was taken in the driveway and the house was clearly visible in the background. The man was smiling and his cap was perched jauntily at an angle on his head. He was hugging his wife and she looked very happy.

Mac looked closely at the photo. The last time Mac had seen the man in the photo was at the airport just before forensics had put a tent over his dead body. He nodded sombrely to Aiden and returned the photo to Maggie.

'Maggie, there's no easy way to tell you this. Jackie's dead,' Aiden said.

She clearly couldn't take it in.

'Dead? Dead you say? Sure, I only spoke to him last week, how on earth could he be....'

She stopped and tried to pull herself together.

'Was it his heart?' she almost whispered.

'No,' Aiden said, 'he was murdered.'

'Mary, Mother of God but you can't be serious?' she exclaimed as she put a hand to her heart.

'This is Mac Maguire. He's a policeman from England. He's the one who found Jackie's body,' Aiden said.

Mac explained what had happened as simply and briefly as he could.

'He was stabbed in an airport? How is that even possible? Was it some terrorist madman like that Isis crowd?' she asked.

'While that's still a possibility, I'd say that it's a remote one. Only Jackie was assaulted. Whoever killed him got away as soon the stabbing took place. It looks like Jackie was the target.'

She shook her head and gave Mac a sorrowful look.

'It was one of his little deals, I've no doubt. I often told him that he sailed far too close to the wind at times and that he'd be sorry for it one day. Oh Jesus, is my Jackie really dead?'

The realisation that she would never see her husband again was beginning to sink in and the tears started flowing.

'Shall I call Theresa and get her to come over and sit with you for a while?' Aiden gently asked.

Maggie nodded without looking up. Aiden got his phone out and made the call.

'Theresa will be here in a couple of minutes. I can see that you're in no state to talk now,' Aiden said. 'Would it be okay if we came back again tomorrow?'

Maggie nodded again. Along with the tears, she started rocking backwards and forwards in her chair. They all sat in an uneasy silence for a time until they heard the front door opening. Aiden stood up and intercepted Theresa. She was a large woman of about the same age as Maggie. She looked concerned.

Aiden spoke softly to her for a while. Mac could see Theresa's expression turned from one of concern to one of shock.

'So, we'll be going now, Maggie,' Aiden said softly.

She just nodded in his direction. Theresa sat down beside her and put her arm around her friend. Maggie seemed to lose even the strength to sit up and her head went down into Theresa's lap. Mac glanced back just before he left the room. Maggie's body had started jerking as the sobs came. Theresa spoke softly to her and brushed her hair with her hand just as a mother does when consoling a heartbroken child.

'She'll be as well as she can be now that Theresa's here,' Aiden said as they got into the car. 'They've been friends since they were at school together.'

Aiden started the car up and turned right back onto the road.

'I take it that you'd like to drop into your cousin's as we're in the area?'

It was exactly what Mac had been thinking.

'Yes please, if it's no problem. Do you know Mick Maguire?'

Aiden didn't reply so Mac left it at that. There was silence for the rest of the short drive. Mac glanced over at Aiden. He seemed to be thinking about something and whatever it was didn't seem to be making him any more cheerful.

A few minutes later they pulled into a narrow lane and Mac saw the sign for 'Three Brothers Farm'. By coincidence his father also had two brothers but the name went back much further than that. The three brothers were Maguires who had bought the land from the Trevithick estate well over a hundred years before. They passed by a derelict stone cottage. The roof had long ago fallen in and it could be seen that it consisted of just three small rooms.

Mac remembered Mick taking him there once when he'd been young and on one of his cousin's 'rambles'. A ramble with Mick could be anywhere between a walk to one of the nearby fields to a ten-mile hike into Ballydove and back. Mick had told him that this humble cottage had housed all three brothers and their families when they first moved onto the farm. The 'big house' hadn't been built until much later.

Mac had stood in one of the rooms and wondered if his cousin had been spinning a tale. He knew that this must have been the case when he added that one of the brothers had eight children. Of course, he found out later that Mick hadn't been joking and cottages of that size had been all that people could afford at the time.

Three or four hundred yards further on they pulled straight into a farmyard. On the left there was a large white house that had the door and window frames painted red. This was the 'big house'. Straight in front of them two large barns stood side by side behind which there stood an assortment of outbuildings. To the right there was a small cottage painted grey that was brightened up by a cloud of multi-coloured plants climbing up the walls. Aiden parked the car outside of the cottage.

This was called the 'wee house' and Mick's father Owen had it built when Mick and his wife Maureen got married. When the children started to arrive Owen and his wife moved into the 'wee house' and gave them the big house. Mick and Maureen had done the same when his son Seamus had his first child.

Aiden sat without moving. Mac assumed that it was him being polite again. He was wrong.

'You'd best go in then. I need to...to get some petrol. I'll pick you up here in half an hour or so if that's alright,' Aiden said.

He never looked over at Mac as he said this. The petrol tank was still three quarters full. Mac looked at the car as it disappeared down the road and wondered at his new colleague's strange behaviour. He heard a door opening behind him and turned. Mick's wife Maureen was standing in the doorway.

She was tall, slim and looked younger than her age. Her hair, once jet black, was now grey but it suited her somehow. She gave Mac a wide smile as he walked towards her.

'I was hoping it would be you,' she said as she gave him a hug. 'Himself will be glad to see you too.'

She led him inside.

'I hope that I'm not interrupting anything,' Mac said.

'Ah and what is there to interrupt these days? He'll only be doing the crossword or playing solitaire on that laptop Seamus bought him.'

His cousin was seated by a large window that looked over the green fields, in the distance the deep grey-blues of the Atlantic Ocean could be seen. He jumped up when he saw who his visitor was and his wide smile showed Mac that he was more than welcome.

They gave each other the firmest of hugs.

'Denny, we were hoping that you'd find time to drop by. How are you?'

Mick pointed to an armchair and they both sat down.

'Tea?' Maureen asked.

Although, this being Ireland, it wasn't really a question but more a statement of fact.

'So, how have you been?' Mick enquired.

'I've been okay, you know trying to keep busy.'

'That was a wonderful service for Nora,' Mick said.

They'd last met at Mac's wife's remembrance service. She'd been dead a year and Mac had been dreading it. However, despite his daughter Bridget telling him that it would just be a small family service, friends and family had come from just about everywhere to be there. Amongst them had been his cousin Mick and his wife Maureen. He'd been surprised and more than grateful that they had come all the way over to England just to be with him.

'I really appreciated that you came. It made all the difference,' Mac said.

'Ah, it was the least we could do,' Mick replied. 'So, you're over for Annie Sweeney's funeral then?'

'I am. I'm not looking forward to it though. I never really liked Aunt Annie much if I'm being honest. Are you going to be there?'

'Yes, Maureen and I will put our best foot forward even though we haven't been invited.'

Mac was puzzled.

'Why is that then?'

'Well, apparently me and Annie fell out over something around twenty years ago or so, although I've absolutely no idea what it could have been. She never spoke a word to me after that and so I never did get to find out.'

'Now don't you be lying, Mick,' Maureen said as she appeared with a tray in her hands. 'You were delighted when she stopped speaking to you. At the time you said that you'd definitely got the better out of that bargain. She was a real funny onion that woman.'

Mick gave Mac a smile.

'Well, I can't lie about that. Every time she opened her mouth, she was running someone or other down.'

Mac nodded in agreement. That was a good description of Annie Sweeney alright.

'So, how long are you here for?' Maureen asked as she handed him a welcome cup of tea.

'I'm not sure if I'm honest. I had planned on just staying for a couple of days after the funeral, mainly so I could spend some time with you, but something's happened. I might well be around for a while longer now as I've got some police business to carry out in the area.'

'I thought that was Aiden who I saw with you in the car,' Maureen said. 'He's gone very strange since he came back from Dublin. Why on earth didn't he come in?'

'I've no idea,' Mac replied.

'So, what are you investigating in Ballydove?' Mick asked. 'Crime around here usually means someone's parked on double yellow lines.'

'Did you know Jackie Connerty at all?' Mac asked.

'Jackie? No, not so much, he's always coming and going, but we know his wife Maggie well. God knows she was around here often enough when the kids were sick. She's a good woman, although what she saw in that waster Jackie is a mystery. Why has he done something?' Mick asked.

'Not that we know of. He's dead. We've only just told his wife.'

'Jackie's dead? What on earth happened to him?' Maureen asked with a look of surprise.

Mac told them.

'The poor man was murdered? May God preserve us all,' Maureen said as she made the sign of the cross.

She had a serious expression on her face as she stood up.

'I'm sorry Denny but I must be off in case Maggie needs anything. The poor woman must be in bits. I'll see you tomorrow at the funeral.'

There was a short silence after which Mac heard the front door slam.

'Now who'd have thought that?' Mick said as he shook his head.

'Is there anything you can tell me about Jackie?'

'No, not really. It might be said that we moved in different circles. He was only interested in a cow if he could smuggle it across the border to make a bob or two. God knows what Maggie saw in him. Maureen asked her once and she said that Jackie made her laugh.'

Mac had known that to form the basis of many lasting relationships. He thought back to the photo. Jackie had looked every inch the cheeky rogue while Maggie had just looked happy.

'So, you thought you were just coming over here for a funeral but the famous Mac Maguire is once again on a murder case,' Mick said in a joshing tone.

'Just in the wrong place at the wrong time I guess,' Mac said with shrug. 'And as for being famous...'

'Ah, get away with you. Sure, we used to follow most of your cases when you were working in London. You were even in the Donegal Democrat a few times. Of course, they never forgot to mention that your family were from Ballydove. I'd guess that's part of the reason why Caitlin wanted to be a policewoman so much.'

Caitlin was Mick's daughter and the youngest in the family. Her elder brother Seamus ran the farm while her other brother Mark now lived in Toronto. He was an accountant and had his own business there.

'Really?' Mac said with some surprise.

'Yes, really and I think that some of it might have rubbed off on Aiden too. I don't think he ever got over the fact that someone from Ballydove could be leading a murder squad in London.'

'How well do you know Aiden?' Mac asked.

He was curious and wanted to find out as much as he could about his new partner.

'He and Caitlin went to school together. I think they were just friends at the time as they decided to go to different universities. They met up again in Dublin a while back when Aiden got a transfer to the Crime and Security Branch. Caitlin had been working for them for some time so she showed him the ropes. Then he started cropping up in some of her phone conversations and letters and we got the idea that there might be more to it than them just being friends. Maureen asked her once straight out and Caitlin never denied it, in fact she said in a roundabout way that things might be getting quite serious. We were both happy about it as we knew that Aiden, while perhaps being a bit on the solemn side sometimes, was basically a good lad.'

Mick paused, shook his head sadly and took a sip from his cup.

'Then, a couple of months ago, Caitlin came back home unexpectedly for a few days. She was very upset, we could both see that, but she wouldn't tell us why. I remember that I went by her room in the middle of the night and I heard her crying. All I could do was stand outside her door and listen. I've never felt so helpless.

Then two weeks later Aiden turns up back here in his old job and he's been avoiding us ever since. I just wish I knew what's gone on between the two of them.'

Mac was now even more intrigued.

'Speak of the devil, that'll be Aiden back now,' Mick said.

Mac had heard nothing. He went and looked out of the window and saw that the car, with Aiden in it, was indeed parked outside.

'Well, there's nothing wrong with your hearing,' Mac said as he returned to the room.

Mick stood up and held out his hand.

'We'll see you tomorrow morning at the church then,' he said.

'Yes, I'll look out for you,' Mac said as they exchanged a firm handshake.

Aiden started the engine when he saw Mac walk out of the house. He had only just sat down in the car when his phone went off. It was his cousins from Dublin. They'd arranged to meet around eight at the hotel but the text said that they were running late and wouldn't be there until ten o'clock at the earliest. Mac was glad as he'd totally forgotten about meeting up with them. A lot seemed to have happened since they'd last talked on the phone just a few days ago.

'Magee's Bar?' Aiden asked.

Mac noticed that he didn't seem to be at all curious as to what he might have learnt from Mick.

'Yes, but I'll need dropping back at my hotel after that as I'm meeting someone if that's okay.'

'That's fine with me. The funeral is at ten tomorrow, isn't it?' Aiden asked.

'Yes, that's right,' Mac confirmed with a sigh.

He couldn't wait until the funeral rites, with all the pretences of sadness and walking on eggshells, were all done and dusted. He would never forget Maggie's

45

reaction to the news of her husband's death and he found that he really wanted to find his murderer.

He didn't know if it would help Maggie that much but it was all he could do.

Chapter Five

Magee's Bar was on the road back into Ballydove. It was coming up to seven-thirty and the sun was about to set. The panorama around them seemed incredibly beautiful to Mac as the sun's rays burst across the green fields from behind the low hills. The sky seemed so huge that it somehow felt surreal and almost spiritual.

He knew this road well. He glanced over to his right. Beyond the fields he looked up at the hill on which the Pauper's Graveyard stood. There was a memorial to the victims of the Great Famine there now but, when Mac had been taken there by his father, it had been just another rocky field on the top of a hill.

'Over a thousand bodies are buried here,' his father had said. 'All of them died in the Ballydove Workhouse in a matter of three years or so during the famine. It seemed that people feared the workhouse so much that they wouldn't go there until they were desperate and near enough dead anyway. A thousand people and Ballydove was a much smaller town back then than it is now. Whole families were wiped out and just about everyone lost someone close to them or so I heard. During that time the only choice many people had was to either starve or go to America.'

Mac remembered his father pausing and looking sadly at him as he added, 'And I believe that they were still exporting food from Ireland at a time when people were so hungry that they were trying to eat grass.'

Mac felt quite sad for a moment. Not because of the famine, terrible as it was, but because he suddenly realised how much he missed his father's presence. The land, the town and its streets were strewn with such memories of his father. Sad as they made him feel, he still welcomed them.

They were now entering the town. A few newly built houses appeared before they passed by a traditional single-storied thatched Irish cottage. It was rendered in a grey colour but the garden walls and windows were painted red, a traditionally durable colour in these parts. It was tiny and around the same size as the derelict cottage on the farm. Mac once again marvelled at how it had managed to house so many of his ancestors.

Ahead, Mac could see the town and a street lined with grey two-storied houses, no two of which looked the same. Aiden pulled into a small car park in front of the first house. It was literally on the edge of town having a street full of houses on one side and a green field dotted with cows on the other. A large painted sign said 'Magee's Bar' in green and gold lettering over the front door.

Mac followed Aiden inside. It had the mandatory bric-a-brac that all Irish pubs seemed to have on display. A seemingly random selection of items accrued over the years; postcards from around the world, a variety of ancient Guinness signs, photographs of Ballydove old and new, a pot-pourri of old agricultural implements and puzzlingly, in proud isolation on one wall, a bicycle wheel was mounted.

It also had something that just about every Irish pub had in Mac's opinion – atmosphere.

The small bar was empty except for a tall grey-haired and red-faced man who stood behind the bar and an old man with a dog who was staring at the glass of Guinness in front of him in quiet meditation. They both looked up when Mac and Aiden came in.

'Ah, so it's you, Sergeant Maguire. Not an official visit I hope?' the barman asked.

'You're alright Mikey. It's nothing to do with you or the pub. How's business?'

'Slow and getting even slower unfortunately,' Mikey replied with a sad expression.

'Were you expecting Jackie Connerty in tonight by any chance?' Aiden asked.

'Well, I wasn't but I think that Wee Tim Mullins and Paddy Geraghty are,' Mikey replied. 'Why do you ask? Has Jackie been up to his tricks again?'

Aiden didn't answer his question.

'What time will Tim and Paddy be in at?'

'Around eight thirty as usual I'd guess,' Mikey replied. 'Can I get you anything while you're waiting?'

Aiden glanced at Mac who nodded.

'Two pints please, Mikey,' Aiden said.

While the pints were being reverentially poured a door opened behind the bar and a woman walked in. The wonderful aroma of cabbage and corned beef came in with her. Mac realised that he hadn't eaten since the morning and he was ravenously hungry. Aiden seemed to have had the same idea.

'That smells great, Annie,' Aiden said to the stout middle-aged woman who was wearing an old-fashioned apron.

She couldn't help but see the hunger in their faces.

'I've enough left for two if you're interested?' she asked with a smile.

'We are,' Aiden said.

They sat down and sipped at their black pints in a comfortable silence. Ten minutes later Annie appeared bearing two huge plates upon which were heaped mashed potatoes and pale green cabbage over which lay several thick slices of red corned beef.

It was honestly one of the best meals that Mac could ever remember eating and he put it away in record time. The corned beef was especially good, red as it should be, succulent and soft enough to cut with a fork.

He and Aiden sat in a comfortable silence for a while afterwards.

'How were Mick and Maureen?' he eventually asked.

Mac glanced over at him but Aiden had his face turned away.

'They were both fine,' Mac replied.

Another silence. This one wasn't so comfortable though. Mac had the feeling that his colleague was plucking up his courage to ask him something.

'And their daughter Caitlin, is she okay?'

Again, Aiden looked away as he asked this but Mac could sense from the tension in his voice that this was a question that he really wanted to know the answer to.

Mac briefly toyed with the idea of telling him that she was fine and was now seeing someone else just to see what his reaction might be. However, he quickly concluded that this might be more than a little cruel and so he dropped the idea.

'I don't know. They didn't really say much about her,' Mac said.

He could see that Aiden was disappointed by his response and, of course, he had lied. He could only assume that what his cousin had told him about his daughter was in confidence. He felt that he couldn't say any more than he had.

Mac's thoughts about his young colleague were interrupted by the appearance of Mikey behind the bar. He pointed with his eyes towards a door on his right.

'Looks like our men have arrived,' Aiden said.

They quickly finished their pints and Mac followed Aiden through the door into a small back room where two men sat side by side on a bench seat. They looked up as he and Aiden came through the door and Mac could read the disappointment on their faces. There was some surprise there too when Aiden pulled a chair up to their table and sat opposite them. There was already another chair at the table so Mac sat in that one.

'Hello lads,' Aiden said with a smile. 'How's tricks?'

The two men looked at each other and then looked a little worried.

They were an odd couple Mac thought. The man on the right was a giant and, although sitting down, Mac guessed that he'd be well over six feet tall and nearly that wide. He was in his fifties and had the weathered looks of someone who worked outdoors a lot. A flat cap was perched somewhat precariously on the top of his head. It was at least a couple of sizes too small for his oversized head.

Knowing how much the Irish loved understatement Mac guessed that this must be 'Wee' Tim Mullins.

The other man, also in his fifties, was small and wiry. He reminded Mac of a ferret. He quickly regained his composure and he was obviously the spokesman for the couple.

'Ah, and if it isn't young Aiden Maguire. We haven't seen you since you came back from Dublin. Too tough there for you, was it?' he said with a touch of spite.

Mac could see that his comment had hit a nerve. The small man saw it too and smiled. Mac had only known him for a matter of seconds and he already disliked him.

'And who's your friend?' the small man asked.

'This is Mac Maguire. He's a policeman from England,' Aiden replied.

'Now and there was me thinking that we had more than enough policemen called Maguire in the district. Are you going to try England now seeing as how you couldn't hack Dublin?' he asked with a malevolent sneer.

Aiden let this pass and carried on, 'You're here to meet Jackie.'

It wasn't a question. Again, the two men looked at each other.

'And if we are?' the small man asked somewhat tentatively.

'Well, Paddy, if you are, it would seem that you'd be wasting your time. Jackie's dead,' Aiden said bluntly.

It was clear that this was news to both men.

'What was it, his heart or something?' Wee Tim asked in a surprisingly gentle voice.

'Well, sort of. It stopped working after someone stabbed him in it,' Aiden replied.

Surprise was replaced by shock on both men's faces. Could Mac detect some fear in their expressions as well?

'I know that you were meeting Jackie here tonight to discuss some sort of deal. What was it?' Aiden asked.

'Now that would be telling,' Paddy said with a forced smile.

'Well, you'll be telling me here or down the station. Which is it to be?' Aiden asked.

'You don't scare us,' Paddy said. 'Now leave us alone to finish our pints and to grieve for our poor dead friend.'

Aiden looked at Paddy for quite a while before he spoke. He took his phone out of his pocket, selected a number and placed it on the table. He then smiled. This seemed to unnerve Paddy a little.

'Is that the best the police can do for a phone these days?' Paddy said trying to make light of the situation. 'I can help you out there if you like, I've got...'

Aiden interrupted Paddy's kind offer.

'If I don't get the answers to all the questions that I'm about to ask I'll be ringing that number. Now, I know for a fact that there's a batch of cows ready to head over the border and I know just where they are. You pair must think we're blind eejits not to notice the trucks coming and going but the truth is we just can't

52

be bothered with your penny-ante smuggling deals. But for you two I'm going to make an exception. If I ring that number, my men will confiscate all those cows and, unless you have clear proof of ownership which I know you don't, you'll never see them again. I've heard that the two of you have quite a bit of cash tied up in this totally illegal operation. So, what's it to be then lads?' Aiden asked with a wide and quite confident smile.

'Ah, you're just having us on,' Paddy said.

Mac noticed that Paddy hadn't denied Aiden's charge and there was definitely some doubt in his expression. The big man wasn't so good at hiding his emotions though and the two policemen could read the panic in his face all too clearly.

Aiden picked up his phone, looked unblinkingly into Paddy's face and said, 'Try me.'

Paddy blinked first.

'Ah now, Aiden lad. You don't have to threaten us. We're law-abiding businessmen and we always cooperate with the Gardai, you know that,' he said in a wheedling voice.

Aiden put the phone down and smiled.

'I just want the truth, plain and unvarnished. If I get anything else then I'll be making that call.'

Paddy looked uncomfortably up at 'Wee' Tim before he spoke. Tim nodded.

'We hadn't seen Jackie for a while when he called us around three weeks ago. He said that he had a business opportunity that we might be interested in.'

'By a 'business opportunity', I take it that you mean a scam,' Aiden said.

Paddy shrugged, 'Well, as it was Jackie talking, we took that as read. Let's just say that he's made us both quite a bit of money over the years and so we were willing to listen.'

'What was this business opportunity?'

'I've no idea,' Paddy said. 'He wouldn't tell us over the phone. He said that he'd need to meet up with us both in person and tell us then. That's why we're here tonight.'

'Is that right, Tim?' Aiden asked the big man.

Tim nodded, 'Jackie also said that it would make us a lot more than the cows and the diesel.'

'Oh, so you're into smuggling diesel as well lads?' Aiden said with a smile. 'Now that I didn't know.'

Paddy gave Tim a searing look before an emollient smile covered his face.

'Ah now, DS Maguire. That was just a slip of the tongue.'

'I'll bet it was. So, is there anything else you can tell me?' Aiden said as he meaningfully picked up his phone again.

'No, that's all we know. Jackie told us nothing at all about the deal. Honestly,' Paddy said trying to look honest and failing miserably.

Aiden looked at the two of them for a while before picking his phone up and getting to his feet.

'Okay, we'll leave you to your evening then,' Aiden said as he turned to go.

'And what about the cows?' Paddy asked with a hint of desperation.

Aiden gave it some thought.

'You've got twenty-four hours to move them on lads. It's just as well for you that I can't stand paperwork.'

They walked back out through the bar, still only inhabited by the old man and his dog, and Aiden waved goodbye to Mikey. Mac stopped halfway to the door and went back to the bar.

'Mikey, can you tell me what that bicycle wheel's all about?' he said pointing to the wall.

Mac had been curious about it since he'd laid eyes on it and he knew he'd only be thinking about it if he didn't ask.

'That's the front wheel from the bike that Shay Kelly rode in the Tour de France in the sixties. He was the first Irishman to wear the famous yellow jersey,' Mikey said proudly. 'He came from six doors down, you know.'

'Thanks,' Mac said as he walked away.

He felt better now he knew. It was as if he'd just scratched an itch.

'So, back to the hotel?' Aiden asked as he started the car up.

'Yes, please,' Mac said.

He glanced at his watch. It had just gone nine so he had plenty of time.

'So, do you think that we're any nearer to knowing what Jackie Connerty was up to?' Mac asked.

'No, not really, apart from the fact that he had a scam coming up. That alone could be useful information though. I'll ask around and see if anyone knows what Jackie's been up to over the last few weeks.'

'I'll ring my boss when I get back and see if they've found anything at their end,' Mac said.

'Ah well, it's early days yet,' Aiden said.

'So, you're really going to let them off so long as they move the cows?' Mac asked.

What Aiden had done just didn't seem right to Mac. However, he knew that this wasn't his territory and that he'd have to trust his colleague on this one.

'Of course.'

Aiden turned and gave Mac the first real smile since they'd met.

'Then again, I might have changed my mind if I actually knew where the cows were.'

Mac laughed.

'You were bluffing, weren't you?'

'Well, I knew that pair wouldn't open up without being threatened so I decided to take the chance. We did have reports of some truck movements a couple of days ago and, knowing their line of business I guessed that Paddy and Tim might be behind it. So, I thought it might be worth a go.'

Mac looked at his new colleague with some respect.

'Well, you fooled me too. Remind me never to play poker with you.'

'Shall I pick you up after the funeral tomorrow?' Aiden asked.

'Yes please. To be honest I could do with a quick get-away so, if you'd wait outside, I'd be really grateful.'

Another smile from Aiden.

'No problem. I've never driven a getaway car before so it will be a new experience for me. I'll meet you outside the church if you like and then drive you to the cemetery.'

'Thanks, that will be great. I'll ask my cousins if they can give me a lift to the church.'

Back at the hotel his cousins had arrived a little early and were waiting for him. He hadn't seen Fiona and Thomas for a few years so the next couple of hours flew by as they reminisced about the old days and caught up with what they were doing and other family news. Fiona was a doctor and worked at one of the big Dublin hospitals while Thomas had now been promoted to vice-principal at a large adult education college. They were both still happily married and both loved their spouses and children enough not to inflict the funeral on them.

Fiona then thanked Mac for the birthday card she had received the week before.

'Oh, it was nothing,' Mac replied.

Which was true as the card had actually been sent by his daughter Bridget. She'd taken over the family duty of ensuring that birthday cards got sent on time after her mother died. Mac had always been useless at remembering things like that.

'Oh, I had a lovely evening, loads of friends came around and, perhaps I shouldn't be telling a policeman, but we even had fireworks!' Fiona said with the face of a naughty child.

Seeing Mac's puzzled look Thomas chipped in.

'Ah now Fi, you're forgetting that fireworks aren't illegal in England like they are here.'

The penny dropped. Mac had forgotten all about Ireland's fireworks ban. Unlike in the UK, people couldn't buy fireworks over the counter in Ireland. So, they had to either use a professional company or buy them on the black market.

'I remember when Roisin was over here a few years ago around Halloween, she said that there was no lack of fireworks going off though,' Mac said. 'In fact, she said that she'd seen one of the best fireworks displays ever and that was in someone's back garden.'

'Well, it seems that the law might be a bit vague in some areas and I can't remember anyone ever being prosecuted for just letting off fireworks so people still do it. If they can get their hands on them that is,' Thomas replied.

Mac suddenly felt very tired. He apologised for being something of a 'damp squib' and headed off for bed. He set his alarm and lay down. He'd planned to do a recap of the case in his head while he waited for sleep to overtake him but, within a matter of seconds, he was unconscious.

He was dreaming about being chased by an old-fashioned police car that used to have a bell instead of a siren when he woke up. It was no police car though just the sound of his phone alarm.

He sat on the edge of the bed and remembered that this was the day of the funeral. He wasn't looking forward to it one little bit.

Chapter Six

Mac suddenly realised that he'd been so busy catching up with his cousins the night before that he'd forgotten to ring Dan Carter for an update on what was happening in England. He looked again at his phone. It was only seven fifteen so he decided to shower, shave and dress before making the call. It wasn't Dan who picked up the phone though but Martin Selby, the team's computer specialist.

'Hello, Mac. I'm afraid that I'm the only one around just now as the rest of the team are working out at the airport. How's the investigation going in Ireland?'

'Slowly, I'm afraid,' Mac replied.

'Probably not as slow as ours though. We've hit something of a problem.'

'What's that?'

'We can't find any evidence of the victim having ever lived or worked in the UK. We've also tried all the name variants around Jackie Connerty that we can think of but, so far, we haven't been able to make a match.'

'That's strange as everyone over here is convinced that he spent quite a lot of time in the UK,' Mac said.

'Well, we've only started looking and I've got a few ideas so we'll keep trying until we come up with something,' Martin said.

Mac wouldn't bet against him doing just that. Martin's 'ideas' had been instrumental in solving several cases that Mac had been involved with.

'Is there anything else that I should know?' Mac asked.

'Well, forensics have discovered that the killer wore latex gloves. There were traces of the powder they use

58

to ensure that the gloves don't stick together on Mr. Connerty's upper back, shoulder and both eyelids.'

Mac could see the murder in his mind's eye. One hand pushing down on the victim's back from behind while the other held the knife. Three quick strikes to the heart and then a hand on the shoulder to pull the body erect again. Finally, the murderer closing both eyes to make Jackie Connerty look like he was asleep. It was clever.

'However, the big news from forensics was around the weapon the killer used. It came as something of a surprise to say the least,' Martin said. 'The blade of the murder weapon was narrow and not very knife-like. In fact, it was sort of triangular in shape having three very short blades. Not only that but traces of ABS were found in all three wounds.'

'ABS?'

'Hang on, I'll get the report up,' Martin said. 'Yes, it's a type of plastic, the full name is 'Acrylonitrile Butadiene Styrene' apparently.'

'Plastic? I've heard of plastic knives but I've never come across one that was used in a murder before,' Mac said.

'Apparently, ABS is also used in some 3D printers,' Martin pointedly added.

'Would such a knife get through security?' Mac asked.

'Well, Dan asked the people who carry out the X-ray screening and they were fairly sure that they'd pick up anything that was shaped like a knife.'

'But this one wasn't though, was it?' Mac asked. 'Not only that but what if the blade was encased in some sort of plastic sheath to disguise its shape?'

'They weren't so sure about that when Dan asked them the same question,' Martin replied. 'The knife was more like a stiletto and would have been thin enough to have fitted into the handle of a large hairbrush for instance. They were quite doubtful about picking that one up.'

Doubtful? Mac thought. Impossible more like it considering the thousands of passengers who are screened every day.

'Thanks, Martin,' Mac said. 'Tell Dan that I'll ring him around five.'

'Will do,' Martin replied.

Mac gave this new evidence some thought. If the killer had gone to the all the trouble of printing a plastic knife then it was obviously a premeditated act. The actual murder itself had been very slickly carried out, indeed it showed a level of technical expertise and daring that Mac found worrying. What were they dealing with here? He immediately started wondering if it might be the type of case that might fall foul of the 'men in suits' as Mac used to call them. MI5, SIS or any other of the alphabet soup of intelligence agencies that existed but were only known by the few.

He sat on his bed thinking for a while until he realised that he had important business to attend to. Breakfast. He'd need something substantial inside him to keep him going through the funeral.

Fiona and Thomas were already seated and tucking into a Full Irish. Mac ordered one for himself. It was basically a Full English plus potato farls and white pudding. It was the white pudding that Mac had been looking forward to most. He couldn't always get it in Letchworth and so it was a rare treat for him.

The pudding was crisp on the outside and meltingly soft on the inside. Its unique peppery taste was incredibly satisfying. Mac promised himself that he'd take back as much as he could and freeze it so he could treat himself every now and again.

'So, when are you going back to Dublin?' Mac asked as they sipped at their tea.

'Straight after the funeral unfortunately,' Fiona said. 'Thomas has an evening class tonight that he has to get back for and I've got a surgery round that I'm supposed to be covering. I suppose that I could have swapped it but I'm ashamed to say that I was glad of an excuse for a quick getaway. I mean the funeral reception will hardly be a barrel of laughs if Declan's arranged it, will it? How about you?'

'I'll be staying in Ballydove for a while yet but, like you, I'll be making a quick getaway after the funeral. I've asked my Irish police colleague to pick me up outside the church so we can get on with our investigation as quickly as possible,' Mac replied. 'Would it be okay if I got a lift to the church with you?'

'Sure, no problem,' Thomas replied.

Declan was there to greet them when they arrived at the church. His face was even more mournful than usual. For some reason Mac found this annoying but then he chided himself. This was a funeral and Declan had, after all, just lost his mother.

The huge church was still more or less empty and echoing. Even so, there were quite a few more people present than there had been the day before. Mac didn't recognise any of them part from Mick and Maureen and his cousins. Of course, Declan had chosen to have a full mass and the longest funeral rites possible. When Mac had been young, he'd first gotten an appreciation of what eternity might be like while sitting through a similarly very long mass. The priest droned on and on in a flat voice for ages until he eventually got to the part where he had to say something about the deceased.

Mac listened closely and he thought that the priest's eulogy was brilliantly non-specific and could have applied to just about anyone. He turned to see Declan nodding his head sadly as the priest spoke. Another period of infinity followed before the rites were finally over and the coffin was wheeled out of the church.

Mac took a deep breath of fresh air when he got outside. He felt like he'd just come to the surface after being nearly drowned in the fusty boredom of the rites. He could see Aiden waiting for him on the other side of the street. He managed to have a quick chat with Mick and Maureen before saying his goodbyes to them. They weren't going to the cemetery and Mac envied them in that. He told Fiona and Thomas that he'd see them at the graveside and climbed into Aiden's car.

'How did it go?' Aiden asked.

'It went, eventually, thank God,' Mac replied as he looked at his watch. 'That's an hour and a half of my life that I'll never get back.'

'Well, it'll only be twenty minutes or so at the cemetery and then it'll all be over. By the way did you manage to ring England?'

Mac told him all about his phone call with Martin.

'Now that's really strange, about not finding any traces of Jackie in England I mean. Although the plastic knife is pretty unusual too,' Aiden said. 'After I dropped you off, I visited another pub and spoke to someone else who's known Jackie for some time. He told me something really interesting, something that might shed some light on why Jackie went to England for the first time some thirty years ago.'

'What's that?'

'Well, it's a long story. I'll tell you when we're on our way to see my father. I've already had a quick chat with him and it seems as if he might be able to tell us a little more about Jackie too.'

Mac would have to wait then. A few minutes later they were driving through the wrought iron gates of the cemetery. Aiden parked the car as close to the grave as he could but it still left Mac with an uncomfortable walk over the uneven grass surface. He took his time before joining Declan, the priest and the two other mourners who were with him. He'd found out that these were Declan's uncle and aunt on his father's side.

They must be in their mid-eighties by now, Mac thought, and they looked pleasant enough.

Mac said hello to all four and got warm smiles back from two of them. He could never remember meeting Declan's father but looking at his brother he wondered what he could have possibly seen in his Aunt Annie. They were soon joined by Fiona and Thomas and the rites finally got under way.

It was thankfully short and Mac breathed a sigh of relief as he walked away from the grave. Of course, Declan had asked everyone if they would have a 'cup of tea' with him. Mac had declined. He once again explained that he was on a police case and pointed to Aiden's car. Thankfully it was still there. He said his goodbyes to Fiona and Thomas and he promised that he'd come and see them in Dublin before too long.

As he walked away, he glanced back at Declan and felt somewhat guilty at leaving him so soon after the funeral. He shook the feeling off and reminded himself that he had a murder to investigate.

'Well, at least that's over with,' Mac said as he climbed into the car.

'I never was that keen on funerals myself,' Aiden said.

'Same here. Now a good wedding is a different thing altogether,' Mac said thinking back to the recent wedding of his colleagues Jo and Gerry which had been a marvellous occasion.

'Perhaps,' Aiden said.

Mac glanced over and saw that vein of sadness once again exposed. He wished he knew what was going on inside his colleague's head. It was becoming like an itch to him now.

They crossed over the old stone bridge and drove up the main street past the town's one and only department store. He always remembered his mother saying that the people who owned the store were some sort of relations of theirs. 'Not that they'd share their money with the likes of us,' she'd added with some bitterness. Mac had always wondered what lay behind his mother feeling that way.

'So, you had a story to tell me,' he asked.

'I'm not sure it'll shed any light on who killed Jackie but you might find it interesting,' Aiden replied. 'Now, Jackie had been a smuggler all his life and in that he followed in the footsteps of his father and grandfather. However, just over thirty years ago, he started smuggling something a little more dangerous than tea or sugar. He started off with replacement parts for pistols and rifles that a certain organisation was using in the North.'

Mac took it that the 'certain organisation' that Aiden was referring to was the IRA or one of its clones.

'Once he'd shown them that he could get away with it, he went on to smuggling guns, Semtex and even people. He didn't exactly do it out of love of the cause though. I was told that he got well paid for doing it.'

'How did you learn about this?' Mac asked.

'That man that I told you about is the ex-leader of that organisation for the area. He laughed out loud when I told him that Jackie Connerty was dead and he even bought me a pint so that I could celebrate with him. Apparently, he and Jackie fell out big time in the early eighties when he found out that Jackie's cross-border smuggling business wasn't confined to the Nationalist cause only.'

'You mean that he was smuggling for the Protestant paramilitaries too?' Mac asked with some surprise.

Aiden nodded.

'That's right. It wasn't guns though or anything like that though. It was tobacco and both he and the para-militaries were making a nice profit on the deal. Jackie swore blind that he hadn't known who he'd bought the tobacco from and he was convincing enough that he managed to keep his kneecaps. He was advised to leave Ireland for a while though and it was advice that he took seriously. He went to Luton originally and the organisation used him for small time stuff there, information mostly. He was forgiven a couple of years later when he made a 'substantial contribution' to the organisation and so he was allowed to come home.'

'How long was he living in Luton for?'

'About three years or so. After he made his peace, the organisation lost interest in him. They never trusted him with anything again though. A 'two-faced gobshite' the man I spoke to called him.'

Mac found this interesting indeed. So, Jackie's first stay in England was for quite some time and yet no trace of him could be found.

'What was he doing in England that enabled him to pay this 'organisation' off?' Mac asked.

'Unfortunately, he didn't know but he did give me the name of someone who might,' Aiden replied. 'There's a man called Jonjo Kerrigan who lives near Coolcholly. He and Jackie went to school together and I was told that he lived in Luton at around the same time that Jackie was there. I'm hoping that he'll be able to tell us something that might fill in a few of the gaps. We'll go and see him after we see my father.'

Aiden's father lived on a road to the north of the town. The single-track lane looked as if it was coming to a dead end when they turned a sharp corner. Around the corner there was a small group of houses. The houses stood on a ridge and looking to his left Mac got the most wonderful view of the town and the sea beyond. Aiden pulled in and parked in front of a small but well-maintained bungalow. It was surrounded by a garden containing shrubs and trees and scattered with brightly coloured flowers.

Aiden knocked on the door before opening it and Mac followed him inside. The house was spotless and, while the furnishings were old, they'd obviously been well looked after.

'He'll likely be in the back garden,' Aiden said.

They walked into the kitchen and through the back door into the garden. There were no showy plants here. The back garden had been sub-divided into several large raised beds where vegetables were being grown. Mac could identify the cabbages, lettuces and carrots easily enough but had some trouble with the rest of the growing greenery. A lean man in his early sixties, who had the same long face as Aiden, stood up and greeted them.

'A cup of tea?' Aiden's father asked.

Mac was more than ready for one. Aiden introduced Mac to his father and told him about the investigation while he made the tea. He gave them each a large mug and then sat down and looked thoughtful for a while.

'Now, Jackie Connerty himself I can't tell you much about as I only met him two or three times at most. However, I can tell you about his letters. It's all texts and emails now but when Jackie went to England after his spot of bother here, he used to send letters to Maggie every week or so. At the beginning anyway, I noticed that the letter writing dropped off somewhat after a few months.'

'Can you tell us anything about where the letters came from?' Aiden asked.

'Oh, of course. I was always a curious man I suppose and, while I obviously couldn't open anyone's mail, you could tell a lot just from the postmark and the envelope alone. If it was from a place that I hadn't heard of before then I used to look it up on the maps that we kept in the main post office. Jackie's letters were all postmarked 'Luton' for the first seven or eight years. I remember Maggie telling me that Jackie had

66

moved from somewhere called High Town to somewhere called Wig...er...'

'Wigmore?' Mac suggested.

'Yes, that's it, Wigmore. Does that mean anything to you?' Aiden's father asked.

'Yes, it does,' Mac replied. 'It probably means that Jackie came into some money as Wigmore's definitely a more expensive area to live in than High Town. Mr. Maguire, may I say that I'm really surprised that you can remember details like that after all this time.'

'Ah, please just call me Paddy. As for the oul memory, sometimes I can't remember what I did last week but, for some reason, when it comes to anything to do with the job, I seem to have no trouble remembering at all. Now, back to Jackie. He came home three years later but went back to Luton again a few months after that. He sent even fewer letters back this time and I remember Maggie stopping me more than once and asking if they could possibly have been mislaid. I told her that I'd look into it but, of course, they hadn't been mislaid. Jackie just hadn't sent her any. Then he'd come back for a bit and Maggie would be happy but it wouldn't be long before he was off again. Jackie had energy, I'll give him that.'

'How long would you say he spent in England compared to here?' Mac asked.

Paddy gave this some thought.

'I'd guess that he spent at least two thirds of his time in England and probably a lot more than that recently. I remember asking Maggie why she stood for it but it was clear that she was mad about him, although God knows why.'

'Can you remember what the postmarks were on the last letters he sent to Maggie?' Mac asked.

'Oh, that would have been some time ago. As I said letters have gone out of fashion these days and it's all email and texting. Now let me see...it must have been around ten years ago, I'd guess. Yes, that's right I remember because it was the same day as the Ballintra races and I was rushing to finish my round as I wanted to make sure that I got over there for the first race. As it turned out I needn't have bothered as my horse came in second last. Anyway, I was surprised as Jackie hadn't sent Maggie a letter for quite some time. I remember the envelope was good quality, embossed too with a sort of flower pattern. I felt that it was a bit strange coming from Jackie as it was more like something that a woman might use. As for the postmark...'

Paddy sat still and deep in thought for a least a minute or so. It seemed a very long minute to Mac.

'Ah yes, that's it,' Paddy eventually said with a smile. 'It was Stevenage.'

'So, he'd moved to Stevenage then?' Mac asked.

'He could have,' Paddy replied, 'but the postmark was put on at the main sorting office so it could have come from anywhere in the area.'

'Did Maggie mention anything else about where Jackie might have recently been living?'

'I'm sorry no. I think she was under the impression that Jackie was still living in Luton but, if so, then why would he be going all the way to Stevenage to post a letter?'

Why indeed? Mac thought.

'When was the last time that you saw Jackie yourself?'

'Oh, that must have been five or six years ago,' Paddy said. 'I met him as he was walking down Main Street and we had a wee chat.'

'Did he say anything about what he was doing in England?'

Paddy shook his head.

'I wish I could help you there but Jackie was a close one. He could talk until the cows came home but he'd never tell you anything that he didn't want you to know. Aiden tells me that you're going over to Coolcholly to see Jonjo Kerrigan. Is that right?'

'Yes, that's right,' Mac replied.

'Well, he might be able to help you more as he and Jackie went to school together and they were good friends when they were young. They both went to England together too but I heard that they had a falling out while they were over there. About what exactly, I don't know. Anyway, Jonjo came home and never said another word about Jackie after that, good or bad, and so I'll wish you luck with that one.'

Paddy said that he'd let Aiden know if he thought of anything else. As they were on their way out the door Paddy shouted to Aiden.

'Will you be wanting some supper tonight, son?'

Aiden looked a little embarrassed at this.

'I got a fair-sized salmon from Gerry Kildare this morning, far too much for just me. It would go grand with some spuds and carrots,' Paddy said hopefully.

'Well, I'm not sure...'

Mac felt suddenly mischievous and interrupted Aiden.

'You wouldn't have enough for three, would you?' he asked hopefully.

Paddy smiled widely.

'Of course, there'll be plenty to go around and it would be nice to have a guest for a change.'

Aiden gave his father a defeated look and said, 'Okay, we'll be back around eight.'

'Around eight will be just fine,' Paddy replied.

As they drove towards Coolcholly, Mac felt that he should apologise.

'I'm sorry if I was a bit forward in inviting myself for dinner but I haven't had any Donegal salmon for quite some time.'

While he did indeed love Donegal salmon, he had to admit that he was also hoping to learn a little more about his colleague.

Aiden gave Mac half a smile.

'No, it's okay. My father will love the company.'

Mac wondered if Aiden was a bit embarrassed about still living at home at his age. If that was the case then it only made him wonder more as to why he was there in the first place. He realised then that he had two cases on his hands, the murder of Jackie Connerty and the mystery that was Aiden Maguire.

He decided that he'd dearly love to solve them both.

Chapter Seven

It only took fifteen minutes to drive to Coolcholly. Aiden was silent for the whole trip and so Mac spent the time admiring the scenery and thinking. They eventually pulled up outside another small bungalow. It was quite similar to the one they'd just left except for the fact that it was badly in need of repair and the garden had gone totally wild.

'We'll just wait for a while,' Aiden said.

A minute or so later the front door opened and the stooping figure of a grey-haired old man came out. He was unshaven and his clothes were old and thread-bare. He used two canes to support himself as his back appeared to be permanently curved.

If this was Jonjo then he must have had a hard life, Mac thought. They were supposed to have gone to school together yet he looked at least twenty years older than Jackie Connerty.

The old man gestured at them to come in and then disappeared inside.

The inside of the house was no better than the outside. It was dark and fusty and smelled as if something had recently died somewhere. Jonjo pointed towards an old broken-down old sofa and gestured for them to sit down. Mac looked at where the springs had worked through the fabric and decided that he had more respect for his back.

'If it's okay Mr. Kerrigan, I'll stand. My back's a bit stiff anyway,' Mac said.

As it was 'a bit stiff' all the time, he technically wasn't lying.

'Ah, suit yourself,' Jonjo replied in a wheezy voice as he sat down in an armchair. 'You're here about Jackie then, I suppose?'

'We are,' Aiden replied as he perched himself on the very edge of the sofa trying to avoid the sharp end of the spring behind him. 'I take it that you've heard about his murder?'

'Oh, I have. Nothing travels fast around here except for news. Stabbed to death in an airport then, was he? I always thought that an airport was supposed to be one of the safest places you could find.'

'Yes, you'd think so, wouldn't you?' Aiden replied.

For some reason what Jonjo had just said started Mac thinking.

'When was the last time that you saw Jackie?' Aiden continued.

The old man looked up to the ceiling as he thought.

'That would be thirty-two years ago next March.'

'You knew Jackie well though when you were both young, didn't you?' Aiden asked. 'What was he doing in Luton when he first went over there?'

The old man smiled. It was not a happy smile.

'What was Jackie doing? He was doing what he always did, screwing as many people over as he could. We started work on the buildings at first, all off the books and cash in hand, of course. However, Jackie never was a fan of hard work and he soon had a couple of schemes on the go. Illegal betting, selling drink and cigarettes, all stolen of course, and anything else that would make him a few bob. Then he hit on something that made him money and it was more or less legal. Meat.'

'Meat?' Aiden asked.

'Yes, sausages, white pudding, corned beef and the like. In those days it was hard to get any Irish food in England. So, Jackie started up a little business importing meat from Ireland that he'd then sell on to local Irish butchers in Luton and North London. He charged quite a bit but people were willing to pay the extra for food from home.'

Mac knew exactly what he meant as he thought of his own periodic cravings for white pudding.

'You said that he had a business. Are you saying that Jackie started his own company up?' Aiden asked.

'Not at all, that wasn't Jackie's way. Just like the building work it was all cash in hand with no records kept. He thought that anyone who paid tax was an eejit.'

'Did you work with him in his business?'

'Ah no. We'd fallen out a month or two before that and anyway, after he was in the money, ordinary Irish hod carriers like myself seemed to be a bit beneath him,' Jonjo said with some bitterness.

'Why did you two fall out?' Aiden asked.

The old man said nothing for a while. Both Mac and Aiden stayed silent and waited.

'I want you to know that I have never said a word about this to anyone. I've wanted to many times but I have too much respect for Maggie. She's a good woman and life hasn't done her any favours in shackling her to a liar and a cheat. I dare say that you'll find out anyway now that he's dead and so I'll tell you. A couple of years or so after we went over, I met a girl called Deidre Kennedy. She was from Dublin and she was training to be a nurse. She was the most beautiful woman that I'd ever met. We were very much in love, or so I thought, but it appears that I'd only been fooling myself. The two of us met up with Jackie one evening and I could see that Jackie and Deidre got on very well. Too well as I found out a couple of weeks later when she broke it off.'

The old man paused and Mac could see tears in his eyes.

73

'She wouldn't tell me why at the time but a month or so later I saw her with Jackie. They were very much the loving couple too. She'd given me up for Jackie, a man who already had a wife. He was my best friend, or so I'd thought, but he turned out to be nothing but a liar and a traitor and may God roast the bastard in hell,' he said with some bitterness.

'What happened after that?' Aiden gently asked.

'Well, I was heartbroken and all for giving up and going home but I couldn't. My mother needed the money and so I had to stay on in Luton and work. I also had to suffer seeing the two of them together. I've often wondered if that was what really led to the accident,' Jonjo said.

'The accident?' Aiden asked.

'Yes, I wasn't born like this you know,' Jonjo said angrily. 'When I was young, I was fit and strong and a good worker but the accident changed all that. They were taking a load of bricks up to the top of the building, about four storeys up, and I was working on the first floor. For some reason the sling broke and I was right underneath it. I don't really remember too much about that day. They say that they shouted a warning to me but it was as if I couldn't hear. I guess that I must have been thinking about Deidre, she'd been on my mind a lot at the time. I was in hospital for three months, lots of broken bones and that, but it was my back that bore the brunt. The bones got better but the back never did. After that all I could do was go home. I've been good for nothing ever since.'

They managed to get a little more information on Deidre before they said their goodbyes. Jonjo didn't move or even acknowledge their existence when they went, he was still lost in the past somewhere. Outside they sat in the car in silence for a while.

'So, what do you think?' Aiden said.

'Well, it certainly tells us a little more about Jackie's character, doesn't it?' Mac replied. 'However, we've now got this meat exporting business we can look into and this Deidre Kennedy might provide us with a lead too. We know that she was a nurse training at Luton and Dunstable hospital, she was from Dublin and we've even got her birth date. If we can track her down then she might be able to tell us something. Then there was something that Jonjo said about airports.'

'What? About them being safe places, you mean?'

'Yes,' Mac said. 'We know that Jackie was murdered in a spot that had no CCTV and one that was often used by airport employees to say goodbye to relatives who were flying out. The thought occurred to me that a meeting might have been arranged there, either by Jackie or whoever killed him. If it was Jackie who had arranged it, did he do so because he thought he'd be safe in an airport? It just makes me wonder if he might have been scared of whoever he was meeting there.'

'Yes, that's an interesting thought alright,' Aiden said as he started the car up. 'I think that we should go and see Maggie Connerty again next. I'm hoping that she might be a little calmer and be able to tell us more about Jackie's business dealings and what else he's been up to in England all these years.'

Mac looked at his watch and was surprised to find that it had gone three-thirty.

'Are you hungry yet?' Aiden asked.

'No, I'm fine. I had a good breakfast this morning,' Mac replied.

In truth he didn't want anything to spoil his appetite for his dinner tonight. He was really looking forward to the salmon.

'Ah, okay. We'll carry on then. After we've seen Maggie there's a man over in Tonery who left a message at the station this morning. He said that he had some information about Jackie but he wouldn't say what it was. It might be something, might be nothing,' Aiden said.

'How far away is Tonery?' Mac asked.

'It's only about five kilometres from Ballydove, just ten minutes drive or so. If all goes to plan, we should have time for a debrief and a few quiet pints at the Bridge Bar on our way back if that's okay.'

Mac smiled as he said, 'Well, that sounds like a plan to me.'

It was clear that Maggie had a few people around as there was no space to park in front of the house. Aiden let Mac climb out and then drove down the road to where there was a sort of layby. He watched as Aiden walked back. From the grim look on his face, he could tell that he wasn't looking forward to interviewing Jackie's widow again.

Aiden knocked on the door and it was Maureen who opened it.

'Hello Aiden, hello Denny,' she said. 'I take it that you're here to talk to Maggie?'

'If she's up to it,' Aiden replied.

'Well, she's not great but I'll go and ask.'

Maureen disappeared and they were left kicking their heels for a few minutes.

Finally, the door opened and Maureen appeared again.

'She'll see you now but, for God's sake, go easy on her.'

'I'll do my best,' Aiden said as they were shown inside.

Besides Maureen three other women were making themselves busy around the house. A priest was seated on the sofa drinking a cup of tea. He nodded at Aiden and Mac as they went past. Maureen showed them into Maggie's bedroom where she lay white-faced on the bed. Her friend Theresa sat by her side. On seeing Aiden, Maggie's hand went out and was clasped tightly by her friend.

'Are you able to talk, Maggie?' Aiden asked gently.

After a pause she nodded and then looked up at Theresa.

'I'd like her to stay, if that's alright?'

'Of course, Maggie, that's no problem,' Aiden said.

They sat down on some chairs that had been moved in there from the dining room. Maggie had obviously been having quite a few visitors.

'We need to know everything we can about Jackie if we're to catch his murderer,' Aiden said. 'We know that he went to work in England some time ago and that he spent a lot of his time there. What can you tell me about that Maggie?'

'Well, when he first went over to England he was working in Luton. He started up a little business over there selling Irish meat products and it took off. Unfortunately, it meant that he had to spend a lot of time in England, too much for my liking, and even when he was back here, he used to travel a lot. He was looking for new suppliers he always said.'

'So, he was still living in Luton at the time of his death?'

'That's right. He had a small flat there in a place called Wigmore.'

She gave them the address and Aiden noted it down.

'Did you ever visit him at his flat?'

She shook her head.

'I asked more than once if I could go over and see what he got up to but for one reason or another the time was never right. I knew he was just making excuses so after a while I stopped asking.'

'Weren't you ever curious about what your husband was doing?' Aiden asked.

'Of course, but one day he told me that I was asking too many questions and if I asked even one more he'd go to England and never come back. I knew that he was up to something but I never asked again after that. I didn't want to lose him,' she said her lower lip trembling.

'Did he tell you anything at all about what he did in England?'

'He'd only ever talk about his meat business and, even then, he didn't say much,' Maggie replied. 'He used to talk to me a lot when he came back but I'm realising now that he never actually said anything.'

'Have you ever heard of someone called Deidre Kennedy?'

Maggie looked at Theresa and then shook her head.

'No, should I have?'

Aiden glanced over at Mac before he said, 'No, there's no reason that you should have. We'll leave it there for now Maggie but if you do think of something then give me a call.'

Maureen showed them out.

'Thanks for keeping it brief, Aiden. She's really not been well.'

'We may have to come back but I could see that she was getting tired,' Aiden replied.

'Will you not come over to see Mick one evening? He's been asking about you. I could do us all dinner,' Maureen asked hopefully.

'I'm...I'm sorry but I can't right now,' Aiden said.

He turned away without looking at her. Maureen sadly shook her head as she watched him walk off.

'I wish I knew what was up with that lad.'

'Me too. I'll see you later,' Mac said.

Aiden was in the car and waiting for him on the road by the time he got there.

'So, who is it that we're seeing at Tonery then?' Mac asked feeling that a change of subject was required.

'A Mr. Flaherty. I don't know much about him apart from the fact that he owns a pig farm.'

'Do you think he might know something about Jackie's meat business then?'

'It's possible. Anyway, we'll find out soon enough,' Aiden said.

After a short trip they pulled into the driveway of a large house. It looked brand new and had at least four bedrooms and a large conservatory on the side. Mac couldn't see any evidence of a farm. He pointed this out to Aiden.

'That's no surprise, let's say that pig farms have a certain aroma about them. You wouldn't want to be living too close to one.'

Aiden rang the bell and a cheerfully plump woman in her forties opened the door. She smiled and shouted to someone inside.

'Dougal, it's the police for you.'

She turned back and held the door open for them. Inside the house was every bit as new and spotless as the outside. They followed her towards the back of the house into a massive kitchen that had wall to wall cupboards and work surfaces of green marble. A man in a pair of brown overalls was standing at the end of a long table drinking from a pint-sized mug of tea. He came towards them and shook hands. Mac caught some of the 'aroma' from the man's overalls and his eyes watered for a moment.

'Mr. Flaherty, I'm DS Aiden Maguire. You called and said that you had some information about Jackie Connerty?'

'Oh yes. The minute I heard about Jackie dying like that I thought that I should tell the police what I know.'

'And that is?' Aiden prompted.

'Well, I've been in business with Jackie on and off for quite a while. We've not only got the pigs but a small meat processing plant too. Have you never heard of 'Dougal's Delicious Puddings' now?'

Aiden smiled, 'Yes, my father swears by them. He always looks out for them when he goes shopping.'

'Your father is a man of taste,' Donal said with a wide smile. 'Anyway, sales go up and down and sometimes I'd be left with puddings that I couldn't sell. When that happened, I'd always give Jackie a ring and sometimes he'd take those puddings off my hands. This was great for us, well, it would have been if Jackie had ever paid on time. Trying to get money out of him could be hard work. I stopped doing business with him because of that. That and the fact that Jackie wanted everything to be off the books. There were no invoices and he paid in cash, when he paid at all that is.'

'How long ago was that?' Aiden asked.

'Oh, it must be six, perhaps seven years ago now.'

'And is that what you wanted to tell me?'

'No, what I wanted to tell you about was something I saw at that factory unit of his that he has in Derry. I always thought that Jackie's business was booming to hear him talk about it but, the last time I made a delivery, it didn't look like that to me. I normally just left the deliveries in the loading bay but this time someone had left the door of the factory unlocked so I went in and had a quick look around. I'd never seen the inside before but, as it was supposed to be a meat processing plant, I was curious to see what equipment they were using. I thought that it would be busy but it wasn't. The only machines that I could see that were working were some automatic packaging units that were wrapping white puddings. It was really strange though.'

'What was?' Aiden prompted him again.

'I could see that the guys loading the puddings for wrapping had been cutting off the original packaging before loading them up,' Donal said.

Aiden thought about this for a while.

'So, Jackie Connerty's meat processing plant wasn't actually processing any meat, they were just rewrapping someone else's. Is that right?'

'Yes, not only that but, around the same time, I heard that a lot of the supermarkets in the area had run out of white puddings as someone had been making bulk purchases. I reckoned that there was some funny business going on but, as I wasn't sure exactly what, I kept it to myself. Once I heard that Jackie was dead, I thought you might be interested,' Donal said.

'Yes, we're interested alright, Mr. Flaherty, very interested. Can you give me the address of this factory?' Aiden asked.

He noted it down.

'Is there anything else you can tell us?' Aiden asked.

'No, that's it really,' Donal replied with a shrug of the shoulders.

'Thanks, you've been of great help,' Aiden said.

Mac was quiet as they drove back to Ballydove. He was thinking about what he'd learnt.

'Penny for them,' Aiden said.

'Oh, I'm sorry, I was miles away.'

'I could see that. So, what did you make of it?'

'I'm not sure if I'm honest,' Mac replied. 'I'd guess that the meat business was a front of some sort but what for? As Jackie was an unreformed smuggler then he might have been using the meat deliveries as a cover but what for? It would have to be something quite small and of high value so the obvious candidate would be drugs. As he didn't seem to be doing much business, I'd almost bet that there was some sort of VAT fraud involved as well.'

'You think that Jackie might have been peddling drugs and fiddling his taxes then?' Aiden said. 'So, fancy a trip to Derry tomorrow? When we get to the pub, I'll call my opposite number in the PSNI and arrange it. We've worked together on quite a few cross-border cases over the years.'

The Bridge Bar was old and it looked it. It hadn't been decorated for decades and yellowed posters giving the details for local events from several decades before and the various ways in which one could enjoy a pint of Guinness decorated the walls. The wood of the bar and tables was black with age having been darkened by years of spilt porter. The bench seats were old fashioned and now slightly shabby. The pub must have been half full yet the clientele talked softly as though they were afraid to break the peacefulness of the place. It had atmosphere to spare and Mac thought that it was perfect.

He and Aiden sat with a pint of black beer in front of them and discussed the case.

'So, I'll need to update my boss Dan Carter as to what we've found so far. He'll need to check out the flat in Wigmore, this Deidre Kennedy and Jackie's meat business, of course.'

'Fine, while you're doing that, I'll call DS Fin O'Kane and arrange for our trip to Derry tomorrow,' Aiden said.

They too didn't want to disturb the quietness of the pub so they both went outside to make their calls. Aiden finished his call first and went back inside.

Mac told Dan what they'd found.

'Well, you've got further than we have,' Dan said. 'We still haven't found any trace yet of Jackie Connerty in the UK which, from what you've told me, is puzzling.'

'So, Jackie's never appeared in the criminal justice system then?'

'It doesn't look like it. Martin has sent his fingerprints and DNA to the Garda headquarters in Dublin to see if they've got anything on him but we've not heard back from them as yet. As we seem to be getting exactly nowhere, I've arranged to go on one of the local TV news programmes tomorrow evening and see if anyone can identify Jackie from his photo. If he's been living in the area then someone must know him.'

'Good idea. That's well worth a try,' Mac said. 'Has Martin had any luck yet with Jackie Connerty's phone?'

'That's something else that's puzzling us. It wasn't the type of phone you'd expect someone like Jackie Connerty to own. It wasn't a smart phone. It was cheap and basic and only useful for calls and texts. It was also brand new. It had no stored numbers on it and he hadn't made a single call from it.'

'Was it a burner then, do you think?' Mac asked.

'It looks like it,' Dan replied. 'Anyway, thanks Mac. I'll pass on what you've told me about this Deidre Kennedy to Martin and see if he can come up with anything. We'll also check out the flat in Wigmore first thing in the morning.'

Mac stood there for a moment thinking. He'd already guessed that, for some reason, Jackie must have been using another name in the UK. However, Jackie hadn't changed his face so he thought it was highly likely that Dan would have some success with his TV appearance. He went back into the calm of the pub, sat down and took a sip from his glass.

He looked over at Aiden who sat unmoving. He appeared to be deep in thought. Mac was quite happy to sit there and bathe in the peace and quiet of the pub.

'So, anything new from England?' Aiden eventually asked.

'No, not really,' Mac replied. 'Jonjo Kerrigan said that Jackie was into some quite dodgy activities when he first went to England, and you said that he's still known to be something of a chancer, yet we can't find a match for either his fingerprints or his DNA in our records. We've sent them to Dublin to see if they can do any better.'

'If they do have anything on him, I doubt that it will be for anything recent. We've suspected him of being involved in quite a few illegal dealings in the area but we've never been able to pin anything on him. He's a chancer alright but he's a clever one.'

'So, how long will it take us to get to Derry tomorrow?' Mac asked.

He was thinking of his back which was now feeling more than a bit tender. A long car ride certainly wouldn't improve it any.

'About an hour and a half depending on traffic. I've arranged to meet DS O'Kane at ten thirty so would it be okay if I picked you up at eight thirty or so at your hotel?'

'That's fine, I'll be waiting outside for you,' Mac said with some relief. A drive of an hour and a half shouldn't be too bad. 'Anyway, they're going to do a local TV appeal tomorrow evening in the hope that someone might be able to identify Jackie. So, we can only hope. Another pint?'

Aiden didn't say no. Mac decided to try and keep the conversation light and asked Aiden what had been going on in the area since Mac had been there last. The time passed comfortably enough until Aiden said that it was time to go. Mac looked at his watch. It was only seven twenty.

'The father always gets the dinner ready early so I told him that we'd be there at eight knowing that he'd have it ready by seven-thirty,' Aiden explained.

That was more than okay with Mac. He was hungry and ready for his salmon.

He was not to be disappointed. The potatoes were waxy and wonderful and smothered in butter, the carrots and broccoli were perfectly cooked being both crunchy and full of flavour but the salmon, oh the salmon was beyond compare! It had been oven baked and then covered with some sort of tangy citrus sauce. Mac had had much worse meals in expensive restaurants.

They ate silently and Mac noticed that Aiden, who must be used to his father's cooking, was enjoying it just as much as he was.

'A cup of tea?' Paddy asked as he cleared away the plates.

'Oh, yes please,' Mac replied. 'That was truly wonderful. How on earth did you learn to cook like that?'

Paddy turned and smiled broadly at Mac.

'Ah, it was just something to do I suppose,' he said before going back to make the tea.

As before he made three big mugs and ferried them to the table.

'When Aiden's mother, Agnes, was alive she was a good cook and so I got used to eating well,' Paddy said as he sat down. 'I used to do a lot of walking in those days and a good dinner at the end of the day was something to really look forward to. When she passed on, I had to get used to doing a lot of things I'd never done before and cooking was one of them. Aiden was only fifteen at the time and studying hard so he could get good grades and go to university. After a few months we both got heartily sick of my cooking...'

'You can say that again,' Aiden said with a smile.

This made Paddy smile too.

'Anyway, we tried some of those convenience meals you can get in the supermarket and we found that they were even worse. So, in desperation, I started asking some of the people I met on my rounds for recipes and cooking tips and they were more than generous. But there was this one chap called Andy MacMahon, who lives up near Ballymacgroarty, and he was a great help. He's retired now but he used to be the head chef in one of those big hotels in Belfast. He was the one who taught me how to cook. I used to get up early to do my round so I'd have half an hour or so for a quick lesson at his house. I still go around there once a week and we have a pint and chat about cooking. Yes, people can be very generous when you've lost someone.'

Mac thought back to when he'd lost his Nora and how generous people had been to him ever since and said that he could only agree.

'Yes, Aiden told me that you lost your wife not long ago. I lost mine nearly fifteen years ago now but sometimes it only seems like yesterday. Tell me, how did your wife go?' Paddy asked.

'Cancer, it was very quick though, too quick for me. And yours?'

Paddy shook his head mournfully.

'It was quick for Agnes too. Where we lived there were only two buses a day and yet she somehow managed to land under one of them.'

Mac glanced over at Aiden. His shoulders were slumped and he was looking down into his mug of tea. His mother's death was obviously still a painful subject for him.

'Now, Agnes was a very religious woman and she used to pray a lot,' Paddy said. 'I often used to see her crossing the road with her beads out while saying the rosary, so it's probably a wonder that she never got run over long before that.'

Mac was still looking at Aiden as Paddy said this. His head jerked up and he gave his father a look that Mac couldn't quite define. Was it angry, sad or hopeless? Mac decided that it might well be all three.

Aiden turned and, noticing Mac looking at him, he quickly turned back to staring into his teacup.

Mac could only think that, for some reason, his new colleague was a deeply troubled soul. Despite some misgivings he found that he still wanted to know why.

Chapter Eight

Mac looked at his phone. It wasn't even six o'clock yet but, as he was wide awake, he sat up and then tested his back. If it was going to be a bad pain day then he'd usually know within the first few seconds after standing up. However, while it felt sore and stiff, he reckoned that he'd be able to make it through another day and that was the important thing.

He thought about what had happened the evening before as he showered. After dinner only a few words had been exchanged as Aiden drove him back to the hotel. Since Mac's pain issues had become life-changing he'd also begun to notice other people who were in pain. Aiden was one of them although, for him, the pain didn't appear to be physical. However, Mac knew from experience that this could be the worst pain of all. Losing his wife had hurt him more than any physical pain could ever do.

He was drying himself off as he played back in his mind the conversation that had taken place after dinner. Aiden had seemed to be in most pain just after Aiden's father had mentioned his mother and how she had died. Was it just a son missing his mother or was there something else? Mac would dearly love to know. Anyway, he'd have his new colleague all to himself for at least three hours as they drove to and from Derry.

Mac had been to Derry once before but he only had vague memories of his visit as he'd only been six or seven at the time. He'd been there with his father and mother but, try as he might, he couldn't remember the reason for their visit. He didn't remember much about the place apart from the fact that it was one of the few times that he'd seen his father looking really scared.

They'd been approached by a group of rough looking men in uniform carrying long truncheons who had started shouting at his father. He found out later that these men were from the much feared 'B Specials'. Much feared if you were a Catholic that is.

He took his time getting dressed but he was still the first one in the breakfast room. He ordered a Full Irish and took his time eating it. He also had two cups of coffee before he finally rose from the table. It was still only seven thirty. As it looked like it was going to be a fine morning Mac went outside and sat on a bench while he had a think.

He went through all the facts of the case as they stood and found himself once again speculating about the murder itself. He decided that the most unusual aspect of the case was where the murder took place. Why was Jackie killed in an airport? With all the security surrounding an airport, and especially the departure lounge, why would any murderer pick such a spot? Mac could only think that, for some reason, Jackie's killer had no choice. Perhaps it was his last chance to get to Jackie before he left the country.

All his thoughts ended up at the inevitable brick wall. He didn't have enough evidence yet to reach even a tentative conclusion and he sincerely hoped that they might find something at Jackie's meat processing factory. He was thinking this when Aiden pulled up right in front of him. Mac looked at his watch. It was only eight fifteen.

'You're early,' Mac said as he climbed in the car.

'So are you,' Aiden replied with a half-smile.

'So, what's the drive going to be like?'

He asked this in the hope that it wouldn't involve any rough country roads. At the moment his pain was bearable but he knew it wouldn't take too much to make it worse.

'Oh, it's easy driving all the way,' Aiden replied. 'It's just straight up the N15 until we get to Strabane where you'll be once again back in the UK. You'll notice the difference when we cross over the Lifford Bridge as the road signs are in kilometres on one side and miles on the other. Once we're over the bridge it's only fifteen kilometres or so to Derry.'

'It must be strange living so close to such a long border.'

Aiden shook his head as he said, 'It's totally crazy. I drove down the Inisclin Road towards a place called Whitehill a few weeks back and, in one stretch that I'd guess might be only five kilometres long, I must have crossed the border at least five or six times. Even I was finding the change in road signs confusing so God knows what the tourists make of it all.'

'There's a lot of talk in the UK at the moment about Brexit and how leaving the EU might affect the Irish border. They're saying that they might have to bring border controls back,' Mac said.

'Well, I wish them luck with that,' Aiden said with a touch of anger in his voice. 'During the troubles they had tens of thousands of British soldiers trying to stop the IRA smuggling weapons and people over the border and they didn't have much luck then, so I doubt that a few border posts now will make any difference now. Ballydove, and many towns like it near the border, are bandjaxed anyway and a hard border could kill them off altogether. It's only the likes of Jackie and his pals who will be happy if that happens. Yes, the smugglers will love it alright.'

Mac thought about what Aiden had said. The on-going argument around Brexit had seemed some-what academic to him from his armchair in Letchworth but here he could see that it was of vital importance to the daily life of the people who lived near the border. He knew that it had taken years and years of sweat and tears to bring the area to some sort of peace and he wondered if endangering that for the sake of a few political slogans would be worth it.

The road was hardly a motorway, consisting of just two lanes, but it was wide and looked like it had been newly surfaced. Easy driving indeed. They passed a sign with an arrow pointing to the left for Rossnowlagh and the memories once again came back. Endless summer days, the sea and one of finest beaches Mac had ever seen. A day out at Rossnowlagh had been a real occasion for him and his sisters when they'd been young. He made a mental note to pay it a visit before he went home.

They passed a brown sign which told them they were now near somewhere called Ballintra.

'If you're still around next week you must go,' Aiden said as he nodded towards the sign. 'The Ballintra Races are always a good day out.'

Although Mac had heard of them, he'd never been to the races before. In fact, he hadn't been to a horse race for ages.

'I'd love to, if I'm still here that is.'

'Now, it's not a fancy racecourse or anything, nothing like Galway for instance. It's just a field that they use for a couple of days of racing but I've always enjoyed it,' Aiden said. 'Everyone in the area goes, in fact you meet just about everyone you've ever known there.'

'Will Mick and Maureen be going do you think?' Mac asked.

Aiden was quiet for a moment.

'I'd guess,' he said hesitantly. 'I saw them there last year when I was back for the weekend. Caitlin was there too...'

Aiden tailed off and appeared to be thinking. His thoughts didn't appear to be pleasant.

'I heard that you and Caitlin were friends at one time,' Mac said hoping to learn a little more.

'Yes, we knew each other at school.'

'No, I meant in Dublin.'

'Yes, well I...I'd sooner not talk about it if that's okay,' Aiden said as he kept his eyes firmly on the road ahead.

Mac could feel the tension emanating from Aiden. An uncomfortable silence lasting several minutes followed.

'I'm sorry if I was bit abrupt just then,' Aiden said.

'No, that's okay. I get the feeling that you're trying to work your way through something. If you ever want to talk about it, let me know.'

'Thanks, Mac,' Aiden said.

A more comfortable silence followed and Mac was happy to just sit back and take in the scenery. Before long they'd left Laghy and Donegal Town behind them. He caught a glimpse of a lake to his left and asked Aiden what it was.

'That's Lough Eske but you'll get a better view of a lake when we go by Lough Mourne. Lakes are one thing we're not short of in this part of the world. Here you can always count on the rain.'

As Aiden said this Mac noticed some blue-grey hills in the distance. The dark clouds above them looked ominous. As they got closer, he could see that the road went through a notch in the hills and that's when the first fat raindrop fell on the windscreen. A few seconds later Aiden had to put the wipers on their highest speed and slow down as the rainfall became more intense. Fifteen minutes later and they had left the clouds behind and were back once again into the sunshine.

The rain reminded Mac of Granny Mulreany, who was his mother's mother. She had a perfectly good house but she preferred to sit outside come rain or shine. It would take a cloudburst just like the one they'd driven through to drive her indoors. She'd sit and knit or shell peas or peel potatoes for the evening dinner. People who walked or drove by almost always stopped for a chat.

She'd visited Birmingham just the once but she soon declared that she didn't like it. She said that 'she couldn't see the weather coming' and, even though he was young at the time, Mac knew exactly what she meant. The view from where she sat was stunning, looking out over green fields to the blue-grey sea beyond.

'See, that's where the weather comes from,' she'd once told Mac as she pointed towards the sea. 'It's nice out now but believe me that can all change in an hour or two. Yes, the weather can be spiteful at times so it's always good to know what it's going to get up to.'

Mac looked to his right and saw Lough Mourne. It ran beside the road for some distance until eventually the road veered away and the lake was left behind. The scenery was spectacular and Mac wondered why he hadn't come back more often. He realised with some surprise that he'd only brought Nora back to Donegal twice, once after they were married and then again to show their new baby daughter off to their respective relatives. They always said that they'd have a long holiday there when they had the time. Unfortunately, time had run out on them.

They were suddenly in a town and driving down a street full of low houses built in the Irish style. Most were of two stories with the odd bungalow appearing now and again. The houses were squat as if they were hunkered down and waiting for some great storm to come. Mac knew this to be true enough. As his Granny had said, the weather did indeed come from the West, straight from the wild Atlantic. He'd only travelled to Donegal in the winter a couple of times and the storms that he had witnessed had been truly spectacular. He remembered one day when he'd sat at his Granny's window watching the rain squalls fly past horizontally carried by the strongest winds he'd ever seen.

'See that wind,' his Granny had said, 'it's so strong because it's had a good run up in getting here. That wind has come all the way from New York.'

Mac had stared in wonder at the gusting movements of the tree branches. Air all the way from New York! He'd only ever seen the city at the cinema and he had the impression that all its inhabitants could either sing and dance or were gangsters or indeed both. His thoughts were interrupted by Aiden.

'We're in Ballybofey now, so only about another fifty kilometres to go to Derry.'

'Where are we meeting DS O'Kane?' Mac asked.

'At Jackie's factory. It's on an industrial estate in a place called Pennyburn just to the north of the city.'

At that moment Mac's phone went off.

All Aiden could hear was Mac saying 'yes' a few times followed by, 'Thanks, Andy. Tell Dan that I'll update him after we visit the factory.'

'That was one of my colleagues, DI Andy Reid,' Mac expained. 'They've just checked out Jackie's address in Wigmore. It turns out that it's a newspaper shop that also doubles as an accommodation address. The owner recognised Jackie straight away as he'd been picking his mail up there for well over twenty years. They gave Andy an email address that they used to notify Jackie of any mail and our computer specialist is having a look at it now.'

'So, possibly another dead end then,' Aiden said. 'That Jackie sure was a slippery one.'

Mac could only agree and wonder what it was that Jackie was hiding. Hopefully, they'd find some clues at the factory.

A little later Aiden turned to Mac and said, 'We're nearly at the border.'

They came to a traffic island and turned right. Within a few yards they were on a bridge crossing over a wide river.

'That's the River Foyle. Here the border runs right down the centre of the river,' Aiden explained as they crossed over to the other side. 'So, you're now back in the United Kingdom.'

Mac looked out of the window with some curiosity. All he noticed at first was that all the road signs looked familiar and that they were in miles and not kilometres. They passed by a garage that had a board outside advertising that it had bottles of milk to sell. It gave the price in both pounds and euros.

Aiden must have noticed him looking at the board as he said, 'It's all dual currency around here and you can even use Euros in some of the big stores in Derry. I wouldn't vouch for what exchange rate you'd get though.'

As they bypassed much of Strabane, Mac still thought it was all very strange. The sky was just as big, the fields were just as green and the houses were just the same. If it wasn't for the road signs, he'd never have known that he'd just crossed over a border from one country into another.

'If some of the eejits in the UK have their way and we get a hard border, you'll be queueing for hours at that bridge,' Aiden said.

The whole border issue seemed to straight out of Alice in Wonderland. It worked well at the moment as the border was almost invisible but, with a hard border, he could easily imagine the problems it would cause. Yet, whatever any government tried to do, such a long and porous border could never be truly managed. Aiden was right, Mac thought, the smugglers would have a field day.

He saw a sign saying 'Londonderry 14' go past and he remembered that it was miles now.

'What's the thing about Derry's name?' Mac asked. 'In our family we've always called it Derry yet the road sign back there said Londonderry?'

'Well, it was originally called Derry until the city was destroyed by Cahir O'Doherty in the seventeenth century after the English Governor had insulted him by slapping his face in public. Then the city was handed over to the London Guilds who rebuilt it and then renamed it Londonderry which a lot of the locals took to be something of an insult. A lot of them still think the same about it today. I honestly think that Derry, and the whole country come to that, would be a lot better off if we could forget the past and just concentrate on the future for a change.'

Mac could only agree. The Troubles in the North had been something of a backdrop to his life. While his sympathies lay more with the Catholic side of the argument, he'd realised long ago that a spot of amnesia on both sides might not be a bad thing. No matter how much you might talk or get angry about it, you can never change the past.

It was a pretty drive into Derry with the wide River Foyle on one side and a massed rank of trees on the other. They passed by an old Irish cottage painted red and then they were in the city itself. They turned left onto a long bridge and crossed over the River Foyle again. The river here was much wider and seemed more like a lake than a river. Mac could see a high church spire and the city buildings lining the riverbank on the other side.

'What's Derry like these days?' Mac asked thinking about the last time he'd been there.

'Oh, it's fine. They get quite a lot of tourists now and there's some really nice pubs. It has a fairly low crime rate too, at least compared to the rest of the UK.'

This surprised Mac and he said so.

They turned right and drove alongside the river again before turning away and into the city. After passing by some neat, and very Irish looking, terraced houses they drove into the industrial area. Here Mac had no sense of being somewhere different as the streets were lined with generic warehouse units and workshops. They could have been in any UK town. They drove until they came to a dead end and pulled up outside a small factory unit with a sign saying 'JayCon Derry Meats – Meat Processors'. Outside the factory a man was sitting on the bonnet of a car.

'That's Fin,' Aiden said.

They climbed out of the car and joined him.

'How's it going, Aiden?' Fin said with a wide smile as they exchanged a firm handshake.

'Ah, not so bad,' Aiden replied returning the smile.

Looking at the two of them together was like looking at the positive and negative of a photograph, Mac thought. They were both roughly the same height and build but where Aiden's face was long Fin's was round, Aiden's hair was black while Fin's was fair and, while Aiden tended to be serious and even downright miserable at times, Fin appeared to be somewhat lighter with a smile being his default expression. Whatever their physical differences, however, Mac could see that they genuinely liked each other.

'This is Mac Maguire who's representing the UK Police on the Jackie Connerty case,' Aiden said by way of introduction.

'Pleased to meet you, DCS Maguire,' Fin said with some deference as they shook hands.

'I'm afraid that I'm just plain Mr. Maguire these days but please call me Mac.'

'Okay Mac,' Fin said as he turned back to face the two of them. 'The factory is all locked up at the moment but I've been asking around and it seems that the key holder is a man called Gerry Morrison who runs a mower repair business just around the corner. I've been to see him and he said that he'd be with us in a couple of minutes or so.'

Aiden turned and looked at the factory unit.

'I must admit that I thought it would be bigger. Not only that but it's Thursday morning and it's all locked up so it's obviously not operating as most businesses would.'

A small van drove up. Mac assumed that it was Gerry Morrison as a sign on the van said, 'Gerry's Marvellous Mowers – Repairs and New'. A man in his fifties got out. Grizzled grey hair stuck out from the sides of an old flat cap of indeterminate colour. He wore a pair of stained overalls that smelled strongly of machine oil. Fin introduced himself and showed Gerry his warrant card before introducing Aiden and Mac. He offered his hand in turn to all three of them.

'Pleased to meet you,' he said. 'I take it that you want to have a look inside?'

'If possible,' Fin replied.

'Well, I'm not sure that I can,' Gerry said as he stroked the stubble on his chin. 'Jackie, the owner, told me not to be letting anyone inside and he was quite firm on the point. You haven't got a warrant, I suppose?'

'Ah, come on Gerry, we just want to have a quick look,' Fin said in a cajoling manner. 'Anyway, I doubt that Jackie's going to mind.'

'What do you mean?' Gerry asked.

Mac got out his tablet and showed Gerry a picture of Jackie Connerty.

'Is that Jackie?' Fin asked.

'Yes, that's him alright. What's he been up to?'

'That's what we'd like to know.'

'Well, why don't you go and ask him then?' Gerry said.

'Well, I would except for the fact that he's now in a fridge in a morgue in England with a tag on his toe.'

'He's dead?' Gerry asked with a slightly puzzled expression.

'Well, him being where he is, I'd hope so. But as he was stabbed in the back three times he's probably in the right place,' Fin said.

Mac watched Gerry's reaction carefully. He seemed surprised perhaps but not shocked. He didn't say anything as he got a bunch of keys from his pocket and went over to the factory. He unlocked the small side door and they all followed him inside.

The factory was somewhat bigger and emptier inside than Mac was expecting. The few pieces of machinery in evidence didn't take up that much of the space. Mac also noticed that there was no office.

'So, what'll happen to this place?' Gerry asked. 'Will I keep getting paid?'

'Paid for what?' Fin asked.

'Well, Jackie gives me a few bob for looking after the place for him and, when he gets an order, me and a few friends help him out with some packing work. He paid well.'

'In cash too, I'll bet,' Fin said as Gerry nodded in confirmation. 'So, how often did you get these orders?'

'It varied,' Gerry replied with a shrug, 'but I'd guess on average we'd get around two a month or so.'

'Business wasn't exactly booming then, was it?' Fin observed. 'When did the last order go out?'

'It was the day before yesterday, around mid-day. Normally Jackie would turn up a couple of hours before it was due to go but, when he didn't, we just got the order ready as usual anyway.'

So, it looked as if Jackie was on his way here first then, Mac thought.

'I can't see an office in here. Where did Jackie do his paperwork?' Mac asked.

'Paperwork? Well, I never saw any of it here so I'd guess that it was all done in England. He'd always email over the invoice the day before to Alex so we'd know exactly what quantity we had to wrap.'

'Who's Alex?' Fin asked.

'Alex Ganson, he's...well, I'm not exactly sure what he is actually. Anyway, he's the one who Jackie always contacts first and then Alex lets me know what's needed and when,' Gerry replied.

'This Alex Ganson, he wouldn't be a big guy, shaven head with a tattoo of a red hand on the right side of his neck and the words 'No Surrender' spelt out on the back of his hands by any chance?' Fin asked.

'Oh aye, that's Alex alright,' Gerry replied.

Mac noticed that Fin looked quite puzzled for some reason.

'So, what happens after Alex lets you know what's needed?' Fin asked.

'Well, I let my friends Ken and John know and then I open up the factory. The white pudding usually arrives the day before and we put it in the cold store over there,' Gerry said pointing to a large metal door. 'The puddings come already wrapped, most times they're from one or other of the big supermarket brands, and we unwrap them and then put them in these.'

He held up a long ribbon of white plastic that had the words 'Mother MacMorragh's Authentic Irish White Pudding' and the picture of a smiling old woman wrapped up in a shawl.

Gerry shrugged, 'I know it looks fishy and I guess that Jackie had some sort of scam going on here but...'

'He paid well and in cash so you thought it best to keep your gob shut,' Fin completed the sentence for him.

Gerry shrugged again.

'So, what happened next?' Fin prompted.

'Well, Alex would tell us the amount that Jackie wanted packing and then we'd do the exact amount as ordered. This was usually around a hundred to a hundred and twenty boxes per order and we always packed fifty puddings in each box. We never wrapped everything that was delivered though. We did that by mistake once and Alex went totally crazy.'

'Why was that?' Fin asked.

Gerry shrugged again as he said, 'I've no idea but take the last delivery that went out. A hundred and twenty boxes of puddings came in but we didn't wrap all of those. We left six boxes in the cold store untouched exactly as Alex had instructed us to. So, once we'd finished rewrapping the other hundred and fourteen boxes in the branded packaging, we put them all back in the cold store and locked up. That would be it as far as we were concerned.'

'You never saw what happened to the puddings after that?'

'Well, I only work around the corner and you have to drive by my workshop to get here. So, being a bit curious, I always kept an eye out for the comings and goings. An hour or two after we'd finished packing an order, I'd always see Alex and Cally drive by. I often wondered what they got up to in here, so once I walked up and had a listen…'

'You never put your head inside for a look?' Fin asked.

'No never, there's no way that I'd chance being seen. That Alex has a bit of a reputation and a short fuse to go with it. I valued my good looks more than that,' Gerry said with a smile that showed off his crooked teeth. 'Anyway, I could tell a lot just by listening. I could hear that they had one of the machines working, not one of the machines that we always used but a special one. That one over there,' Gerry said as he walked towards the back of the factory.

He waved towards a smaller version of the other machines. It looked very clean.

'So, what's the difference between this machine and the others?' Fin asked.

'Well, the others are set up just to wrap the puddings but with this one you have to put the white pudding mix into this hopper here and then it shapes it and packs it as well.'

The three policemen looked meaningfully at each other.

'Did you ever see who came to pick up the boxes of white puddings?' Fin asked.

'Oh yes. Well, I saw the lorry anyway. I never got a good look at the driver though. It was usually quite a small lorry, a refrigerated one it was too,' Gerry replied.

'Did it have any markings on it?'

'No, but I can tell you that it was white,' Gerry said in the hope that this might help. Seeing the exasperated look on Fin's face he quickly continued. 'Oh, and it wasn't local either, it always had a UK number plate.'

'And I take it that you know the number?' Fin asked with some expectation.

'Ah now, I'm not all that good at remembering numbers and things but I do remember that it started with an 'L'. Now that should be some help to you,' Gerry said hopefully.

Fin and Aiden looked at Mac.

'That means that it was registered in London. So, we're looking for a white lorry from London then,' Mac said.

'Great,' Aiden said under his breath.

'So, how often did you see Jackie then?' Fin asked.

'I only ever saw him on the day that the lorry came to pick up the delivery. After it had gone, Jackie used to come by my workshop, pay me and he'd also leave the lads' money with me too. Which reminds me that we still haven't had any money yet for the last lot we did,' Gerry replied with some feeling. 'Anyway, that's honestly all I know. Jackie and Alex only ever told us what we needed to know to get our bit of the job done.'

'Thanks Gerry, you can get back to your lawn-mowers then,' Fin said, 'but drop by the station tomorrow to make a statement and bring your two pals with you.'

Gerry nodded and had turned his back to go when Fin continued.

'Oh, and leave the keys here. Don't worry we'll lock up when we're finished.'

Gerry returned and handed the bunch of keys to Fin.

'Well, I suppose you might as well have them. Jackie Connolly won't be needing them where he is, that's for sure.'

Chapter Nine

The three policemen looked at each other in surprise.

'Jackie Connolly? Is that the name that you knew him by?' Fin asked.

'Of course, and why not? It was his name after all,' Gerry said. 'I remember him once telling me something about his real first name being John but that everyone had called him Jackie since he'd been a child.'

Fin thanked Gerry who touched the peak of his cap by way of goodbye and scuttled away as quickly as he could.

'I'll need to ring England,' Mac said.

He managed to reach Dan and told him why they probably hadn't found anything on Jackie Connerty. Dan said that he'd get Martin looking for anything on a John or Jackie Connolly straight away.

'Who's this Alex Ganson?' Aiden asked as Mac put his phone away.

'He's an ex-UVF thug, a Protestant and Unionist who was so patriotic that he went straight into drug dealing and protection rackets once peace had been declared,' Fin replied.

'UVF?' Mac asked.

'It stands for the 'Ulster Volunteer Force',' Fin explained. 'I suppose they're the opposite numbers of the IRA Provisionals. They were responsible for a fair few bombings and murders during the Troubles. Alex's dad, Sandy Ganson, was a celebrated thug who was rumoured to be directly responsible for at least five murders, mostly unarmed Catholics who were kidnapped after being picked out at random. He's a nasty piece of work is Alex and, from what you've told me about this Jackie, I'm quite surprised to hear that they were working together.'

'And who's Cally?' Mac asked.

'His full name is Alistair MacAllister, believe it or not, but everyone calls him Cally,' Fin said. 'He's a petty criminal, we've done him for burglary, shoplifting, credit card scams and the like in the past. I've arrested him twice myself. Then he got into drugs a while back and got caught dealing. He did a year inside for that. After he came out, I heard that he'd hooked up with Alex Ganson after which he seems to have fallen off our radar. That was a couple of years or so ago, I'd guess.'

Fin took the keys and went over to the door of the cold store. He opened the door and looked inside.

'Empty,' he said as he shut the door again.

Mac walked over to the smaller machine. He stood and stared at it. Aiden went over and joined him.

'So, what do you think Jackie was up to?'

'Drugs would be my best guess,' Mac replied. 'From what Gerry told us it's possible that they were putting whatever it was they were smuggling straight into the white pudding mix itself. They'd probably mark the boxes so they could separate them out when the load was delivered in the UK. I presume whoever they were smuggling the drugs for had some sort of process for separating the drugs from the white pudding at the other end. If that's the case then it's really clever. You could cut one open and you wouldn't see anything even if you were lucky enough to pick one of the boxes that had the drugs in the first place. Six out of one hundred and fourteen. So, what's that then, a one in nineteen chance?'

'What about sniffer dogs?' Aiden suggested. 'Wouldn't they be able to detect the drugs?'

'Well, there's a lot of meat there, isn't there? Anyway, we don't have all that many and I'd guess that most of them are deployed at airports right now,' Mac replied.

He turned to face Fin.

'Can you get a forensics team in here?' Mac asked. 'I think it might be a good idea to get them to do a detailed examination of this machine. It looks like it's been well cleaned but there's bound be some traces of whatever it is that they've been putting in the white puddings.'

'Sure, no problem,' Fin replied as he got his phone out. 'I'll get some uniformed police over here too. Once they're here, I think that we should go and pay Cally a little visit.'

They only had to wait a few minutes before two uniformed policemen from the Police Service of Northern Ireland turned up. Once Fin had given them their orders Mac and Aiden followed him outside.

'We can take my car if you like,' Fin offered.

Aiden got in the back leaving the front seat for Mac for which he was thankful. There was always a little more leg room in the front.

'So, where are we off to?' Mac asked.

'The other side of the river, a place called Waterside,' Fin replied. 'That's where Cally lives. I haven't had much to do with him for a while but I saw him going into his flat a month or two ago so I'm hoping that he'll still be living there.'

'Waterside?' Mac said. 'I haven't heard of that area before but, to be honest, the only place name in Derry I can really remember is the Bogside.'

'Well, Waterside's not just on the other side of the river but it's also on the other side politically as well. It's mainly Protestant and Unionist while the Bogside is mainly Catholic and Republican.'

'And that's still the case? I mean, even now after a few years of peace?' Mac asked.

This got a wry smile from Fin.

'It'll take more than a few years for divisions as deep as we've got to disappear. We're still in the business of frantically papering over the cracks and the cracks seem to be getting ever wider. I mean we're supposed to have our own devolved government but they all squabble so much that it spends more time being suspended and with its doors shut than actually doing any work,' Fin said in an exasperated tone of voice.

'Ah, but you notice that the politicians on both sides are still drawing their wages even though they're not doing a tap. I even heard that one of them was on the radio not long ago moaning about people who are unemployed and drawing benefits,' Aiden pointed out.

This made Fin laugh.

'But you know what? There are more than a few people who think that things are running much more smoothly without a government anyway. If I'm being honest, it's a bloody mess but somehow people still seem to have the knack of getting by.'

That's the thing that keeps us all sane, Mac thought. The ability to get by when we have to.

They crossed back over the river, turned left and drove down a street lined with shops on both sides. The lower part of the street had ordinary shops that sold things but a little further on up it was mostly betting shops, pubs, food takeaways, taxi offices and tattoo parlours. It reminded Mac of several streets he'd visited in the less salubrious parts of Luton. They pulled up outside a pizza delivery shop that was closed. Judging from the rust on the metal shutters it looked as if it had been closed for some time.

'He's upstairs,' Fin said as he made his way to a door that was next to the shuttered-up shop.

Mac slowly followed Fin up the stairs. The banister moved when he put his weight on it and the stair carpet looked worn and was sagging in some places. Mac went even more carefully. He was grateful that Aiden, who was following, didn't put any pressure on him to go any faster. By the time he reached the small landing Fin was already banging on an unpainted door.

'Cally! Cally, open up. It's the police.'

Fin stopped and listened. There was a faint sound from the other side of the door.

'Cally, open up! We're not going away until you do,' Fin shouted.

Another faint noise was followed by a thud that was swiftly followed by an 'Ouch!'. Mac could almost see someone's toe colliding with a piece of furniture. The door opened a crack.

'Oh, it's you Sergeant O'Kane. Come in.'

Fin pushed the door open and the musty aroma of sweat, urine and food that was on the turn made Mac wrinkle his nose. Cally proved to be a tall skinny man in his late thirties with long dark hair and a scruffy beard. He was wearing nothing but a black T shirt and a pair of underpants that had probably been white once. He sat down on an old sofa and tried to light a cigarette but his hands were shaking too much. Fin took the lighter from him and held it to his cigarette.

Cally took a long drag before looking up at his visitors. He had a truly puzzled look on his face.

'Have I done something?' he asked.

It was a genuine question.

'Having memory problems then, Cally?' Fin asked.

'Well, I've been out of it for a few hours. What day is it?'

'It's Thursday.'

Cally looked even more confused.

'Thursday? What happened to Wednesday then?'

He tried to put the cigarette to his lips but it fell from his fingers. His eyes went up into his head and he started shaking violently. It took a few seconds before they realised that he was having a seizure.

'Aiden, quick, help me to get him to the floor and in the recovery position,' Fin said.

Mac could only stand and watch as they quickly manoeuvred Cally onto the floor and then onto his side ensuring that he wouldn't choke himself if he vomited. They were just in time as Cally's stomach emptied itself onto the carpet. There wasn't much of it but in the yellow mucus Mac thought he could make out what looked like small pieces of undigested food.

Fin got out his phone and rang for an ambulance. They could all see that Cally was in a bad way but they had no idea what to do for him. They could hear the sirens in the distance when things got suddenly worse.

Cally had stopped breathing.

Fin quickly put him on his back and started doing CPR. He then pinched Cally's nose and, despite the traces of vomit around his mouth, he breathed deep and gave him two breaths before returning to pumping his chest.

'I'll run down and make sure they know where we are,' Aiden said just before he flew out of the door and clattered down the stairs.

Mac had rarely felt so helpless. All he could do was stand by and watch. It seemed an age before he heard footsteps running up the stairs. Two paramedics carrying big black bags came into the room followed by Aiden.

'It's okay, we'll take over now,' one of the paramedics said to Fin.

'He's not stopped breathing for long and I've been giving him the kiss of life as well as CPR,' Fin said before suddenly turning green.

He looked desperately around and ran through a door to his right. Mac could hear the sound of retching followed by the sound of running water. He turned back to the paramedics who had continued the CPR. They stopped for a few seconds while one of them checked Cally's heart with a stethoscope and then felt for a pulse. He shook his head. Then CPR was continued as the paramedic pulled a bright yellow defibrillation unit out of one of the bags.

The paramedic attached the two electrodes to Cally's chest and said 'Clear'. A few seconds later his body jerked as the electricity was discharged. He once again checked Cally's heart with a stethoscope and then felt for a pulse and once again he shook his head.

Mac turned as Fin came out of the toilet. He still looked a little green. When he looked back, they were trying CPR again. Then they tried the defibrillator. Then more CPR.

Then they gave up.

'I'm calling it at twelve oh two,' the older of the two paramedics said as he looked at his watch. He stood up and turned towards the three policemen. 'Were you here when he collapsed?'

'Yes, yes we were,' Fin replied.

'What happened?'

'I don't know. He talked to us for a few minutes but he seemed to be a bit confused. Then he started shaking violently so we got him in the recovery position. I thought that he must be having some sort of epileptic fit or something. Then he just stopped breathing.'

The paramedic shook his head as he turned to his colleague, 'Looks like we've got another one.'

'We've seen this a couple of times now,' the younger paramedic explained. 'So far, they've all turned out to be heroin users but the heroin itself wasn't the problem. The drugs they were taking were heavily laced with fentanyl. That means that it's much easier to kill yourself through an overdose than just with heroin by itself.'

'So that's what it is!' Fin said. 'I've read the reports but I've not come across a case myself yet. Where they're getting the stuff from is still a mystery though.'

Mac looked around. On a small table in the corner, he saw that a small white package that had been opened. He went over. All he could read was 'Mother MacMorragh's Auth...' but it was enough.

'I think the mystery's just been solved,' Mac said. 'Fin, you better get forensics up here straight away. I need to phone England immediately. I think that we might have a major problem on our hands.'

Chapter Ten

Dan stood in front of the white board waiting impatiently for Andy Reid and Gerry Dugdale to turn up. They'd been the team that had been the furthest away when he'd sent out the call. Three of the detective teams were already there; Jo Dugdale and Leigh Marston, Tommy Nugent and Kate Grimsson, Adil Thakkar and himself.

Once he'd gotten the news from Mac, he'd alerted his bosses and all the neighbouring police forces. His team would now be responsible for co-ordinating the Hertfordshire end of the investigation. They all waited silently until finally the door burst open and Andy and Gerry rushed in.

'Sorry Dan, we made it back as fast as we could,' Andy said breathlessly. 'I take it that something's happened?'

'You could say that. I had a phone call from Mac an hour or so ago and it looks as if we could have a major incident on our hands. He's been investigating Jackie Connerty's activities in Derry in Northern Ireland where he found that Mr. Connerty, using the name of Connolly, had a meat processing plant. While Mac's convinced that Mr. Connerty was operating a VAT scam, it appears that he was also supplementing his income by smuggling drugs in meat products. However, instead of hiding packages of drugs as we'd normally expect, they were actually mixing the drugs straight into this meat product so it would be virtually undetectable.'

'What is the meat product exactly?' Andy asked.

'White puddings,' Dan replied.

'White pudding?' Jo asked with a puzzled look. 'I've heard of black pudding, horrible stuff, but I've never heard of white pudding before.'

'It's a little bit like liver sausage I suppose,' Tommy explained, 'and it's a sort of beige colour rather than white. Mac loves it. I tried it once but I wasn't sure what I made of it.'

'Apparently, it's a very popular food item with some of the Irish community,' Dan continued, 'and we believe that there's a consignment of it heading our way right now, if it isn't here already. There are one hundred and twenty boxes, each of which contains fifty of these white puddings. We think that six of these boxes contain the contaminated puddings. So, that's three hundred in all.'

'I take it from the urgency of this meeting that the drug involved isn't cannabis then?' Gerry asked.

'No and that's why we've got a problem,' Dan replied. 'We've just had a quick initial analysis from the forensics team in Derry and they've confirmed that the pudding they analysed was laced with a fairly pure form of heroin that has been heavily cut with fentanyl.'

Dan could see that the expressions on the team's faces became more serious.

'Why is it a major incident though?' Leigh asked. 'I take it that this smuggling has been going on for some time.'

'Yes, we believe it has but Mr. Connerty was due to fly back to the UK yesterday and Mac thinks that he was planning on being here when the drug shipment arrived. Now, we know that he used to supply Irish meat products to a lot of local butchers and even some in London, so that's where we think that the bulk of these white puddings will also be going. Mac also thinks it likely that Mr. Connerty might have been the type who kept his cards close to his chest. If that's true then it's possible that he might be the only one on this side of the Irish Sea who knew about the drugs and who could identify which boxes they'd be in.'

Dan let this sink in.

'So, you think there's a chance that some or all of the white puddings containing heroin and fentanyl might make their way into shops here in the UK?' Kate asked.

'Yes, that's exactly what we're afraid of.'

'How much of it would you have to eat for it to be fatal?' Jo asked.

'Very little, a thin slice would do it,' Dan replied. 'As I said the heroin is pure and the proportion of fentanyl is much higher than we'd normally expect. It's the fentanyl that appears to be the main problem as you don't have to ingest much for it to cause you to stop breathing. We think that the reason that the levels of fentanyl are so high is because the drugs were going to be heavily cut again before they went out on the streets. We know for a fact that the contaminated white pudding's deadly as it's already been identified as the cause of a fatality.'

Dan let them think about this before carrying on.

'So, there'll be an item on all the TV and radio news programmes right about now warning people not to use or even touch these puddings. They'll also be appealing for anyone who knew Mr. Connerty to come forward and that means that I won't need to go on TV myself tonight. So, there's always a silver lining, I suppose. In the meantime, all the police forces in the South-East are mobilising to cover every butcher's shop in their area just in case. The main problem is that the shipment left Northern Ireland two days ago which means that these puddings could have hit the butcher's shops some time ago.'

'What do you need us to do?' Andy asked with some urgency.

'The uniforms are checking all of the butcher's shops in the area but we suspect that Mr. Connerty had some sort of factory or premises here in the South-East where meat products could be delivered and stored and it might just be in our area. It's a long shot but if we can get our hands on a list of where all of these puddings were delivered then that would help immensely. So, it's our job to try and find the list, if it exists that is. We're covering all of Hertfordshire and the local detective teams in Cambridgeshire and Bedfordshire will be doing the same in their areas. Are you ready, Martin?'

Martin nodded and brought over some sheets of paper.

'I've tried the names Connerty and Connolly when searching for meat companies in the South East but I've come up with nothing so far,' Martin said. 'So, I'd guess that the murder victim might have been using yet another alias. I've put the meat companies all in separate lists by area so it will make it easier for you to get around them all. Here's the priority list you asked for,' he said as he passed Dan a printout.

'Okay, we're going to check these ones first as they're all in Stevenage or close by,' Dan said. 'The last letter that Mr. Connerty sent to his wife had a Stevenage postmark. It's a long shot I know but let's try anyway. There are eight in all so each team will take two addresses each. If you don't find anything then immediately start working on the sheet that Martin's going to give you now. These lists cover all of the rest of Hertfordshire but I'm hoping that we won't need them.'

Martin handed each team a sheet of paper.

'What if the premises are locked and nobody's there?' Kate asked.

'We're not going to be messing around today. Get inside by whatever means you can and, if you have any problems, call for an entry team and force your way in. Normal rules don't apply today, just do what you have to. If you find anything call me immediately and then phone Martin. He'll make sure that any information is shared with the other forces as required. He'll also update us if they come across anything that we need to know so keep your phones handy. Come on, let's go!'

The first company that Dan and Adil tried was open and happy to talk to them. Once they'd established that the company only dealt in local meat products, they sped off to the next one. They had no luck there either as they were just sausage manufacturers and they said that they had never handled white or any other type of pudding. The list that Martin had given them covered the part of North-East Hertfordshire from Royston to Bishop's Stortford. As they sped up the motorway towards the next factory just outside Royston, Dan said a little prayer that the other teams might have better luck. He kept his phone out in case he got a call. He hoped fervently that it would come sooner rather than later.

Andy and Gerry's first call took them to a large factory where bacon, sausages and black puddings were being processed and packed. However, the manager assured them that they only packed British meat and that they had never handled white pudding. The second factory also looked like a dead end as it was locked up tight and several minutes of ringing the bell and banging on the roller shutters got them exactly nowhere. They walked around the outside of the factory unit but, except for a small window high up at the back of the building, there appeared to be no other way to get in.

Andy was about to call for an entry team when he noticed that Gerry was deep in thought and looking up at the window.

'I could climb that,' Gerry said very matter-of-factly.

'What?' Andy said in some disbelief. 'That window must be at least twenty-five feet straight up from here. How on earth would you get up that high? It's just a sheer wall.'

'Not quite,' Gerry said pointing to the brickwork.

The walls of the factory unit had a pattern made by blue coloured bricks that had been inserted into the wall at intervals. Each of these bricks protruded from the wall by about an inch or so.

Andy didn't look convinced.

'Believe it or not but I've done much harder climbs than this,' Gerry said. 'I used to be part of the Army Free Climbing Team when I was younger. I could be up that wall, smash the window and be inside in a matter of minutes. If you call for an entry team we could be waiting here for ages.'

Under normal circumstances he would never have allowed Gerry to take such a risk. However, these were not normal circumstances and the situation being so serious tipped the balance.

'Okay but, if you fall, I'm not going to catch you,' Andy said only half joking.

'Don't worry, you won't need to,' Gerry said with a confident smile.

He took his jacket off and put it in the car while at the same time he retrieved a hammer from the boot. It was a special hammer that had a pointed head. They kept this handy in case of any car crashes where they might need to break a window to get people out. He put the hammer in his trouser pocket and wedged the haft under his belt so it wouldn't fall out. He took his shoes and socks off and he was ready to go.

Andy could only watch and wait while he literally kept his fingers crossed. Gerry started off slowly but soon picked up speed. Two minutes later he had the hammer in his hand and a shower of broken glass landed a few yards from where Andy was standing. Gerry carefully knocked out any pieces of glass that were left in the frame before climbing inside. Andy grinned and shook his head as he picked up Gerry's shoes and socks and went around to the front. He got two pairs of latex gloves out of the car.

A few minutes later the side door opened and a smiling Gerry emerged.

'That was amazing!' Andy said as he handed Gerry his footwear and a pair of gloves.

'I must admit that I haven't done anything like that for quite a while. It was fun. I really should take it up again,' a smiling Gerry said.

Andy laughed as he said, 'I guess that we should call you Spiderman from now on.'

While Gerry was putting his socks and shoes back on Andy turned on the lights and had a quick look around. While the factory unit had a few machines scattered about it was more than half empty and his footfalls echoed eerily as he walked around. He noticed a few pieces of white packaging material lying on the floor near one of the machines and picked one up.

It read 'Mother MacMorragh's Authentic Irish Black Pudding' and had a picture of a smiling old woman wrapped up in a shawl.

'Yes!' Andy said excitedly as he pulled out his phone.

He handed the packaging to Gerry as he told Dan what they'd found. He next phoned Martin and gave him the news. While they waited for Dan, they had a look around the unit. There really wasn't much to see. Apart from the machines, which Andy assumed were for packaging, there was only a big metal box set in one of the far corners. Andy opened the door and looked in. It was a cold store. It was still cold inside but it was also very empty.

'What's upstairs?' Andy asked pointing to where Gerry had been.

'Just a small kitchen and an office I think,' Gerry replied.

'Come on, let's have a look,' Andy said.

Once upstairs Andy looked in an open door and saw that this was the kitchen. He opened the cupboards but they were all empty as was the fridge. He crossed

117

the hallway and opened another door which led into a small office containing a desk, three chairs and an old metal filing cabinet. They looked in all the drawers but these too were totally empty. There was a last door in the hallway but this just led into a small toilet.

'Not much to go on, is there?' Gerry said.

'You'd have thought that at least some paperwork would be kept here, wouldn't you?' Andy said looking exasperated. 'Anyway, hopefully Martin will be able to identify who owns the business and that might give us a start at least.'

Hearing noises they went downstairs and saw that Dan and Adil had arrived.

'Well?' Dan asked hopefully.

'We've had a quick look around but we've found nothing. It was this that led me to make the call,' Andy said as he produced the white wrapper.

'Well, that's definitely the right brand but this says black pudding,' Dan said looking puzzled.

'I've been thinking about that,' Andy replied. 'You can only get white pudding from Ireland but black puddings are made locally, in fact, we've just come from a factory where they were packing thousands of them. If Jackie Connerty was as much of a con man as we think then I'd bet that he's been buying local black puddings, rewrapping them and then adding a bit on for them being authentically Irish.'

'That sounds likely but I was hoping we'd find more,' Dan said looking disappointed. 'Anyway, I'll get a forensics team in perhaps they'll find something...'

Dan was interrupted by his phone. He listened for a while and then pulled his notebook out and made a note. Andy knew it was good news as Dan's usually grumpy expression was gradually replaced by a smile.

'Martin, God bless him, has identified the owner of the factory as a John McCormack whose official address is the same as the newspaper shop in Wigmore,' Dan told them when he'd finished talking. 'However, we've also had calls from several people in Preston who have identified him as a local resident also called John or Jackie McCormack. We've got his address.'

'Preston?' Gerry asked.

'Oh, it's not the one in Lancashire. It's a small village a couple of miles south of Hitchin,' Dan replied. 'It's quite nice and quite expensive too. Jackie must have had some money if he was living there. Okay, Adil and I will go and check this out. Can you and Gerry stay here until the forensics team arrives. I'll call and let you know what to do next.'

Adil put the siren and blue lights on as they sped towards Preston. It was country roads all the way and Dan had to hold on tight as the car whipped around the numerous corners and then sped up again. He still managed to call for a forensics team and for a couple of uniformed officers to relieve Andy and Gerry at the factory. He then rang Martin and asked him to contact the rest of the team. They were to join him in Preston and start interviewing everyone who had called in and identified John McCormack.

It didn't take them long to get to Preston. Adil pulled into the expansive drive of a house just a half mile from the church down a pretty country lane. They parked in front of a huge Porsche four-by-four and a Mercedes sports car. The house was massive and must have had six bedrooms at the very least. Dan had often gone for drives through pretty little villages like this with his wife who loved looking at the houses. He'd always wondered how the people who lived inside them got the money for such places.

In Mr. Connerty's case he now knew.

He rang the doorbell and saw a figure approach him through the patterned glass. They'd been thwarted at every turn so far in their attempt to find out where the deadly white puddings had gone. He could only hope

119

that whoever they were about to interview might hold the key.

He had his fingers crossed as the door opened.

Chapter Eleven

Mac stood outside on the street leaning against the shutters of the pizza shop. Even though it was early days he was wondering how Dan and the team were getting on with the hunt for the deadly white puddings. Even in his head the words 'deadly' and 'white puddings' sounded ridiculous when put together but he knew that it was far from being a joke. The manner of Cally's dying had shown him that and his last few minutes on earth were something that Mac would never forget.

Fin and Aiden were still upstairs with the forensics team but Mac had felt the need for a breath of fresh air. He took his phone out and willed it to ring. Although he knew that Dan would call and update him when he could, he was still impatient for news. He was hoping against hope that, when it came, it would be good news and that they had found the white puddings in time. He didn't want to think of the consequences if they failed.

He watched as Aiden and Fin came out together. They were laughing at some joke of Fin's. Mac smiled. He'd discovered long ago that humour was the most important weapon they had in combatting madness. The darker the situation, the blacker the humour.

'So, what's next?' Aiden asked.

Mac had been thinking about this.

'We desperately need to find where those white puddings were being delivered to,' Mac said. 'From what we've learnt, besides Jackie, only Alex Ganson and Cally knew what was going on with the drugs. We need to find Alex Ganson.'

'I was thinking the same thing,' Fin said as he produced his notepad. 'While we were upstairs, I phoned the station and got his address. Strangely enough, it's only a few streets down from where I used to live. I doubt that he'll be there after what happened to Jackie, especially if his death was related to this drug dealing, but you never know. I've also asked some of my team to help. They'll be checking out their informants and following up any leads. We can only hope.'

They drove down a busy main road lined with supermarkets and retail outlets before they turned off into an older area of the city. Here the streets were narrow and Fin had to weave in and out to avoid the parked cars. On either side there were rows of terraced houses that looked as if they'd been some-how squashed together. Mac got an idea of which side of the divide he was on as the kerbstones were painted red, white and blue and Unionist flags adorned every lamp post. They passed a mural that showed men in some sort of uniform wearing black balaclavas. They were waving a large Union Jack with the words 'No Surrender' in bright orange. The mural seemed to be fading a little and Mac could only hope that such divisive images could be left to fade out altogether.

The thing that was strange to Mac was that the houses and the streets still looked typically Irish to him. While a few of the houses could only be described as scruffy, most were well looked after and rendered different shades of grey with tidy little gardens in the front. They pulled up outside one of the scruffiest ones.

Fin knocked and eventually the door opened an inch at the most.

'What do you want?' a woman asked in a slurred voice.

Fin showed her his warrant card and the door opened a fraction wider so that Mac got a look at her.

She was in her forties and had a top on that was far too small for her ample figure and track suit bottoms that had seen better days. He caught a whiff of the smell of raw alcohol.

'I'm looking for Alex Ganson. Do you know where I can find him?' Fin asked.

She just shrugged her shoulders as an answer.

'Who are you exactly?' Fin asked.

'I'm Donna, Alex's wife,' she replied.

'When did you last see Alex?'

She looked behind her before she answered.

'About three days ago now. He said he had something to do and that he wouldn't be home for a while,' she replied.

'And what was this thing that he had to do?' Fin asked.

'God knows. He never tells me anything, after all I'm only his wife,' she said with a hint of anger.

They heard a sound from inside and she looked behind her again.

'Is there anyone else in the house?' Fin asked.

'No, no, there's just me,' she replied in a manner that was far from convincing.

The policemen were even less convinced that she was telling the truth when they distinctly heard a voice say, 'And where's my sweet little kebab then? Daddy wants to give her some good loving.'

Donna looked up to the sky and held the door open. The living room was dingy and had several empty vodka bottles and a half a dozen empty pizza cartons strewn over the floor. It wasn't made any tidier by the man who stood in the middle of the room in just his underpants. He was in his forties, fat, bald headed and heavily tattooed. He was also in the process of going very red.

'Christ!' he said in surprise.

'No, not quite,' Fin said as he showed the man his warrant card. 'And you are?'

The man sat down on a battered sofa and held his hands over his crotch.

'Jimmy, Jimmy Ganson,' he replied.

'So, you're Alex's younger brother then I take it?' Fin asked.

'Yes, that's right but I'm not like Alex honestly. I haven't done anything,' he protested.

'Donna sit down next to Jimmy,' Fin ordered. 'Now, I've got just two questions for the both of you but first here's a warning. Something incredibly serious has happened and I need to find Alex urgently. If I find that you've been holding information back then I'll do my absolute level best to make sure that you both do time for it. Do you understand?'

They looked at each other and then nodded.

'So, first question. Where's Alex right now? Donna, you go first,' Fin said.

'I've no idea. He went out on Monday and said he wouldn't be back until late tonight at the earliest.'

'And that's all he said?' Fin asked.

'Yes, but I heard him on the phone saying to someone that he'd guard it personally.'

'It?'

'Yes, but I've no idea what he was talking about,' Donna hastily added. 'I asked but Alex just told me to shut it.'

Unfortunately, Mac believed her.

'Same here,' Jimmy said. 'I asked him if he wanted to go out for a drink during the week but he said he had something to do. He wouldn't say what it was though.'

Unfortunately, Mac believed him too.

'Okay then, have either of you ever heard of a Jackie Connerty or Connolly?' Fin asked.

They looked at each other and shook their heads.

'What about John McCormack?' Fin persisted.

'Oh, aye,' Jimmy said with a smile.

All three policemen were suddenly very interested in what he was going to say.

'He was a singer, wasn't he? Opera and stuff like that. My grandad loved him, even though he was a taig.'

Fin put his face close to Jimmy's and said, 'Believe me Jimmy when I tell you that you didn't get you any brownie points for that one.' He pulled back and turned to Donna. 'Have you got Alex's phone number?'

Donna pulled her phone out and showed the number to Fin. He rang the number but got no reply.

'If you think of anything else call me immediately. Here's my number,' Fin said as he gave her a card. 'I can't stress how important it is that we find Alex so, if I find that either of you have been lying or holding anything back, you'll be in serious trouble.'

Fin then gave them both a stern glare which Mac thought was quite good. They both looked as if they sincerely believed him.

As she showed them to the door she stopped and gave Fin a hopeful look.

'Now, if you find Alex, you won't be needing to be telling him about Jimmy being here, will you? He can be a bit, well...'

'Violent?' Fin suggested. 'Don't worry, I'll keep it to myself as it will be one less domestic for us to deal with but just remember what I said.'

As soon as Donna shut the door Fin had his phone out. From what Mac and Aiden could hear he was ordering a trace on the phone number that Donna had given them.

When he'd finished the call Fin said, 'They can't find a location so he's probably turned the phone off. They said that they'll keep monitoring just in case.'

Fin looked at his watch. It was now after five o'clock.

'Fancy a pie and a pint?' Fin asked.

Mac and Aiden didn't say no.

125

'There's a pub a few streets away,' Fin continued. 'It used to be my father's local at one time and I still know a few of the regulars. There's one in particular who might just be able to tell us what Alex has been getting up to.'

That sounded like a plan to Mac and he said so.

The pub was called The Paisley Bar but, as it was painted green and had a Guinness sign outside, it could have been a pub anywhere in Ireland. Inside it was all dark wood and peace and quiet. A stocky middle-aged barman stood behind the bar chatting to a couple of builders who were leaning against the bar, the brick dust still clinging to their overalls. In the corner a group of three elderly men were jointly trying to complete a crossword puzzle. From their exasperated looks Mac guessed that they weren't getting very far with it.

Mac and Aiden sat at a table in the other corner. Fin had a chat with the barman before ordering three pints and three pies. He brought the black beers over and Mac gratefully took a sip.

'Well, today hasn't gone quite as I expected it to,' Aiden said.

'You can say that again,' Fin said just before he took a giant gulp from his glass. 'I've just been asking Tom the barman about a regular called Budgie Campbell. He used to make it his business to know everything that goes on around here and, according to Tom, he still does which might be lucky for us. He's usually in around seven.'

'Good,' Mac said. 'After what's just happened, an hour or so in some peace and quiet won't do us any harm at all.'

The pies arrived.

'Meat and potato, home made by the missus,' Tom said with some pride as he placed them on the table.

Mac opened a corner of the pie and a wonderfully meaty aroma literally made his mouth water. Mac took a taste and thought it was amongst the most wonderful pies he'd ever eaten. Of course, that might have been down to the fact that he was ravenously hungry, but, whatever, he enjoyed every morsel of it. Aiden and Fin must have felt the same as not a single word was said until the plates were clean.

'Now, that's what I call a pie!' Mac said with some feeling.

'Oh, the Paisley's famous for its pies,' Fin said with a smile. 'I haven't been here for quite a while and I'd almost forgotten how good they were.'

'While we've got a bit of time would you mind if I asked you a question?' Mac asked.

'Sure,' Fin replied.

'How come your family's Protestant with a name like O'Kane?'

This made Aiden chuckle.

'They're all 'Soup Protestants' that's why. Isn't that right, Fin?' Aiden said with a wide smile.

Fin laughed too. He could see that Mac was puzzled so he explained.

'During the Great Famine, and the many other times when people were hungry, the country was under English rule so, in some places, they made sure that the Protestant hungry got fed first. So Irish Catholics would 'take the soup' as they called it and become Protestants, usually to make sure that their children didn't starve. Some of them stayed Protestant afterwards as it meant that they usually had better job prospects and so on. However, I'd be careful using the term around here as you might well be missing a few teeth afterwards.'

'I can see that. I must admit that I'm finding it difficult to get a handle on things around here,' Mac said a shake of his head.

'You've got lots of company in that believe me,' Fin said. 'Both sides like to think that their communities

127

are totally different to the other but they're more alike than they'd ever want to admit. During the troubles I remember my dad saying that it was strange that one of the leaders of the IRA had a Scottish surname while one of the top Unionists had an Irish name, a Gaelic name come to that. Anyway, I decided at the age of fourteen that all this Catholic-Protestant religious stuff was absolute nonsense and I haven't changed my opinion since.'

'What happened when you were fourteen?' Mac asked getting genuinely interested.

'I used to go to judo classes and there I met a girl called Sinead, who is of course a Catholic, and that was that. We kept it a secret from our parents and even some of our friends for quite a while. We 'came out', as it were, when Sinead was eighteen and, I must admit, it wasn't anywhere near as bad as we thought it would be. We got married a few years after I joined the force but we both felt that we wouldn't be comfortable living in either community. So, we moved out of town altogether to a little place where people tend to mind their own business and no-one gives a damn whose side you're on.'

Fin stopped and looked a little pensive before he went on.

'You don't realise how tense this place can be at times until you leave it. When I go home, I can truly relax and, believe me, that's something you can't always do around here.'

Mac could well believe it. Indeed, he'd felt quite tense ever since he'd arrived. However, he knew that could be as much down to the investigation as anything else, not forgetting the funeral which now seemed a long time ago. He decided that he'd give the place a proper visit some time when he had nothing on. After all, he'd found at least one pub he liked.

'So, what's it like being a policeman in Northern Ireland?'

It was a question that Mac had wanted to ask since he'd met Fin.

'It's what it is, I suppose. I've never worked anywhere else so I've not really got anything to compare it to. I'd guess that we spend ninety nine percent of our time doing what every policeman does; investigating punch-ups in pubs, thefts, domestics, vandalism and so on but we've had a bit less of that lately as crime rates have been at their lowest for quite a while. The only problem is that we still get some sectarian related crime, mostly assaults these days with the odd firebomb thrown in. They're hate crimes but I dare say that you get plenty of those in London too.'

Mac had to admit that they did.

'And, from what I'm hearing, they've been on the rise since the Brexit vote,' Mac conceded.

'I'll bet that you don't get mothers taking their own sons to get kneecapped in London though,' Aiden said.

'There's a sort of shadow justice system in force here as there are people on both sides who don't trust the police. To one side we're an enemy occupying force while to the other we're traitors to the Unionist cause. I'd guess that, so long as they both keep thinking that, then we're probably doing something right,' Fin said with a sigh.

'Those punishments, they're not so strange really,' Mac said. 'I've known members of street gangs who've dragged their friends and even relatives to get beaten or have arms or legs broken for some perceived crime against the gang. I'd guess that was mostly because the only other alternative available was a bullet in the head.'

'So, from everything I'm hearing, it's not all that different then. Apart from the crime rates being vastly higher in London of course,' Fin said with a wink. 'It must be such a lawless place.'

This made both Mac and Aiden laugh.

'Another pint?' Aiden asked.

Neither Mac nor Fin refused.

While Aiden was at the bar Fin asked, 'So what are you going to do? I take it that you'll not be driving back to Ballydove tonight?'

Mac hadn't really thought past what they might learn from Budgie Campbell.

'What about that place I stayed at last time?' Aiden said as he placed the drinks on the table.

'I'll give them a ring,' Fin said. 'I'd better ring the wife too. It might be a late night.'

He took his phone out and went outside.

'It's a really nice little hotel near the bridge. They do a fantastic breakfast there too,' Aiden explained.

That was more than enough of a recommendation for Mac. He always felt that he could face almost anything so long as he'd had a good breakfast to start the day off.

'All booked up for you,' Fin said when he returned. 'I told them that you might not get there until quite late.'

The door opened and a short but stocky man came in. Mac guessed that he might be in his late fifties as the hair that peeked out from under his flat cap was turning grey. He had a horse racing paper sticking out of his jacket pocket so Mac guessed that he'd been spending some quality time in the bookies.

'That's Budgie,' Fin said as he stood up. 'Keep your fingers crossed that he knows something.'

While he watched Fin as he bought Budgie a pint Mac's thoughts were with Dan and the team back in England. He checked his phone once again but there were no messages. It was taking too long and he was starting to get more than worried.

Chapter Twelve

The woman who answered the door was somewhat younger than Dan had expected. She was in her late forties, slim and elegantly dressed. She looked at Dan with some apprehension as he introduced himself. She didn't ask why they were calling but her red eyes and the damp tissue she clutched in one hand provided the answer. She'd obviously already heard the news. She asked them to come inside.

Her voice was light and her accent was Irish, perhaps Northern Irish, Dan thought.

The interior of the house had obviously had some money lavished on it and Dan would admit that he had seen much worse show homes. He was certain about that as he and his wife had started house hunting recently and he'd been dragged around enough show homes to last him a lifetime. His wife would have definitely liked this place but it would have been way outside their limited budget.

He and Adil sat down on a sofa that could have seated six in a light and airy living room. Original works of art decorated the pale walls while the room was dominated by a huge marble fireplace.

'Can I ask you for your name?' Dan asked.

'It's Diane McCormack, Mrs. Diane McCormack.'

Dan's expression didn't change even though he was surprised. Did Jackie Connerty really have two wives? He took a photo out and showed it to her.

'Is this the man who you knew as your husband?'

She looked at the photo for some time before returning it.

'Yes, that's my Jackie,' she replied her bottom lip shaking as she said the words. 'Is it true? Is he really dead? I only saw it on the news a few minutes ago. How...'

Dan interrupted her as he didn't want to get into a lengthy explanation of how her husband had died. Time wasn't on their side.

'Yes, I'm afraid that he's dead. We'll explain all the circumstances surrounding his death to you a little later,' he said a little more abruptly than he'd meant to. 'Do you know anything about your husband's meat business? Who he delivered to and so on?'

'I've no idea. He never involved me in any of his business dealings,' she replied.

Dan wasn't quite sure that he believed her but he didn't pursue it. Trying to pry the truth from a reluctant witness might take more time than they had.

'Did your husband have an office in the house? Somewhere that he'd keep his business papers perhaps?'

'Yes, it's just down the hall.'

They followed her down a short hallway. She opened a door and then stepped back.

'Is it okay if we have a look around?' Dan asked.

'Well, I don't know...' she said.

'I'd like you to agree but we're going to search this house whether you like it or not. I can't give you any details but people's lives may be depending on it.'

She looked quite stunned at this news and she thought for a moment before replying.

'In that case of course. Would you like a cup of tea?' she asked attempting a smile.

'Oh, yes please,' Dan said.

As soon as she had her back turned, he and Adil started opening drawers and skimming through some files that were lying on top of the desk. They were mostly property related. It seemed that Jackie had been investing quite heavily in real estate. They had just started looking in some cupboards when she arrived with the tea. Dan opened one of the cupboard doors to reveal a safe.

'Do you have any keys to this safe or know the combination for it?' Dan asked.

She looked at the safe, shrugged and then shook her head. Dan could see that she was close to tears.

'No, I've no idea of how to open the safe or what's in there,' she replied. 'That was Jackie's business.'

'What about this laptop?' Dan said. 'Do you ever use it?'

'Oh no, that's Jackie's. Only he ever used it,' she replied.

Dan turned it on. It needed a password.

'I don't suppose that you know what the password is?'

She just shook her head by way of reply.

'Thanks for the tea,' Dan said.

As soon as she left, he phoned Martin and told him that he'd shortly be receiving a laptop that needed looking at. He also asked for a phone number from the records. While he was looking it up Martin gave him the latest update. As soon as Martin rang off, he called the number.

'Hello, is that Jimmy?' Dan asked. 'It's Dan Carter from the police. I urgently need a safe opening. If I send a car over straight away, would you be able to come?'

Dan's grin told Adil that Jimmy had agreed to help.

He then rang DS Jo Dugdale.

'Jo, can you drop everything and pick someone up from this address. He'll be waiting for you.'

Dan read out Jimmy's address.

'Once you've got him on board then get over to the McCormack house as fast as you can. I'll need you to keep someone company for a while after that.'

'She's on her way,' Dan said as he put his phone away.

'I take it that was Jimmy Stourton that you were talking to just before Jo?' Adil asked.

'Yes, it's quite handy that we've got one of the best safecrackers in the country living on our patch. I just hope that he can get this one open. To be honest, it looks quite impregnable to me. By the way Martin's said that altogether they've located forty-two of the white puddings so far, all in North London, and they're being tested as we speak. That means that they've got as far as the butchers' shops then. So, forty-two down and just under another six thousand or so to go,' he said bleakly. 'Anyway, let's get this laptop bagged up and get it off to Martin.'

While they waited Dan thought back to the first time that he'd met Jimmy Stourton. He'd been a suspect in the murder of a soap star's chauffeur but, although there seemed to be clear proof of his involvement, Mac had a suspicion that the evidence had been planted and that Jimmy was being framed. It turned out that he'd been right. Mac had later used Jimmy to success-fully open a safe in the Pierson case so Dan was more than hopeful that he might be able to help him now.

While they waited, they continued searching but they didn't find any list.

Just over half an hour later the doorbell rang. Dan reckoned that Jo must have used the sirens to get there so quickly. Mrs. McCormack already had the door open by the time he got to it.

'Mrs. McCormack,' Dan said, 'this is Detective Sergeant Jo Dugdale who'll look after you for a while. If you need anything just ask her.'

Jo flashed a look of surprise to Dan as he spoke her name. She said nothing though and quickly wrapped an arm around Mrs. McCormack before steering her towards the living room. Jimmy just stood there calm and unmoving as was his way.

'Jimmy, thanks for coming. I'll take you to the safe,' Dan said as they shook hands.

While Jimmy was examining the safe Dan explained why they needed to see its contents so urgently. Jimmy gave this a little thought.

'Okay, it seems that time's an important factor but we'll still need to do this by the book. If we rush and miss something then we might never get it open. It's new, a top of the range Chubb security safe with an electronic combination lock. That means that it's got a six-figure key. Cracking it might take too long and, even then, it might damage what's inside. I need to speak to Mrs. McCormack.'

Dan was surprised at how gently Jimmy spoke to her. She looked in shock as she wrote down hers and Jackie's birth dates as well as those of her daughters. He also asked for any other important dates. She wrote down the date that Jackie proposed to her and the date that they were married.

'Where are your children?' Dan asked.

'They're both at university. Julia's in her last year while Marie's just started,' she explained.

'I think that you'd better call them,' Dan said.

'Yes, I hadn't thought about that but I suppose I should. Oh God, what will I tell them!' she said as she dissolved into tears.

Jo held her as they quietly left the room.

Jimmy sat with the list of numbers in front of him and stared at them. He looked a little puzzled.

'You might as well leave me to get on with it,' Jimmy said. 'I'll work more quickly if you're not looking over my shoulder. By the way, you'll probably be getting a call from a security company within the next few minutes.'

'What do you mean?' Dan asked.

'This house has got a top of the range security system installed and I'd be surprised if it didn't include the safe,' Jimmy explained. 'Trying several different passwords will probably make their alarm bells ring.'

Dan and Adil went outside. While he waited, he rang around the team and then called Mac. When he'd finished, he looked at Adil and shrugged.

'We're still in bloody limbo. For all we know half the Irish population of Hertfordshire might be sitting down right now and eating a nice piece of fentanyl laced white pudding for supper and there's nothing we can do to stop them,' Dan said in exasperation. 'We can only hope that everyone's been watching TV today.'

'Mac's come up with nothing then?' Adil asked.

'Not yet. They're trying to track down one of Jackie's accomplices but he seems to have disappeared on them.'

'Something will break,' Adil said trying to sound cheerful.

'Let's hope you're right. I'm beginning to get a very bad feeling about this one.'

Dan's phone went off. Adil could see the anticipation on his face as he answered. It was soon replaced by his usual glum expression.

'That was Martin again,' Dan explained as he put his phone away. 'Jimmy was right. We've just had a call saying someone's trying to break into the safe. You've got to admit he's good, isn't he?'

Fifteen minutes later Dan and Adil were still chatting outside when Jimmy came out and joined them. From the look on his face Dan assumed that he wasn't having much luck with the safe.

'No luck yet?'

'It's open,' Jimmy said.

'You what?' Dan asked not quite believing what he'd heard.

'It's open,' Jimmy said again.

Dan remembered Mac once saying that Jimmy was a hard person to read. He now knew exactly what he meant. He and Adil hurried inside to find the safe door wide open. Most of the space inside was taken up by large wads of cash. Dan put some latex gloves on and started pulling them out and placing them on the table. They were all either pounds or euros and all were high denomination notes. However, Dan wasn't interested in the money, he needed information.

'How did you do it?' Dan asked as he took more wads of cash out.

'It ended up as being a sort of combination of his two daughters birth dates backwards,' Jimmy said. 'It was fairly straightforward really or it should have been.'

'What do you mean?' Dan asked.

'The birth dates that Mrs. McCormack gave for her daughters weren't right. She was a year out on both.'

'How on earth did you know that?'

'I noticed her hesitate a little when it came to writing down the years they were born. When none of the dates worked, I tried putting a year on the daughters' birthdays and that did the trick.'

Dan stopped for a moment and looked at Jimmy with real respect.

'What on earth made you think of doing that?'

'Most people go to university when they're eighteen or nineteen, don't they? According to Mrs. McCormack her youngest would have only been seventeen so I thought it was worth a try,' Jimmy explained.

Dan shook his head in wonder. Was it merely a mistake made by a woman who was very upset or might it have been an attempt to stop them opening the safe? Dan decided to find out later. He needed to find that list first.

He and Adil continued removing wads of cash. Once the money had been removed all that was left was a pile of documents.

Dan started leafing through the documents. There were several VAT tax returns in the pile but the rest of them made no sense to him. He assumed that the numbers must be money but the names, if that's what they were, were in code or abbreviated in some way. Dan guessed that Jackie used his own version of shorthand for security purposes. He was almost despairing until he came to the last few sheets. They were lists of addresses, most of which were in North London, Hertfordshire and Bedfordshire. Although it was just a simple list Dan could tell from some the business names that they were butcher's shops. He breathed a sigh of relief.

'Adil take photos of these and send them off to Martin straight away,' Dan said as he moved the money out of the way and laid out the three sheets on the desk.

While Adil was doing this Dan rang Martin.

'I'm going to send you three photos that are lists of addresses. Can you make sure that they go out to all the relevant forces and tell them to check out every one of these butcher's shops straight away,' Dan said.

At least they should now be able to contain the situation and stop it from getting any worse.

'Also Mr. Connerty's laptop is on its way to you. See what you can do with it.'

'Will do,' Martin said. Then there was a pause. 'Dan, we've had some news.'

Dan knew from his tone of voice that it wasn't going to be good news.

'Go on.'

'We've just had our first confirmed death related to the white puddings, well, two I suppose if you count the dog.'

'A dog?'

'Yes, it belonged to a Mrs. Aileen McGurk. She was a sixty-five year old widow who lived in Cricklewood,

North London. She was found dead by her friend this afternoon. She'd luckily seen the TV appeals and recognised the brand of white pudding. She called the police immediately.'

'Okay,' Dan said with a sigh. 'I'm really hoping that these addresses might help. Let's also hope that the people who bought the white puddings are all regular customers.'

Dan ended the call with a sinking feeling in his stomach. Mrs. McGurk may have been the first but he knew that she wouldn't be the last. He turned and saw Jimmy waiting patiently in a corner of the room.

'I'm sorry,' Dan said. 'I'll organise a lift home for you. Thanks Jimmy, you've really helped us out, in fact you could have just saved quite a few lives.'

Dan shook Jimmy's hand warmly.

After Jimmy had gone Dan sat down and looked at the sheets of paper more closely hoping that he could glean a little more from them. They needed every crumb of information they could get. However, he still couldn't make head nor tail of them. He glanced over the VAT returns and noticed that Jackie had reclaimed over half a million in tax in the last tax year after claiming that his company had a turnover of some eight million pounds a year. From what he'd heard from Mac about the factory in Northern Ireland and what he'd seen for himself he knew that this had to be a scam. Mac had been right then. He'd make sure that he'd take it up with the tax people when he had more time.

Jo poked her head around the corner. Dan waved at her to come in.

'She's just gone to the loo,' Jo said. 'Is she really Mr. Connerty's wife?'

'Yes, it looks like our victim was a bigamist on top of everything else. How is she?' Dan asked.

'Shocked and upset, I suppose, but she's not saying much which I find a bit strange.'

'What do you mean?'

'Well, I've done this a few times before when I worked as a Family Liaison Officer in Stevenage and people usually talk about the person they've lost, even if it just to say that they can't believe they've gone,' Jo replied.

'Do you think she's hiding something?' Dan asked.

'Well, she started talking about her husband and then had to bite her tongue a couple of times. So, if I had to guess, I'd say yes, she's hiding something.'

That was good enough for Dan.

'Adil, can you photograph every one of these sheets and send them to Martin, perhaps he'll have better luck trying to decode them,' Dan said. 'After that get in contact with forensics and see how soon they can get a team here. I want them to go through this place with a fine-toothed comb. They're probably going to be busy for a while so get a couple of uniforms in to guard the place in the meantime. Bring the sheets to us when you're finished. I want to show them to Mrs. McCormack. Come on Jo, let's see what she's got to say.'

Diana McCormack was just sitting down again as Dan and Jo entered the living room.

'I know that this is a difficult time but I need to ask you some questions,' Dan said. 'You said that you know nothing at all about your husband's business activities?'

'No, I never wanted to get involved and he never asked me to. He was the breadwinner and I looked after the house and children. We're both happy with that...' she stopped and looked down. 'I suppose I should say we *were* both happy with that.'

'When and where did you meet your husband?'

Dan couldn't help noticing that she hesitated slightly before answering.

'We met in Luton nearly thirty years ago now. I was just nineteen and I'd come over here to work. He was ten years older than me but I didn't care about that. He'd already started his business and he was doing well.'

'You're from Ireland originally then?' Dan asked.

'Well sort of, I was born in Dunstable but my parents took me back to Ireland when I was young. It was the same for Jackie.'

Dan looked puzzled.

'Do you have yours and Jackie's passports handy?' he asked.

'Of course,' she said as she left the room.

She returned with two purple UK passports and handed them to Dan. He opened her passport and turned to the photograph page. It stated that she was a British citizen who was born in Dunstable. He then opened Jackie's and was surprised to find that he was also a British citizen having been born in Luton.

'Your husband was found at the airport with an Irish passport in the name of Jackie Connerty. Can you explain that?' Dan asked.

She shook her head.

'He told me that he had an Irish passport as he had dual citizenship but I never saw it. He said that it was useful for his business but I just assumed that it was in his name.'

'From what we've discovered so far it appears that your husband was leading a double life. Were you aware that he had a wife in Ireland?'

She shook her head again but she didn't look as shocked by the news as Dan would have expected.

'I knew that he'd been married but he said that his wife had died.'

'Well, she didn't. In fact, she's very much alive. He used to go and stay with her whenever he went over to Ireland.'

'No!' she said as she stood up her fists clenched.

Dan was convinced that this was the first truthful reaction he'd had from her. She quickly regained her composure though and sat down. She started biting her nails.

'Do you have any idea who might have wanted your husband dead?' Dan asked.

She looked up at Dan and shook her head.

'Was it quick?' she asked in a low voice.

'Yes, it would have been quick. He was stabbed in the back three times and one of the thrusts went straight into his heart.'

Adil came in with the sheets of paper from the safe. Dan showed them to her.

'Now, please don't touch them Mrs. McCormack. Our forensics team will need to process them. I'm showing them to you in the hope that you can tell us what they mean.'

Dan showed her each sheet in turn and every time all he got was a shake of the head.

'It's our belief that your husband was smuggling class 'A' drugs into this country in Irish meat products. Can you tell us anything about that?'

She looked at him as though he'd just spoken in a foreign language.

'I saw that on the news. No, my Jackie would never get involved in anything like that. You're getting it all mixed up. Maybe the man that you found dead wasn't my Jackie after all, just someone who looked like him,' she said in hope.

'Well, our forensics team will soon prove that one way or the other,' Dan said. 'We've already had one death associated with these white puddings. Is there nothing you can tell us that might help?'

She didn't look at him. She just shook her head by way of an answer.

He gave up. She obviously wasn't going to tell him anything. He decided that he'd be better off leaving her to Jo in the hope that she'd let something accidentally slip.

'So, not much luck there then,' Adil said as they walked outside again.

'Well, thanks to Jimmy, at least we've got the list,' Dan said. 'However, despite all her denials, I've got the feeling that Mrs. McCormack is hiding something and that she knows a lot more than she's letting on. Oh well, perhaps she'll let something slip to Jo. As soon as the uniforms arrive let's get back to the station and see what's going on there.'

As they waited Dan thought of Mac and his lead. He hoped that he was having more luck.

Chapter Thirteen

While Fin was at the bar chatting to Budgie, Mac noticed that Aiden wasn't looking at all comfortable. He asked him why.

'I'm on the wrong side of the river, I suppose,' Aiden said in a low conspiratorial voice. 'If people here knew that a member of the Gardai was sitting amongst them, well, who knows how they might react.'

'It's still that bad even this long after the peace agreement has been signed?'

'Don't kid yourself about that,' Aiden replied. 'Peace here is only skin deep and I don't think it would take that much for it to kick off again. If you doubt the depth of the hatred then you should visit Derry in July when the Protestant marches celebrating the Battle of the Boyne take place. If the marches weren't bad enough, they also take great delight in burning effigies of the Pope and Irish flags on their bonfires.'

'They still do that?' Mac asked.

'They do and the bonfires get bigger every year. Just a few months ago during the 'celebrations' there were shots fired at the police and vehicles were hijacked and set alight. Of course, the Catholic thugs on the other side of the river couldn't stand by and watch that happen so they chipped in by throwing petrol bombs into a Protestant area by way of a reply and at an old people's home too, if you can believe that. As far as I can see, peace here is skating on very thin ice and it wouldn't take much to break it.'

Mac could only shake his head sadly in reply. Like many people in England, he'd assumed that, after years of 'peace', Northern Ireland would be just like in the rest of the UK. It clearly wasn't and he wondered if

Brexit and the border issue might just be the rock that would shatter that very thin ice.

Fin said his goodbyes to Budgie and patted him on the back before returning to Mac and Aiden.

'Budgie's told me something that might be worth looking into. A friend of his who works for one of the housing associations told him that Alex Ganson has been renting some garages located in a small housing estate just off the Dungiven Road. Unfortunately, Budgie wasn't sure exactly where but he gave me the name of the man who told him and where I might find him,' Fin said.

'Garages?' Aiden said. 'I take it that Alex Ganson had something that needed storing then?'

'That's what I'm thinking and you can bet your life that it won't be anything that's legal,' Fin replied. 'So, if whatever needs guarding is in those garages, then Alex might well be in there with it. Anyway, I think that it's worth a shot. I need to go to a pub in town to meet Budgie's friend but I was thinking that I could drop you both at the supermarket in case you wanted pick up any toiletries. They sell clothes there too.'

'That sounds like a good idea to me,' Mac said.

'God yes, it would be nice to have a clean shirt to start the day with tomorrow,' Aiden said.

The supermarket was bigger than Mac had expected and he had no problems in getting everything he needed. Aiden had done the same and they both stood outside with a couple of carrier bags in their hands waiting for Fin to turn up.

'It's been a strange day,' Aiden said.

Mac looked at his watch and found that it wasn't too far off nine o'clock.

'A long day too,' he said as he watched the very last glimmers of sunlight disappear into the black night sky.

He realised that they hadn't even been in Derry for twelve hours and yet he was already feeling tired and ready for his bed. Aiden's phone rang.

'Yes...yes...okay. No problem. We'll see you later then.' Aiden put his phone away as he explained, 'That was Fin. He's been having some trouble finding the man he's looking for. However, he's just learnt that he should be in the pub around ten so he's going to hang around until he turns up. He's ordered us a taxi and he said he'll meet us in the hotel bar a little later.'

The man at the hotel reception was very pleasant as was the room. Mac stowed his few purchases away and sat on the bed to test it. Luckily it was quite firm and that suited him or at least his back. He gazed down at the bed and was tempted to lie down for a while but instead he stood up, went to the bathroom and threw some water on his face in the hope that it might wake him up a little. He looked at himself and sighed. He looked even worse than he felt.

Aiden was already sitting in the bar and hadn't noticed Mac come in. He seemed to be very absorbed in a news story being shown on a large TV screen on the wall. Mac stopped halfway into the room and looked at the TV too. There was no sound but he could get the gist of the story from the titles that were displayed prominently across the bottom of the screen. Mac moved closer so he could get a good look at Aiden's face. He was surprised at what he saw there. It was a look that could not be mistaken.

It was raw and unfettered hatred.

Mac looked again at the TV screen and the penny then dropped. He would have to ask some questions once they got back to Ballydove, just to be certain, but he was fairly sure that the idea that had just popped into his head was right. This new theory certainly explained why Aiden had been behaving as he had and perhaps even why he and Caitlin had broken up. As he couldn't do anything about it right away Mac decided to park the thought until later. He coughed so that Aiden would know that he was there.

'Oh Mac, I didn't see you there,' Aiden said looking flustered and forcing a smile as he stood up. 'Fancy a pint while we're waiting?'

'As much as I'd like one, I think that a coffee might be the better choice. I'm already feeling a little tired and I might need waking up a bit if Fin comes up with anything.'

'That's a good idea. I'll get two then,' Aiden said before making his way to the bar.

While he waited, Mac thought back over all the conversations he'd had with Aiden. He knew that he was basing his theory on very little evidence but, nevertheless, he still knew that he was right.

They managed to make some small talk while they waited and Mac found out that Aiden had another dark and terrible secret. He supported Liverpool who, Mac had to admit, were having a little more success lately than were his club Aston Villa. Mac was almost getting used to the sympathetic looks he got every time he mentioned which football club he supported. Eventually Aiden's phone rang.

'Fin said that he's found out where the garages are and he'll pick us up outside in five minutes,' Aiden said as he put his phone away.

Although it was now nearly ten thirty the tiredness that Mac had felt suddenly disappeared. They had a lead!

'We're on our way to a place called Altmore Gardens,' Fin explained as they drove off. 'It's just off the Dungiven Road and it runs along the back of the houses there. I've never noticed them before but I've been told that at the bottom of the road there's a row of six garages. The residents no longer seem to need them as they've all built parking areas at the front of their houses and so they've now been made available to rent. Around a month or so ago Alex turned up and rented all six of them. He said that he was moving to a new house and needed somewhere to store furniture for a few months.'

'I'll bet that it's not furniture he's keeping in there. Any idea what it is?' Aiden asked.

'Unfortunately, no. Derek, the man I spoke to, said that he was curious as to what Alex was up to and so, when he was in the area a few days ago, he dropped by the garages to have a look. A car was parked outside and he could hear a radio on inside one of the garages so he assumed that someone must be inside. He guessed that Alex might have been using the garage as a workshop of some sort,' Fin said.

The Dungiven Road turned out to be a wide and busy dual carriageway. They turned right at an island and right again down a small road that ran between two houses. They found themselves on a narrow lane that ran down the back of a long row of terraced houses on one side while on the other there was a view over the houses that cascaded down the steep hillside below. He also noticed that most of the back gardens had a big green plastic storage tank in it and guessed that oil heating must still be quite popular in this part of the world.

Fin pulled up a good distance before the end of the road.

'I think that we'd better have a quick look first,' he said.

They closed their car doors as quietly as they could and then Mac and Aiden followed Fin as he kept close to the wooden fence beyond which the roofs of the houses below seemed to be almost close enough to touch. After a hundred yards or so the road came to a dead end. A row of six prefabricated garages stood a little back from the road to allow enough room for cars to turn around in. The garages were somewhat larger than Mac had expected. Fin stopped where the fence turned at ninety degrees and they all peeked around the corner.

A car was parked in front of the nearest garage but it one of the middle garages that got their attention. A sliver of light could be seen from underneath the garage door and a faint noise could be heard. They backed off a bit and discussed what they should do next.

'If Alex is in there then we haven't got any time to lose,' Mac said. 'Is he likely to be on his own?'

'I've no idea,' Fin replied. 'To be honest Alex would be a bit of a handful even by himself. Let's take no chances, I can get an entry team up here in less than half an hour.'

They all agreed that this was the most sensible thing to do. Even so, Mac chafed at having to wait. It seemed like three hours had passed before he saw a group of six men dressed in uniform silently making their way towards them. He looked at his watch, it had only been twenty-five minutes. They had been quick alright.

Fin explained the situation to the commander of the entry team and they had a brief discussion.

'We've decided to give Alex a chance to give himself up first. If he doesn't respond then they're going to take the garage door off,' Fin said.

This made sense to Mac. They followed the entry team as they positioned themselves in front of the garage door. They could hear the radio quite clearly now.

'This is Radio Ulster and this is the Late Show. Next up, it's Rosanne Cash, daughter of the late great...'

The commander banged loudly on the metal garage door, 'Police! Open up,' he shouted.

The radio stopped. There was a short silence in which they heard a few indeterminate sounds from inside the garage.

'Police! Open up,' he shouted again.

Another short silence. Then they heard the sound of something breaking followed by a few choice swear words. This was quickly followed by a loud, 'Jesus!'

The policemen all looked at each other. Then they heard an even louder shout.

'JESUS!' This was then followed by a long drawn out scream, 'JEEESSSUUUUSSS!'

Mac smelt it before he noticed smoke seeping out from under the garage door. He had an immediate flashback. He was in a street in Paris and his colleague Kate Grimsson lay unmoving on the ground before him.

He didn't think, he just shouted, 'RUN!' as loudly as he could.

Luckily no-one stopped to argue and the team all ran back the way they had come. This proved to have been the correct decision.

They watched as smoke poured out of every crack around the garage door and then from under the roof. A few seconds later there was a loud 'whump' and the metal garage door flew right through the space that they had been standing in. It drove straight through the wooden fence and ended up in someone's back garden. A body had also been thrown out by the blast. It lay halfway between the fence and the garage. It was charred black and there was no movement.

The smoke got worse, it hung in the air like a thick fog now. Then they were all shocked by the sudden sounds of whooshes and whistles as a barrage of rockets screamed out of the garage. Luckily, nearly all of them were stopped by the wooden fence. They lay on the ground moving erratically while spewing red, yellow and green sparks until finally their fuel ran out.

'Fireworks!' Fin shouted. 'The bastard's been storing fireworks in there.'

Another batch of rockets screamed out of the garage but these seemed to be much larger than the first. Once again most of the rockets were stopped by the fence but this time more than a few screamed through the gap in the fence that had been made by the garage door. They watched helplessly as the fireworks smashed straight through the downstairs windows of two houses before they exploded. A few seconds later they saw yellow flames spring up inside.

'Come on!' Fin shouted with urgency. 'We need to get everyone out of those houses.'

The team didn't hang around and all but Mac broke into a run. Fin had his phone out and called for help as he ran.

Mac hobbled along as fast as he could knowing that he would suffer for it tomorrow but not caring. Before he reached the street, he heard a sound from behind him. He turned and looked. The roof of another garage had been blown off and a series of glowing balls hit the sky and exploded. He said a little prayer hoping that no more of the garages were crammed with fireworks.

With a loud 'whoosh' a group of eight or nine rockets that seemed to be tied together went straight up and then started to fall back to earth as only a couple of the rockets had been ignited. Then the rest of the rockets started firing and the bundle flew at an immense speed at a downward angle straight towards the buildings further down the hill. Mac watched helplessly as they screamed towards a house and crashed straight through a ground floor window. As before yellow flames were visible a few seconds later.

He walked as fast as he could. Once he was back on the street, he noticed that a car had just arrived. It was flame red in colour and had the word 'Fire' on the bonnet. He guessed that the fire station couldn't be too far away. A man got out and Mac dragged him down the road until he could see the house that was on fire down the hill. The Fire Captain got straight on his radio and ordered a fire engine to go to the location. Mac could do no more.

Neither could Aiden or Fin. Once they had explained the situation to the Fire Captain, they were all pushed back behind a cordon well up the road along with the residents. Roman candles were popping now, bright balls of colour cascading into the sky and exploding with loud bangs. Another garage went up and ranks of colourful rockets flew skywards. The firemen had just started spraying a stream of water on the garages but it didn't seem to be having much effect as fireworks were still exploding in every direction. Mac had never been in a war zone before but he felt as if he was in one now.

All he could do now was stand with the men, women and children of Altmore Gardens as they stood watching their homes go up in flames while a mad firework display played loudly out in the background. Mac looked around him. Most of the crowd standing with him looked as if they had just gotten out of bed. Some had dressing gowns and slippers on while a few were only dressed in pyjamas. One middle aged man only had a T-shirt on and a pair of underpants that had the Manchester United badge on the front and the words 'Red Devil' in large red letters on the backside.

There was another loud 'whump'.

Another garage going up, Mac thought. He also noticed a thick column of oily smoke rise into the air and surmised that one of the heating oil storage containers had caught fire. He guessed that it wouldn't be the last.

They all looked up as another mass of rockets shot straight up into the black sky and then exploded in a shower of red, green and gold sparks.

A little boy near Mac with a rapturous look on his face couldn't help jumping up and down and shouting, 'That was a good one!'

His mother had her arms around him, holding him tightly, but her eyes were not on the sky. She was looking straight ahead at the home that she'd abandoned just minutes before. Tears fell as she watched everything that she owned in this world going up in flames.

Chapter Fourteen

Mac first felt the pressure of the explosion on his skin. The sound followed sometime later. She lay there on the ground and he needed to get to her. She lay unmoving while the flames burned all around her. He tried and tried but, as hard as he ran, he couldn't get any closer. He shouted at her to get up and run, run from the flames. He looked up and there she was hanging out of a window. She was screaming in fear as the yellow flames licked all around her. Her face started to melt...

Suddenly he was standing in a dark space. Even though he couldn't see anything he knew that it was a strange space too. What had happened? What was he doing here? For a few seconds he had no idea as his brain was still full of explosions and fire. Gradually the dream faded away and he realised that he was awake and in the real world. He felt blindly along the wall for a light switch but it took him some time to locate it as he had absolutely no idea where he was. Eventually he found the switch and turned the light on.

He looked around the hotel room and he remembered. Somehow, the memory seemed stranger than the dream he'd just had. He sat on the end of the bed and rubbed his face with his hands. He held his right hand out in front of him. It was shaking quite badly. He gripped it hard with his other hand. His back didn't feel too bad but he knew that it was too early to tell whether he'd done himself any damage. It usually took between eighteen to thirty-six hours before his pain levels started to increase.

He looked at his phone. It was only five-thirty. He was wide, wide awake so he showered and dressed.

Before he went downstairs, he held his hand out again. It had stopped shaking. Even so, he was aware that he might have a problem. It would have to wait for now.

The breakfast room was empty as it was so early but it had a coffee machine in one corner and some paper cups. He filled up a cup, put the closure on the top and went into reception. He ordered a taxi.

He stood outside while he waited and looked eastwards towards the rising sun. The clean nascent light contrasted with the several dirty plumes of smoke that were clearly visible on the skyline. He thought that it had been bad last night but he now realised with a sinking heart that it might be even worse than he'd thought.

The taxi driver dropped him as near the cordon as he could. Even at this early hour a small group of people were standing watching the firemen scurrying around while huge arcs of water were being directed on the still smouldering garages. The dawn light showed the damage all too starkly. On Altmore Gardens itself six houses had been burnt to the ground while another ten or so had been badly damaged with the roofs having caved in. He sincerely hoped that everyone had managed to get out in time. Mac remembered that houses on other streets had been damaged too and wondered if they looked the same. He turned and saw two familiar figures walking towards him. It was Fin and Aiden. It seemed that sleep had evaded them too.

'Have they any idea how bad it was yet?' Mac asked with urgency as they approached him.

'We had a word with the Chief Fire Officer not long ago and we told him what we knew,' Fin said. 'There's no definitive body count yet. They're still damping down so they haven't been able to get into all of the buildings yet to check for casualties.'

'What do they think though?' Mac asked.

He knew that they'd have a rough idea as people would have been reported missing by family or friends.

'As I said they're not sure but they think it could be as high as ten,' Fin replied with a downcast expression.

'Ten dead?' Mac said in disbelief.

'The Fire Officer told us that it might have been a lot worse if we hadn't acted so quickly,' Fin said. 'Most of the fireworks were Chinese and designed to be used in professional shows so they were really powerful. So powerful, in fact, that in one house a single rocket took the whole window frame out rather than just break the glass. He said that once they got inside a house, they were worse than a firebomb and, with so many fires starting at the same time, the firemen didn't have much of a chance. They had to concentrate on the garage and could only cover those house fires where they knew that someone was in danger. That's why so many of the houses are so badly damaged. It took quite some time before they had enough crews and fire engines to attend to every fire.'

'There was a house on fire down the hill. I told the fire officer about it. Do you know what happened there?' Mac asked.

Fin and Aiden looked at each other. Mac knew that he didn't really want to hear the answer.

'There were four people living in one house, a father, mother and two young kids and there were two in the house next door, an elderly couple we've been told. As far as they can tell no-one got out. They said that they had no chance. When the rockets hit, they exploded setting fire to everything. They reckoned that the smoke would probably have got them first,' Fin replied with some sadness. 'If I'm being honest, we're lucky it's not a lot worse.'

'I couldn't sleep at all last night, I just couldn't stop thinking about what had happened here and about the bastards who had caused it,' Aiden said angrily.

'However, one thought occurred to me,' he continued. 'If Jackie Connerty and Alex Ganson were dealing in dodgy fireworks then there's only one place that they'd be headed with them and that's over the border where the sale of fireworks is illegal. If they had the right connections, and you can bet that Jackie did, then there was a nice profit to be made. So, they'd need quite a big truck to move that many fireworks, wouldn't they?'

Mac was beginning to see where Aiden was going.

'That's right and we know that Paddy and 'Wee' Tim had a truck full of cows going North so you're guessing that, after the cows were delivered, they were going to carry on up to Derry and fill the truck up with fireworks?'

'That's my guess,' Aiden said. 'I'll be having a serious word with that pair when we get back.'

'We'll have to make a formal statement on what happened yesterday so fancy going to the station and getting it over with?' Fin asked. 'There's nothing we can do here.'

Mac and Aiden nodded gloomily.

'The only bright spot is that we do have a decent canteen there and we can get some breakfast afterwards if you're up for it,' Fin added.

'I hope they do sausage and egg sandwiches,' Mac said hopefully.

'And here was me thinking that you'd want some nice white pudding,' Fin replied with a wink.

It wasn't the greatest joke perhaps but, standing in the ruins of people's lives and on the very spot where lives had been lost, they all laughed. It was all they could do.

The police station was protected on all sides by high walls which were festooned with CCTV cameras. On one side of the high blank black metal gates there was an observation post that looked down on the street below. It was protected by a massive wire cage. The building looked more like a military blockhouse in a war zone than any police station that Mac had ever seen before. He felt a shiver go up his spine as they drove inside.

Fin took them to an interview room and a young policeman took their statements. While Aiden was giving his, Mac phoned Dan and told him what had happened. Dan, sounding even grumpier than usual, had some bad news of his own. There were now three confirmed deaths due to the fentanyl contaminated white puddings. Mac had been hoping against hope that they might have somehow stopped them reaching the public. He couldn't help feeling a little depressed by the news.

After the formalities were completed, they made their way to the canteen which, to Mac's delight, they did indeed do sausage and egg sandwiches. After everything that had happened, he desperately felt the need for some comfort food. They had to wait a minute to get a table as the canteen was full of uniformed officers who were getting some breakfast before going on duty.

'So, what now?' Mac asked a little later as he wiped his mouth with a napkin.

He felt a little better now. The sandwich had been a big hit with him.

'Well, there's not much you can do here for now,' Fin said. 'We'll be investigating what happened last night for quite a while.'

'That's good because I'd quite like to...'

Aiden was interrupted by a couple of uniformed sergeants who had come over to join them. One of them placed a hand on Fin's shoulder.

'Is that you really you, Fin? Hanging out with your little taig buddies again, are you? You should fancy these two for last night's fireworks as I hear that they're pretty good at blowing things up,' he said with a smile that wasn't a smile. 'Don't get too fond of them now, you may have to shoot them one day. With any luck that is.'

The two sergeants walked away laughing. Mac could see that Fin was seething.

'Just a minute,' he said before getting up and going over to the two sergeants.

Mac could see him talking to them and then pointing towards himself. The smiles suddenly disappeared from their faces.

'I'm sorry Mac. As you can see, we still have some dinosaurs in the force,' Fin said as he sat back down.

'I take it that 'taig' is not a term of endearment in these parts?' Mac asked.

'You can say that again,' Aiden said. 'It's a word that they use up here for Catholics and basically anyone from the South. Think of black people and the 'N word' and you won't be too far off.'

Mac had already gotten the idea well before he heard Aiden's explanation.

'What did you tell them?' Mac asked.

'Well, while I admitted that Aiden here is, in actual fact, a taig,' Fin said with a wink, 'I pointed out to them that you were in fact a very senior British police officer who had been sent over by the Home Office to have a look around. I hinted at possible job losses.'

'You lied then,' Mac said with a laugh.

'Yes, that I did,' Fin admitted with a wide smile. 'Sorry Aiden, you were saying something before we were so rudely interrupted?'

'I was just going to say that I'd like to get back to interview two characters called 'Wee' Tim Mullins and Paddy Geraghty who might just be able to shed some light on where those fireworks were heading.'

'Okay then, I'll drop you back at your car,' Fin said.

Mac had almost forgotten that they'd left their car at Jackie's factory just the day before. It seemed a lot longer. An awful lot had happened since then.

As they left the canteen Mac glanced over at the two sergeants who looked back at him nervously. He stopped, got out his notepad and scribbled some nonsense in it. He noticed with some amusement that they had both turned quite pale.

As they drove back to the factory Aiden made a call. He told someone to pick up Paddy and 'Wee' Tim and throw them in separate police cells until he got there.

They both shook hands with Fin before they left.

'Mac, I hope that those eejits haven't put you off Derry. Come and look me up if you're ever in these parts again,' Fin said.

Mac promised that he would. In truth though, he was glad to be heading back to Ballydove. There was a tenseness in the city that he found tiring.

'Does it upset you when they call you a taig?' Mac asked as they drove off.

'No, not really,' Aiden replied. 'I don't like it but I expect it. Still the police here have come a long way since the days of the 'B' Specials.'

Mac thought that some of them still had a bit further to go. Then he remembered the casual racism he'd often heard against black and Asian people by members of the London police and wondered if they were really any better.

'Would it be too far out of our way if we went back through the Bogside?' Mac asked.

He was curious to see what the Catholic side of the river looked like. He soon found that it had flags and murals enough and, apart from the colours, it looked exactly the same as the Protestant side. Mac found it just as depressing too. He'd only come across this marking of territories before with street gangs, where sometimes a gang member might be killed just for being in the wrong postcode. However, he also noticed that, as with the Protestant side, the flags were just in a few small areas. Most of the city was thankfully devoid of sectarian markings.

Then they were back over the river again. They called into the hotel and picked up their plastic bags and then they were on their way back to Ballydove. Mac felt quite relieved. He wasn't sure if this was down to the city or to the all too exciting events of the previous evening.

Probably both, he concluded.

'So, what do you think?' Aiden asked as they left the city behind them.

'It's a beautiful place but I must admit that I didn't like the flags,' Mac replied.

'I can see that but it's changing Mac and mostly for the better. Twenty or thirty years ago it was basically a war zone. Give it time.'

The River Foyle once again accompanied them on their way and it looked peaceful and serene behind a line of green trees. Mac wasn't taking in the scenery though, he was still thinking about Derry. While the schizophrenic nature of the city was bad enough, it was the police station that had unsettled him most. It wasn't the 'banter' with the sergeants so much as the station itself that had bothered him. He remembered something that his old boss Rob Graveley had said a few years after he'd joined the London murder squad. There had been riots in one of the sink estates and one of their colleagues had been killed.

'It's always good to remind ourselves that we can only do our job if we have the consent of the public. If we don't have that then we might as well give up.'

It was something that he'd borne in mind ever since. Somehow that fortified police station didn't speak to him of consent but of the imposition of power.

Aiden could see that Mac was deep in thought.

161

'Those sergeants didn't upset you now, did they?' Aiden asked.

'No, God knows I've been called worse things in my time. It was that police station. I found it quite chilling for some reason.'

'Yes, it's not exactly welcoming, is it?' Aiden said. 'You'd think they'd have scaled it all back a bit by now but I reckon that the high walls and all the security features are there to make the policemen feel safe more than for any other reason.'

Mac thought that Aiden might well be right. Either that or they were waiting for another war to break out.

He watched the scenery go by until it turned into a blur and then went black. When he woke up, he could see a lake on his left with some low hills in the distance. He rubbed his face with his hands.

'Is that Lough Mourne?' he asked.

'It is,' Aiden replied. 'Did you enjoy your nap?'

Mac's neck felt stiff and it clicked as he moved his head around in a circle.

'I'm not sure that enjoyed is the word. I still feel as if I haven't slept in a week.'

'Yes, me too. I'll drop you back at your hotel and then I'll be going home myself for a long sleep.'

'What about Paddy and 'Wee' Tim?' Mac asked.

'They'll keep. Giving them a little time to think about their sins before we interview them won't hurt.'

'We?' Mac asked.

'If you want to that is,' Aiden replied.

Mac did. A little later they passed by the sign for Ballintra once more.

'When did you say that the races were on?' Mac asked remembering something that Aiden had said on the way up.

'A week tomorrow,' Aiden replied. 'Why are you thinking of staying until then?'

'Yes, I think I just might. I'll need to check with my neighbour first though as she's looking after my dog. After all we still haven't got any idea who killed Jackie yet so there's still some digging to do but, I must admit, I'd love to see the races.'

'You'll enjoy it. It's a grand day out.'

It had gone eleven by the time that Aiden had dropped him back at his hotel. They agreed that he'd come and pick up Mac around five o'clock. Before he went up to his room, he made sure that he extended his booking until a week on Monday and, luckily, they had room for him. He then phoned his neighbour Amanda and, luckily, she was happy to look after his dog Terry for a little while longer. He'd have to do something really nice for her when he got back.

Before he went to sleep, he rang Dan and gave him a quick update. He could tell that Dan was even grumpier than usual and found that it wasn't just his news that led to it. Despite all their efforts, the hunt for the deadly white puddings didn't seem to be going too well. It was obvious that Dan was fearing the worst.

He sat on the edge of the bed for a while and wondered if Jackie's murderer realised what he'd done. Jackie's death sentence had led to the deaths of so many more on both sides of the Irish Sea. He sighed and set his alarm for four. He was still thinking about the white puddings when he fell fast asleep.

He heard a loud bang and felt the world move. He felt incredibly anxious and his heart was beating very fast. He opened his eyes, sat up and looked around for the source of the sound. The hotel room was quiet and still and he realised that the sound must have come from some dream he'd been having. He tried to remember what it had been about but it slipped away into a dark corner of his mind. The anxiety lingered for a while longer.

He eventually summoned the energy to look at his phone. It was nearly four o'clock and his alarm would be going off soon anyway.

He sat up and only then noticed that his hand was shaking again. The anxiety was like a hard ball in his stomach. What was happening to him?

A shower, shave and a change of clothes made him feel a little better. He was on his way outside when he had a thought. He went back inside and spoke to the receptionist. He needed to ask her a question.

'I see that Bishop Crotty is in the news. In fact, they're saying that he might be the next Cardinal of Ireland. I believe that he used to be a priest here at one time. Is that right?'

'Oh yes, he was here about twenty years ago or so, in fact he was the priest who baptised me,' she replied with a smile. 'My mother's a terrific fan of his. She said that he's a lovely man and she's praying every day that he gets picked.'

He thanked her and then waited outside for Aiden. His theory had been all but confirmed. He thought about what he should do next.

There would be no easy way to do it, he knew that. He remembered that it was still Friday and he figured that the weekend might give Aiden the time he needed, if he followed his suggestion that is. He needed to do it now. The only problem was Mac couldn't be sure how he'd react. By the time Aiden pulled up he had a plan sketched out in his mind.

It was the simplest approach possible, Mac thought, and therefore probably the right one.

'Did you get some sleep?' Aiden asked as Mac climbed in the car.

'Yes, and you?'

'It was more like going unconscious if I'm honest. Anyway, let's see what these pair have to say for themselves.'

164

'How are you going to do it?' Mac asked.

'Well, Tim, for all his size, will definitely be the easier nut to crack. I'll tell him that we've already spoken to Paddy and that he's told us everything. It might work.'

The police station was on the outskirts of town. It was a modern building rendered white. It had no high walls and no obvious security features. It also had actual doors that you could actually walk through. It was as unlike the police station in Derry as it could be.

Aiden's plan worked. He was very convincing and when he passed Tim a tablet showing the news story with some very graphic pictures of the devastation in Derry, he was almost blubbering. He told them everything.

Paddy, on the other hand, was closed-faced and obviously determined to tell them as little as possible. Aiden told him that Tim had already spilled all the beans.

'I don't believe you. You're just telling me that to get me to snitch. Well, I'm not saying a word,' Paddy said with determination.

Aiden sighed and then played him a small part of the interview he'd had with Tim.

'The rat!' Paddy said with disgust. He quickly regained his composure. 'Well anyway, we might have been planning to do something but we didn't. You can't bang us up for not doing something, can you?'

'I can actually,' Aiden said with a little smile.

This seemed to unnerve Paddy. Mac thought he was starting to sweat a bit.

'What do you mean?'

'Well, I asked you and Tim a straight question when I spoke to you both in the pub,' Aiden said as he took out his phone. 'You both lied to me. You knew that the deal that you and Jackie were cooking up involved fireworks, didn't you?'

'Well, perhaps but I'm sure I must have mentioned it when we spoke. Yes, I'm sure I did,' Paddy said with confidence.

Aiden touched the screen of his phone.

'So, is there anything else you can tell me?'

'No honestly, that's all we know. Jackie told us nothing at all about the deal. Honestly.'

'You were recording us!' Paddy said in something like shock.

Mac turned and gave Aiden a respectful look. He hadn't noticed it either.

Paddy's shoulders slumped as he asked, 'Okay what are we looking at here? Wasting police time?'

'Not this time Paddy. I'm afraid that you've told one lie too many,' Aiden said as he passed the tablet over to Paddy.

He read the headlines and looked up at Aiden. All the colour drained from his face.

'Were those the fireworks that we were supposed to be picking up?' he asked in a quiet voice.

Aiden nodded.

'Jesus,' Paddy said softly to himself. 'It says here that there are ten people dead. Is that true?'

'As far as we know but I'm hearing that it might be more as they are still some burned out houses that haven't been properly investigated yet. The fireworks were being guarded by someone called Alex Ganson in a row of garages...'

Aiden stopped and looked at Paddy.

'Ganson, you've heard that name before, haven't you?'

'Well, I might have and I might not,' Paddy said.

Aiden gave him his best glare.

'Well, perhaps I heard that it was someone called Ganson who Jackie partnered up with quite a while ago when he was smuggling tobacco.'

166

'That would have been Sandy Ganson, Alex's father then?' Aiden asked.

'Spot on. Anyway, when the lads found out they weren't happy with Jackie at all, kneecapping would have been the best he could have hoped for. It was lucky for him that, only a few weeks before, Maggie had been called in to have a look at the Commandant's young son who was sick. It was lucky for them that Maggie had come so quickly. She drove the wee thing to hospital herself just in time for them to save his life. She didn't know it but she saved Jackie's life too when she did that.'

This was a piece of information that explained a lot, Mac thought. Not just how Jackie had weaselled his way out of a severe punishment from the IRA but also how he and Alex Ganson knew each other in the first place.

'That's interesting,' Aiden said. 'Anyway, when we knocked on the garage door it looks like Ganson knocked over a table lamp he'd been using to light the place and broke the bulb. It seems that some of the fireworks had been damaged and had leaked onto the garage floor. The hot bulb ignited the gunpowder and a few seconds later the whole lot went up.'

'So?' Paddy asked. 'All that has nothing to do with me.'

'No? Well, do you think we'd have been knocking on the door like eejits asking to be let in if we knew that Ganson was sitting on top of what was basically a massive bomb?' Aiden said angrily.

Paddy gave this some thought.

'Well, perhaps not. Still, it was just a little lie,' he said in a wheedling voice.

'If you'd told us the truth then those lives might have been saved,' Aiden said pointing to the tablet. 'You can be sure that I'll be pointing that out to the judge.'

Aiden ended the interview and stood up.

'Are you not going to give us bail then?' Paddy asked hopefully.

'No way. I'm not going to give you even the slightest chance to do a runner. You can ask the judge for bail when you see him on Tuesday,' Aiden replied.

'Ah but it's only Friday now,' Paddy pointed out with a pained expression.

'That's right, it is, isn't it? Thanks for reminding me about that. I'll be off to the pub then to have a few pints and a bit of craic. Have a nice weekend,' Aiden said by way of parting.

Outside the station Aiden said, 'So, what's next then?'

'With the case? Well, we've found out a lot about Jackie and hopefully it might have even led to a few lives being saved. We just keep plugging on.'

'I guess you're right. Fancy a pint?'

Mac was thoughtful for a moment.

'I think I'd like to go back to my hotel, if that's okay.'

'Yes, sure, of course,' Aiden replied looking slightly puzzled.

As they drove back Mac was deep in thought. He was still turning over what he was planning to do in his mind. While he was mostly sure that he would be doing the right thing there was still a little seed of doubt in his mind.

'Are you feeling okay? Is your back playing you up?' Aiden asked with some concern.

He'd been so wrapped up in his thoughts that he hadn't noticed that the pain had started to ramp up a little.

'Well, it's not great...' Mac replied.

The hotel came into sight. Mac had butterflies in his stomach and could feel his palms sweating.

He had to do it though, he told himself.

'Here you are,' Aiden said as he pulled up outside the hotel.

'Can you drive over there for a minute?' Mac asked as he pointed to the far side of the car park.

Aiden gave him another puzzled look but did as he asked.

'Can you turn the engine off?' Mac asked.

Aiden did.

'What's going on Mac?' he asked.

'I'd like to ask you a question and I think it might be good if you answered it truthfully.'

'Why sure, of course I will,' Aiden replied having no idea where this was going.

Mac licked his lips and then dove in.

'I know that something's on your mind and I think it's the same something that made you leave Caitlin and move back from Dublin. Do you want to talk about it?'

'What?' Aiden asked his expression a mixture of puzzlement and surprise. 'Mac, I've absolutely no idea what you're talking about.'

'I'm talking about Bishop Crotty and you.'

Chapter Fifteen

Aiden looked at Mac with wide eyes. It was clear that he didn't quite believe what he'd just heard.

'What?' he said with a look of utter disgust on his face.

He opened the car door and almost fell over getting out. He turned and shut the door so hard that it made the car rock. Mac could see him walking up and down behind the car in the rear-view mirror. He kicked the car's back wheels angrily a few times before he finally calmed down a little. He leant against the back of the car and didn't move for a good five minutes.

Mac was not a religious man but he found himself saying a little prayer that he'd done the right thing.

Eventually Aiden opened the door and sat down, shutting the door softly behind him. He rested his forehead on the steering wheel and closed his eyes.

'How on earth did you find out about that?' he asked in a near whisper.

'Well, I think just about everyone has noticed how miserable you are and it had me wondering why. I noticed you looking at the church with some disgust when you dropped me off for the funeral and that got me thinking. My suspicions were only confirmed that night at the hotel in Derry when we were waiting for Fin to pick us up. There was a news story on the TV about a Bishop John Crotty who was favourite to be the next Cardinal of Ireland. I also found out that he used to be the parish priest in Ballydove when you were a child. Aiden, I've dealt with quite a few people in my time who were abused as children so, when I saw such bitter hatred on your face, I knew.'

There was a silence that seemed to last forever.

'I was nine,' Aiden said softly. 'I was nine when that bastard first raped me.'

'And you've never told anyone?' Mac asked.

He turned and gave Mac a despairing look.

'I told my mother when I was fifteen.'

Now it all made sense to Mac. He'd not only been carrying the burden of being sexually abused as a child but also the guilt for his mother's death. Mac thought that he must have immense mental strength, a life experience like that would have driven many people towards drugs or madness.

'Tell me,' Mac said softly.

Aiden did.

He told him how his mother was such a devout Catholic that she'd insisted that her only son become an altar boy when he'd have much preferred to have been playing football with his friends. The parish priest back then was a young Father Crotty who was the darling of all the congregation, especially the women. However, Father Crotty had a dark side and Aiden found out all about that after his second mass as altar boy.

He'd gone back to the presbytery to take his robes off when he noticed Father Crotty lock the door behind him. He had a strange look on his face. He then physically turned Aiden around and forced him to bend over the desk. He pulled his trousers down and raped him. There were some mass cards on the desk with a picture of Jesus on the front. He was smiling and showing his sacred heart off. The pain was unbearable. He prayed to Jesus with all his heart for it to stop.

It didn't.

When the priest was finally done, he pulled up Aiden's shorts and trousers and then started talking to him as though nothing had happened. As he walked home, he started to wonder if it was indeed something that he'd just dreamed up. The pain told him that it was real.

He had tried to stop being an altar boy but his mother wouldn't hear of it. She even dragged him there physically to make sure that 'he did his Christian duty' as she put it. He tried to tell her several times what had happened but he couldn't. He was too ashamed and she wasn't listening anyway. Like most of the parishioners she wouldn't hear a bad word said about Father Crotty. So, it turned into something of a cat and mouse game in trying to avoid the Father, one he lost more often than he won. This went on for three very long years until finally Father Crotty was given a new parish.

When he was fifteen his mother suggested that he should become a priest himself. It was the last straw. He exploded and told his mother what one priest had done to him. He told her in some detail. The very next day she walked under a bus.

'And you think that she committed suicide, don't you?' Mac asked.

'I know she did. It was the guilt. It was her that had insisted on me becoming an altar boy after all,' Aiden said.

'She might not have though. Your father said that she was often distracted as she crossed the road. Now, I'm not saying that she didn't feel guilty, just that she might have had her head full of what you'd told her and that she might not have been paying full attention.'

Mac could see that this hadn't convinced Aiden.

'Anyway, if she was such a devout Catholic as you say, then there was no way that she'd kill herself,' Mac argued. 'Suicide, after all, is a mortal sin.'

He could see that this argument carried a little more weight with him.

'You might be right Mac but I just don't know what to think any more. I'm so tired of it all. Ever since I saw him again on TV all the feelings of anger and shame that I thought I'd buried have come flooding back. I even found myself getting angry at Caitlin. That's why I left Dublin. I couldn't stand to see her hurt.'

'But she's hurting anyway. Her father told me that she's been really miserable since you left Dublin but she wouldn't tell him why. You need to tell her Aiden,' Mac said.

'I'm...I'm not sure I can Mac,' he said bleakly. 'I don't think I have it in me.'

'You've told me and that wasn't so hard, was it?'

'No, I suppose not,' Aiden said trying to raise a smile and failing. 'I'm afraid Mac, what if she...what if she doesn't want me once she knows?'

'Well, you'd be no worse off then, would you? Look, I doubt very much that will be the case but you have to tell her. The very least you owe her is an explanation as to why you left so suddenly.'

Aiden still didn't look totally convinced.

'I suppose...I'm so ashamed of it though, Mac. It feels like an acid that's eating me away inside.'

Mac turned, grabbed him by the shoulder and looked him straight in the eye.

'You have nothing to be ashamed of, for God's sake you were only nine years old. You did nothing wrong. It was that monster Crotty who should be ashamed not you,' Mac said fiercely. 'Believe me, Caitlin will say the same thing too if you can just summon up the courage to tell her.'

Mac crossed his fingers as Aiden silently gave this some thought.

'You're right, I can't go on like this anymore,' he said almost to himself.

'It's seven o'clock now, you can be in Dublin in three hours or so. If she's not in then sit on her doorstep until she arrives. You have to tell her everything and you have to tell her tonight,' Mac said.

173

'I will Mac, I will.'

He smiled as he detected something in Aiden's expression that he hadn't seen before. It was hope.

Mac climbed out of the car and said, 'Drive safely now and text me if everything goes okay.'

'What about you?' Aiden asked.

'Oh, I'll be fine. I was planning on spending some time with Mick and Maureen over the weekend anyway.'

Mac wished him luck and shut the door. He said another little prayer as he watched the red taillights disappear into the distance.

He went into the hotel and had a bite to eat. He'd planned to sit and have a few quiet pints while he mulled things over in his mind but after just one drink he gave up. The mixture of tiredness and the increasing pain in his back had gotten the better of him. He brushed his teeth and tried to get some sleep. It eluded him. Every time he felt like he was about to drop off a sharp spike of pain woke him up again.

It was nearly midnight and his back still hurt even though he was trying to keep as still as he could. He decided that it was time for the little blue knockout pills. He tottered painfully into the bathroom and washed them down with water. The bitter chemical taste of them stayed in his mouth as he lay down again and prayed for oblivion. By one o'clock sleep still hadn't come. The pain was getting worse and he was beginning to despair. Then he woke up and it was bright morning.

He looked over at the clock. It was actually bright afternoon as it had already gone two o'clock. He tried to move onto his side and a raw bright pain ran down his left leg making him yelp out loud.

So, it's going to be one of those days, Mac thought despondently.

He lay there for a while wondering what he should do when there was a light tap on the door. Then another tap. Then it opened. A woman in her late thirties poked her head in.

'Oh, I'm sorry. I can always come back,' she said with a smile.

Mac could see her trolley in the hallway through the open door. It was stacked with bedsheets and towels and cleaning materials.

'I wouldn't bother if I were you. I think I'm likely to be stuck here all day,' he said glumly.

She gave him a concerned look.

'Are you not feeling well?' she asked.

'It's my back,' Mac explained.

'Oh,' she said with a nod of understanding. 'My Danny suffers with the sciatica something terrible at times. When it happens, all he can do is lie down until it goes away.'

'Well, that's exactly the same with me,' Mac said.

'Is there anything you need?' she asked.

'Well, some water by the bed might be good, just in case I need to take any more tablets.'

She went into the bathroom and came back with a full glass of water.

'What about some breakfast?'

'Isn't it a bit late for that?' Mac said.

'Not at all. I'll go and tell them at reception. I'll see you later then,' she said giving him a warm smile.

'See you.'

Her little visitation and her kindness really cheered Mac up. He lay back and tried to think about the case but the pain kept interrupting him. Then there was another light tap on the door. The door opened and the girl from reception came in. She had a tray in her hands and on it were a glass of orange juice, a cup of coffee and a sandwich. Mac's nose told him what was in the sandwich.

White pudding!

'I'm afraid that we've stopped cooking full breakfasts but the cook made this for you,' she said brightly. 'One of the waitresses said that you really liked white pudding.'

'Oh, that's perfect,' Mac said as he tried to sit up. 'Thank you.'

'If you need anything else just give me a ring and I'll come straight up.'

'Thank you, you've been more than kind,' he said with gratitude.

'Oh, it's nothing,' she said as if she really meant it.

Mac tucked into the sandwich thinking it was the best breakfast he'd ever had, mostly perhaps because it had been so unexpected. Afterwards he drifted in and out of a light sleep. He was aware of the door opening at one point and then softly closing again. They were keeping an eye on him and he was once again grateful that he'd picked this hotel.

He finally got some sleep. When he woke up it was evening. He needed the toilet and braced himself as he sat up. So far so good. Leaning on the bedside table he stood up and a flash of pain ran down his leg making him wince.

So still there, he thought.

There was nothing else for it. After he returned to his bed, he took two more blue pills and twenty minutes later he was deeply and blissfully asleep.

Chapter Sixteen

As they headed back to the station Dan got a call from Martin. A man had turned up at Stevenage Police Station saying that he'd been the driver of the refrigerated van that had picked up the white puddings from Derry. Instead of going straight on for Letchworth they made a screeching right turn and headed for the motorway, blue lights flashing and sirens blaring.

The man was waiting for them in an interview room. He was thin, in his early forties and wore a scruffy beard and hair tied back in a ponytail. He looked hollow eyed and wasted. He stood up as they came in.

'Can you check on my sister?' he asked with some urgency. 'I stopped at her house in Birmingham on the way down and I gave her a couple of rolls of white pudding. I've tried calling her but she isn't answering her phone.'

He gave Dan the address. He wrote it down and added a note that the police in Birmingham should be contacted immediately. He handed it to the policeman standing outside the door.

Dan turned on the recorder.

'Can you please give me your name and address for the record?' Dan asked.

'James Murphy, but everybody calls me Jimbo though,' he said.

He tried to smile but, on seeing Dan's expression, it evaporated instantly. He gave Dan his address.

'Can you confirm that you picked up a consignment of white puddings from JayCon Meats in Londonderry, Northern Ireland on Tuesday last?' Dan asked.

'Yes, that was me,' he replied as he shifted nervously in his chair.

Dan showed him the list of butcher's shops that they'd found in Jackie Connerty's safe.

'Mr. Murphy, I want you to read this carefully and let me know if you've supplied any shops that weren't on this list.'

Jimbo took him at his word and took over three minutes to read through the list. Dan didn't try to rush him though. It was too important.

'Yes, that's most of them. I had a few boxes left over so I went around some local shops in Stevenage and Welwyn that I know and they took them off my hands.'

Dan asked him to write down the names and addresses of the shops. As he wrote Dan noted that not all them were butcher's shops. As soon as he'd finished writing Adil snatched the list and hurried outside. They'd have officers at all of the shops within minutes. Dan stopped the recording and waited as patiently as he could until Adil returned. He looked over at his interviewee. He was sweating and he looked extremely uncomfortable.

'Can I get you anything?' Dan asked.

'Some water would be good. I'm afraid that I went on a bit of a bender once I'd got paid,' Jimbo said.

That explained his wasted look, Dan thought. He poked his head out of the door and asked the uniformed officer outside to bring some water.

Adil and the water came in together. Jimbo downed the plastic cup in one go. Dan started the recorder off again.

'Can you tell me who instructed you to make the pickup?' Dan asked.

'It was Jackie.'

Dan showed him a photo.

'Yes, that's Jackie McCormack alright.'

'And that's what you knew him as?'

'Yes, well that was his name, wasn't it?' he replied looking puzzled.

'What were you told to do?'

'I was told that it was just the usual pick up. I must have done it at least twenty times before. I hired the refrigerated van in London and then drove it to Derry. Once there we'd load it up...'

'Who is we?' Dan asked.

'Well, me and a guy called Alex and another guy whose name I can never remember.'

'Was Jackie usually there?'

Jimbo gave it some thought.

'No, not every time but they told me that he always turned up a bit later to pay the guys off.'

'Carry on,' Dan instructed.

'So, we loaded up and I drove to Belfast and then I caught the ferry over to Stranraer. It was basically straight down the M6 after that. I was feeling a bit tired so I stopped at my sister's house in Birmingham for a cup of tea and a few hours sleep. She said that she fancied a bit of white pudding so I gave her a few rolls. I guessed that no-one would miss them. I was back in this part of the world early Wednesday morning. Jackie always met me at the factory in Stevenage where he'd take a few boxes out for a 'special delivery' or so he said.'

Dan and Adil looked at each other.

'Go on,' Dan said.

'I waited for quite a while but, when Jackie didn't turn up, I started doing the rounds. I couldn't wait too long because I only had the van until that evening. So, I went around all the butcher's shops and eventually managed to get rid of the lot.'

'Did they pay you cash?'

'Yes, Jackie insisted on that. The deal was that I'd collect all the money and then I'd take a thousand pounds out as my cut. I've still got his share of the money but I'm afraid that I've already spent a good bit of mine at the pub...'

179

They were interrupted by the door being opened and a note being passed to Dan.

'You'll be glad to know that your sister's okay. She luckily hadn't opened any of the white puddings you gave her and they've now been taken away for testing.'

Jimbo visibly relaxed at the news.

'Thanks a lot, that's a real weight off my mind.'

'When did you first learn about the drugs?' Dan asked.

'Just today on the news. As I said I've been on a bit of bender and then I had to sleep it off. When I heard about it on the radio I came straight here.'

'So, you're saying that you had no knowledge of the drugs before today?'

'Look, I knew that Jackie was up to something dodgy but I honestly had no idea that it was drugs. I wouldn't have touched it with a bargepole if I did. I just thought they were rewrapping stuff that had gone out of date or something,' Jimbo replied.

Dan believed him.

'We may have a few more questions so I'd like you to hang around for a bit if you don't mind.'

'Normally I'd say okay but, if I'm honest, I'm totally shattered. I need to lie down for a bit,' Jimbo said.

Dan could see that he wasn't lying. He looked totally drained.

'Shall I see if I can get you a police cell for a while? I promise we won't shut the door.'

'That would be great,' Jimbo replied with half a smile. 'Anywhere horizontal will do right now.'

Dan asked the policeman outside to arrange it and then asked where the communications room was. The room was surprisingly quiet. Eight uniformed officers in crisp white shirts sat at semi-circular desks looking at multiple monitor screens while talking softly into their headset mics and gently tapping at their keyboards. A sergeant got up and approached them.

Dan introduced himself and Adil and then asked, 'Is there any news from the shops yet?'

He was getting worried. The fact that some of the shops weren't butchers meant that they wouldn't have received a visit from the police yet.

'Officers should now be at all of the addresses that you gave us. We think that we might have visited one or two of them already but we've assigned men to each address anyway just in case. They'll call in as soon as they get the details of any customers who might have bought the contaminated items,' she said. 'It shouldn't take too long...'

The sergeant stopped and began listening to a nearby operator. Dan listened too but couldn't make out what the officer was saying.

'We're getting some names in now from one of the shops,' the sergeant said.

She left Dan and Adil and went over to the operator. She came back with a list of five names and addresses.

'These are the first in. The butchers only knew the names but we've been able to put some addresses to them using the Electoral Register.'

Dan scanned the addresses. One of them leapt out at him.

'Have you assigned any officers to these yet?' Dan asked.

'No, we're in the process of doing that now,' she replied.

'We can take this one if you like,' Dan said as he pointed to an address.

The sergeant looked slightly puzzled as she said, 'Yes, if you want to, but we have enough men on the ground.'

'It's just that I'd like to have a look for myself if that's okay,' Dan said.

While that was true, he also knew that he'd feel better if he was doing something rather than just hanging around the comms room waiting for the bad news to come in.

'So, where are we going then?' Adil asked as they climbed into the car.

'I'll direct you. It's only about five minutes from here,' Dan replied.

'I didn't think that you knew Stevenage that well,' Adil said as they pulled away from the station.

'I don't but I know this particular street,' Dan said. 'I used to take my daughter to violin lessons in a house not far from there until a few years ago. Every other Tuesday evening from seven to seven thirty for nearly two years. It's not something you forget.'

They drove around a huge roundabout and took the road towards Hertford. They drove past the super-store and turned left into a housing estate. A few lefts and rights later and they were on the street looking for number fifty-two. It proved to be the middle house in a small row of terraced houses. The little garden in front was neat and tidy and a porch had been added around the front door so you wouldn't get wet when fumbling for your house keys on a rainy day.

Dan rang the bell. On getting no answer he knocked the door as loudly as he could. He then rang the bell again. And again.

There was still no answer.

'We might need those size twelves of yours to open the door if no-one comes,' Dan said to Adil.

As soon as the words had left his mouth Dan saw some movement through the frosted glass panel in the door. The door opened and a flustered looking young woman peered out at them. She looked tired and had obviously just gotten out of bed. She had one hand on the door while the other was holding the two sides of a blue dressing gown together. She had pink pyjamas on underneath.

'Yes?' she asked clearly annoyed at being woken up.

Dan showed her his warrant card. She squinted at it through half-open eyes.

'Is Mrs. O'Dwyer in?'

She looked up to heaven and said, 'Obviously not or she'd have answered the bloody door, wouldn't she?' She looked at them and shook her head. 'You'd better come in, I suppose.'

They followed her into a small living room full of old-fashioned furniture and porcelain ornaments.

'What you want with nan anyway?' she asked.

'And you are?' Dan asked.

'Cassie O'Dwyer. I'm her grand-daughter.'

'And you live here?'

'Yes, while I'm working at the hospital anyway. I'm a nurse there.'

'I take it that you're working on the night shift?' Dan asked with some sympathy.

'Yes, twelve until eight and I hate it. So, what do you want with nan then?'

'I just need to check something. Are you sure that your nan's gone out?'

'Of course, your banging would have woken the dead and, even though she's in her seventies, there's nothing wrong with her hearing.' She thought for a moment. 'It's Saturday, isn't it? She always goes into town on Saturday and meets up with some friends for a drink.'

'Can you check anyway?' Dan asked.

She gave him a puzzled look before leading them out into the hallway. She opened the door to the kitchen and then went as still as a statue. Dan looked over her shoulder. An elderly woman sat in a chair at the kitchen table. Her head was resting on a plate and her left cheek was smeared with baked beans. Her dead eyes seemed to be looking straight at them. Her right hand was down by her side. It was still clutching a fork.

They all just stood there just looking for a few seconds.

'Nan!' Cassie shouted and broke the spell.

She felt for a pulse and her face told Dan that she hadn't found one. Dan felt her skin. It was cold. She'd obviously been dead for some hours. He checked for a pulse too just in case. There was nothing.

'Adil, can you take Miss O'Dwyer back into the living room?' Dan asked.

Cassie was having problems taking it all in and she had a strange disassociated feeling, as though she might still be in bed and having a bad dream. She didn't resist Adil's prompts and followed him out of the room.

Dan looked around the kitchen. Failing to find what he was looking for he put a latex glove on one hand and opened the fridge. There it was right in front of him, three quarters of a roll of 'Mother MacMorragh's Authentic Irish White Pudding'. He closed the fridge door then ensured that the back door of the house and all the windows were locked before leaving the kitchen. He closed the kitchen door behind him. He called it in before joining Adil and the girl in the living room.

Dan knew that the forensics teams had been working overtime so it might be quite a while before anyone would be able to process the crime scene. They were sending two uniformed officers over to guard the house in the meantime.

Cassie sat on the sofa next to Adil. Her head was bent forward and her long ash blonde hair covered her face. Her head went up when Dan walked in. She looked pale and frightened.

'Is nan really dead?' she asked still hoping that it was all just a bad dream.

'Yes, I'm afraid she is,' Dan replied.

184

'I don't understand. I wake up and you're banging at the door and then nan's dead. What's going on?'

'We've only just learned that your nan had purchased some white pudding from a shop in the town...'

'White pudding?' she said interrupting Dan. 'I know she likes it and I've often heard her moaning that she can never get it around here but I still don't...'

Dan could see the realisation dawn on her face.

'It was on the news, wasn't it? I remember now. God, what was it? Yes, they were warning people that they were dangerous or something. I never thought twice, I mean I can't stand the stuff and nan hasn't bought any for ages.'

'A shop that your nan goes to had received a delivery of white puddings recently and unfortunately they included some contaminated ones,' Dan said.

'What was it? It wasn't food poisoning that's for sure.'

Dan thought for a moment and decided to tell her the truth. It would all come out soon and, being a nurse, he'd find it difficult to concoct a lie that she'd believe anyway.

'The white pudding was adulterated with drugs. Heroin and fentanyl to be specific.'

'Fentanyl?' she said in disbelief. 'Some bastard is putting fentanyl in white puddings? My God, what's the world coming to?' She thought for a moment. 'That would explain why she died with her head in her breakfast. She just stopped breathing.'

'I'm sorry Miss O'Dwyer but I'll need you to get dressed and then pack a small bag,' Dan asked. 'I'd like you to come to the station and make a statement. In the meantime, the forensics team will need access to the house to process the scene and to safely remove the white pudding. Do you have anywhere that you can stay for a few days?'

'Yes, I can stay with my mum. She lives just outside Peterborough so it will make for a long commute. That's why I started living with nan really, she lived so close to the hospital, but I really liked it here. She was a lovely woman.'

A single tear rolled down one cheek.

'I'll go pack that bag,' she said as more tears started to come.

They heard Cassie's footsteps as she ran up the stairs. While they were waiting for her the two uniforms arrived. Dan briefed them on what had happened and what they needed to do. By the time he'd done that Cassie came down the stairs clutching a small suitcase. She looked both fearful and nervous. It was a look that Dan remembered seeing on his own daughter's face when he'd dropped her off for the first day at her new school.

'I've just rang my mum,' she said.

Dan guessed that it had been something of an emotional conversation as her eyes were red and watery. She managed to keep herself together as she made her statement. After she'd signed it, Dan offered her a lift but she said that she'd sooner catch the train. Her mother would pick her up at Peterborough.

Dan checked in on the communications room again. Besides Mrs. O'Dwyer three more deaths had been reported. Adil could see that the news hadn't improved Dan's mood any.

'Let's go and see if Jimbo's remembered anything new,' Dan said.

They went down to the cells and only one had its door open. Dan looked in and Jimbo was fast asleep. He looked peaceful and had a half-smile on his face. Dan didn't have the heart to wake him up.

'Let's leave him. I'll get one of the local detectives to question him when he wakes up,' Dan said as he looked at his watch. It had gone five. 'Come on, let's get back to Letchworth. There's nothing more we can do here.'

Dan was silent all the way back. For some reason a picture of the baked beans on the old woman's face came back into his mind. The man directly responsible for it was dead too. Was it just events that had conspired to kill the old woman or were there others out there who had her blood on their hands? If there were, Dan promised himself that he'd do his absolute best to bring them all to justice.

Chapter Seventeen

Mac awoke gradually as the light edging the curtains grew brighter. He finally found enough strength to turn and look at the clock. It was seven o'clock. In the morning, he hoped. The need for the toilet forced him to eventually get up. He gingerly sat up and then, even more gingerly, stood up.

His back was still sore but there was no flashing pain and, for that, he was grateful. Every time he had a severe pain episode, he always had the worry at the back of his mind that it might stay like that forever. As it was, he wouldn't be doing any sprinting but, with care, he should be able to get through the day.

He checked his phone and found two messages and a text. The text was from Aiden. Mac had asked him to let him know if it went okay with Caitlin. He smiled when he read it.

It simply said –

Went very very very okay! See you Tuesday Aiden

Good for you! Mac thought feeling instantly cheered up.

One of the voice messages was from Mick inviting him around for Sunday lunch. The other one was from Dan. He was asking Mac if he could attend a conference call at nine o'clock on Monday morning. He sounded worn out and more than a little depressed. Mac guessed that the news on Monday wouldn't be good but he decided that it could wait until tomorrow. Until then he'd think about Aiden's good news and the prospect of lunch with one of his favourite relatives.

A shower, shave and a change of clothes increased his feeling of well-being. He stopped by reception on his way to the breakfast room and thanked the girl again.

'It's nice to see you up and about again,' she said cheerily.

Breakfast was wonderful and he couldn't help noticing that he seemed to have a little more white pudding on his plate than any of the other guests. This too made him smile. Afterwards he went outside. It looked as if it was going to be a lovely day so he sat and thought about what he could do between now and one thirty when dinner was going to be served at Mick and Maureen's house. He settled on going for a drive.

He didn't consciously think about going anywhere in particular but he somehow ended up on the road to Rossnowlagh. He drove past the big hotel and parked his car as close to the sea as he could. Even this early in the day he was not alone. He managed to find a quiet spot where he could sit on a rock and watch the waves gently crash onto the beach and then ebb away again. He found it quite relaxing. Although he tried not to think the memories still percolated upwards into his head.

His mother had loved this beach and she'd brought them there as often as she could when they were over for the summer holidays. She always told people that she thought that the exercise and being out in the sun were good for the children but, looking back, he suspected that she too had good memories of the place.

Back then each day had seemed to last forever. There were sandcastles to make and then destroy, rock pools to explore and foot races with his sisters on the firm sand. There was a blanket to sit on when it was time for sandwiches and, with luck, an ice cream for afters. Then there was the limitless sea to paddle in, to sit in, to splash in and to swim in.

A big wave hit the beach and the smell of the salt spray brought him back in time as a movie played in his head. It was a bright, sunny summer's day and he and his sisters had gone up the beach to explore and there they'd found a jellyfish stranded on the sand. It was round and translucent with veins of bright colour running through it. They talked about what they should do with it for some time until Roisin insisted that they should tell their mother about it.

She'd always had been the most sensible of them all and still was, Mac thought.

Of course, when their mother saw it, she warned them to keep well away from jellyfish as they could sting even when they were dead. The only time Mac could remember being stung was when he had fell into a bed of nettles. He hadn't liked it one little bit. He remembered being nice to Roisin for the rest of the day.

He smiled at the memory as he watched a car drive onto the beach. It was another day now, a blustery rainy October day, and their car was the only one there. Mac had wanted to show Nora the beach even though the weather was awful. They sat in the car eating sandwiches and looking at the grey-black sea and the squalls of rain that came streaming in from the west.

Sitting in a nice warm, dry car listening to the rain battering down on the roof was quite wonderful. The waves, whipped up by the strong winds, were exciting to watch as they pounded the beach and disintegrated into white foam. Then cries from the back seat of the car, weak at first and then quickly growing to a shrill crescendo. Mac had to kneel on his seat and lean over to undo the baby seat. He lifted his new daughter up, who was still a miracle to him, and handed her to Nora. She lay Bridget on her knee and then popped out a breast and suddenly the grizzling stopped.

He sat there holding his wife's hand as she fed their new child while the elements howled wildly outside. It is often said that one is only happy in hindsight but

Mac knew in that moment that he was truly, truly happy.

He shed a tear. It had been over a year but there was still a massive hole in his life now that his Nora was no longer with him. He knew that it would be there until his dying day. Just after she died, the sadness had been overwhelming and debilitating. He couldn't function, all he could do was sleep and be sad. Gradually, he'd learnt how to control the sadness so that he could start doing things and get back to work. Even so there were still times when it came back with full force and today was one of them.

He reminded himself of her last words. She'd looked him in the eye and said, 'Live for me.' He would do his best to do just that.

He stood up and made his way back to the car. He still had a couple of hours to kill so he decided to head for Ballintra. He couldn't remember having been there before so it would be somewhere new for him to explore. It turned out to be basically one long street with a church, a pub and a shop. In a few seconds he was out the other side. All he remembered was the different colours that the squat solid houses had been painted, pink, green, blue, yellow, grey and white. It was certainly colourful.

He looked at his watch. It wasn't even twelve yet. Mac had had enough of his own company and decided to head towards Mick's place. He'd said in his message that dinner was at one thirty but that Mac was to come whenever he was ready. He was more than ready.

He parked outside the 'wee' house and knocked on the door. He got no answer. He heard a sound from behind and turned. A young woman was waving at him from the doorway of the big house.

'We're over here,' she shouted.

He couldn't place her at first but, as he came nearer, he recognised her. Her name was Siobhan and she was

Seamus's wife. She looked like a farmer's wife too, tanned and robust, and with no airs and graces. Mac had liked her a lot when he'd met her for the first time some years ago. She smiled and gave him a hug.

'You're just in time for a cup of tea,' she said as she led him inside. 'Seamus has just finished work and he'll be with us in a few minutes once he's cleaned up.'

Some wonderful smells were coming from his right so he turned and looked through the open door into the large kitchen. He waved at Maureen who was hard at work. She smiled and waved back as did her little helper who was carefully peeling carrots with a scraper. He realised with a start that this must be Aisling, Seamus and Siobhan's daughter.

She must be about eight or nine now, Mac thought. The last time he'd seen her she'd been a dot. He felt a little sad at letting so much time slip by and promised himself that he would visit more often in future.

'Mick is in the living room,' Siobhan said as she joined Maureen in the kitchen.

He turned to his left and entered a room dominated by a large fireplace on the wall opposite that had a massive mantel piece made from a single piece of oak. Mac remembered being told the story by his uncle about how Mac's grandfather had come by that piece of wood. He'd found it washed up on the beach one day after a Dutch ship had been wrecked just off the coast. To his left there stood a huge traditional Irish dresser that was festooned with cups and milk jugs hanging from hooks and massive plates with old-fashioned ornate designs shown to their advantage as well as a scattering of ornaments and souvenirs of long-gone holidays. The room seemed to be somewhat brighter than he remembered when he used to visit as a child and he wondered if this was due to the large French windows that had replaced the single window that used to be in the wall to his right. There was a spectacular view through the windows across the green fields that sloped down to a slate grey sea and the hazy blue line of land on the other side of the bay.

Mick was sitting with a young boy and both were engrossed in a game of snakes and ladders. From the exasperated expression on Mick's face, it looked as if the boy might be winning.

His face broke into a smile when he spotted Mac, 'Ah Denny, I'm glad you could make it. You're just in time. I'm in need of a bit of help as young Michael here is thrashing me.'

Michael looked shyly up at the stranger. Mac reckoned that he must be seven or so by now. At Mick's prompting he took Michael on in the next game and suffered the same fate as his cousin had, a resounding defeat. The game seemed to have broken the ice somewhat as Michael felt that he could do a little victory dance in Mac's presence.

Seamus joined them a little later and brought in a tray with steaming cups of tea and handed them around. They chatted lightly and caught up with the family news from both sides of the Irish Sea and the time flew by. Mac was surprised when Maureen came in and told them that dinner was ready.

They all trooped into the dining room next door and he once again saw the table. He remembered being in some awe of it when he'd been young as it was the largest table that he'd ever seen. It filled the long room and could seat at least sixteen people. Mac remembered his dad explaining that in his father's time not just the family but most of the men who worked on the farm would eat here and that's why it had to seat so many. There was just the seven of them eating there today.

Siobhan came in with a massive joint of beef and placed it in front of Seamus who was seated at the head of the table. He started to slice the meat as

Maureen and young Aisling brought in the vegetables and placed them on the table. They all went out again and came in with yet more bowls of vegetables. Mac thought it a veritable feast.

'Will you say grace please, Denny?' Maureen asked.

Mac felt a moment of pure fear. He hadn't said grace or even heard it said for quite some time. He made himself relax and closed his eyes. He thought of his father and what he used to say before every meal and the words somehow came back to him.

'Bless the food we eat today and bless the hands that made it. May it give us strength and health. Bless us all.'

'Amen,' they all said in unison.

They all smiled, especially Mick.

'My father used to say those exact same words too,' he said with just the hint of a tear in his eye.

Plates were passed up and down and filled to the brim with slabs of roast beef and an assortment of vegetables.

'How's the beef?' Mick asked after Mac had sampled it.

'Wonderful!' he said with utter sincerity. 'Just like beef used to taste like when I was young.'

'The cow that beef came from was fed on the grass in those fields you can see out of the window,' Seamus said with some pride. 'You won't get better beef anywhere.'

Mac could well believe it. He could have cut his meat with a fork it was so tender and it had a succulent flavour that he'd almost forgotten existed. By the time he'd put his knife and fork down he was full to the neck, yet he somehow still found a little room for some home-made apple pie and ice cream.

He had been seated next to young Michael and opposite Aisling. After a little awkwardness Mac soon got them talking and they competed as they told him all about their schools and hobbies and all the various chores that they did around the farm. He found that their enthusiastic chatter really cheered him up after the darkness of the past few days.

When everyone had finished Seamus stood up and nodded at young Michael. They started stacking the plates and dishes and taking them towards the kitchen.

'Whoever does the cooking never washes up,' Mick said as he stood up and started helping too.

'Yes, and don't forget a nice cup of tea for the cooks too. We'll be in the living room,' Maureen said as she winked at Mac. 'Come on and join us. I'd like to have a chat and, don't worry, guests are definitely exempt from the washing up.'

Once they'd gotten themselves comfortably seated Mac asked about Maggie Connerty.

'She's still in bits of course but at least she's started to think about what needs doing, the funeral and so on.'

'I think she's going to need her friends,' Mac said with a shake of the head.

He heard a phone ring in the hallway.

'Oh, Mick will get that. Denny, I heard a rumour that's going around from someone after mass. She said that Paddy Geraghty and Tim Mullins have been arrested by Aiden Maguire and that it had something to do with that fireworks tragedy in Derry. She also said that it had something to do with Jackie Connerty as well. Is that true?' Maureen asked.

Mac hadn't been planning on saying anything about his trip to Derry as it was an ongoing case but it would appear that word had already got out. He reminded himself that Ballydove was, after all, a small town.

'Well, the rumours aren't wrong, I'm afraid to say. I was in Derry with Aiden and another policeman when it all went up. We were there looking for one of Jackie Connerty's associates and we tracked him to a set of garages. Of course, we weren't to know that every one of the six garages he'd rented were stuffed to the roof with professional grade fireworks, bombs basically and a lot of them flying bombs at that. I've honestly never seen anything like it before.'

'They're saying that fourteen people died in the fires it started. Is that right?' Siobhan asked.

'Fourteen?' Mac asked. 'It was only ten the last I heard.'

He realised that he hadn't caught up with the news since he'd gotten back to Ballydove. He also realised that there was probably a good reason why. He knew that the casualty count would rise. It always did.

'Oh yes, I heard it on the news this morning just before I did the milking,' Siobhan replied.

'Jesus, Mary and all the saints!' Maureen exclaimed as she crossed herself. 'And that was Jackie's doing?'

'It looks like it,' Mac said.

'Maggie will take that hard, poor woman,' Maureen said.

Wait until she hears about the white puddings, Mac thought. He decided to keep that to himself for now.

Mick came in with a tray full of teas and a puzzled look on his face.

'Who was that on the phone?' Maureen asked as her husband handed the teas around.

'That was Caitlin. She said that she's coming down on Friday and she's staying for the weekend,' Mick replied.

'Oh, so she'll be here for the races then. I was hoping that she would be. Did she sound alright?' Maureen asked the anxiety clear in her voice.

'Yes, she sounded very much alright to be honest. I'd go so far as to say that she even sounded happy,' Mick said. 'She said that she'd have some news to tell us when she arrives although she wouldn't say what it was.'

'News?' Maureen said with a thoughtful look. She turned to Mac. 'Have you seen young Aiden recently?'

'No, not since Friday,' Mac said innocently.

He was determined not to give anything away.

Maureen gave Mac a penetrating look. She knew that he knew something but, luckily, she was polite enough to leave it at that. Mac suspected that she'd make a good detective.

'Well, it's nice that she's feeling happy,' Maureen said looking a little more relaxed. 'The way that she's been moping around these last few months has had me really worried. I suppose that we'll just have to wait until Friday then.'

Once Seamus and Mick had finished the washing up more tea was served and more family news caught up on. By five o'clock Mac was flagging and had to say his goodbyes. After taking the little blue pills, he sometimes got what he called a 'hangover' from them, a feeling of exhaustion that couldn't be argued with. Of course, he realised that the massive dinner might have something to do with him feeling so tired as well. Mick saw him to the door and luckily Mac remembered the question that he'd been wanting to ask him.

'I was just wondering if there was anyone in the town that I could speak to who might know something about Jackie Connerty's past. We're still looking for a motive for his murder and I could do with finding out as much about him as I can.'

While this was true, he also realised that he had a week to fill before he went home. Finding out about Jackie's past would fill it as well as anything else. He found that he was curious to find out more about the man anyway.

'Oh, you'll want Johnnyboy McGloin then,' Mick replied.

'Johnnyboy?'

'Well, he's in his seventies now but his father was also called John so they called him that when he was young to tell the two of them apart and the name stuck.

He makes it his business to know everything that happens in Ballydove and he's got a great memory,' Mick said. 'If he can't tell you then no-one can. You'll find him most days across the river in the Bridge Bar around lunchtime.'

Mac said goodbye and was thankful to be heading for the hotel. Aware of his tiredness he drove carefully and he was grateful to see the hotel come into view and more than grateful at the sight of his freshly made-up bed. He brushed his teeth, climbed in between the sheets and fell instantly asleep.

Chapter Eighteen

Mac had set his alarm for seven o'clock, just in case he slept in. This proved to have been a wise move as he was still deeply asleep when it went off. He sat up and then, with some trepidation, stood up. The pain was within his normal limits for which he said a little prayer. He also felt well-rested and ready for the day ahead. He held his hand out, it wasn't shaking. He sighed with relief and wondered what that had been about.

He reminded himself that he had a conference call at nine. After getting showered, shaved and dressed he went downstairs, got a coffee to go and returned to his room. He sat in an armchair and tried to marshal his thoughts while he waited for nine o'clock to come. Apart from digging into Jackie's past he wasn't sure what else he could do from this end. Wasn't it much more likely that Jackie's murder had been related to his drug smuggling activities in England? The thought came to him once again that a professional hit might still be the most probable explanation.

At one minute to nine he rang the number that Dan had texted to him and entered the password. He could hear chairs being dragged and papers being shuffled in the Major Crime Team's room in Letchworth.

'Hello Mac, how are you?' Dan's voice asked.

'I'm fine, Dan,' he replied.

'Well, the whole team's here so I'll kick off. Martin has managed to get the latest updates on all the casualty figures so far. The Fire Service in London-derry have said that the latest figure there is fifteen dead and they're now fairly sure that will be the final figure. They're saying that it was so high because there were four major fire sites besides the garages themselves and they had to get help from other fire stations which took some time to arrive. Unfortunately, a lot of elderly people lived on that estate and quite a few of them were hard of hearing. They said that by the time the smoke would have woken them up it would have been too late for them to escape. Now, as for the fentanyl laced white puddings...'

Mac had been dreading this piece of news.

'All of the police forces in the area have been working on this together and, so far, we've managed to account for all the puddings except for around sixty or so but we don't think that any of those are likely to contain fentanyl. We've established that so far that thirteen people have died as a direct result of eating the drug-laced white puddings and four of these were in the Stevenage and Welwyn area. Oh, and two dogs as well.'

Mac had been hoping that it might have stayed at three but he wasn't surprised. Even so he reminded himself that if they hadn't found out about the white puddings when they did the death toll would have been vastly higher. That still meant that twenty-eight people on either side of the Irish Sea had died directly as a result of Jackie's murder. Mac wondered if his killer had ever thought of what the consequences of his act might have been beyond the ending of one man's life.

'Those figures may still go up as at least five of the people who died were elderly and living by themselves. Their bodies were found by friends or relatives but if someone was unlucky enough to have neither then, for all we know, they may still be lying there undiscovered. However, I'd like to say thanks to you all for working so hard over the past few days. Without that, and all the work the other forces have put in, the death toll would have been much higher. Talking about other forces, the Met have also told us that a minor gang war seems to have broken out in North

London between the McInerney gang and the Steeley Boys,' Dan continued. 'It seems that the drugs may have been destined for the McInerney gang who used the route from Northern Ireland to top up their supplies at times when it was difficult to get them through Europe. They had a deal with a Dublin gang who like to heavily cut their heroin with fentanyl and that's why it was so lethal. So far there have been three shootings, one of which has proved to be fatal.'

So, make that twenty-nine then, Mac thought.

'Anyway, one good thing that came out of it was us finding out how the gang were moving shipments of drugs by mixing it with sausage meat and then chemically reclaiming it. We're going to be inspecting all shipments of meat products from Europe in the future and we're working with some scientists who are trying to develop some sort of test kit so we can use to make the process quicker,' Dan said. 'The emergency's over for now but we find that we're still no nearer catching Jackie Connerty's murderer. So, we'll all need to start focussing on that again. Mac, have you come up with anything at your end?'

'Nothing much as yet, I'm afraid. I'm here for another week though and I'll keep digging,' Mac replied.

'Thanks Mac, it's really appreciated. On this side we've got a lot of evidence that was seized from the McCormack house that we've still got to go through. Forensics will send us a report later on. Meanwhile, Martin's trying to crack the shorthand, or whatever it was, that Jackie Connerty was using in the documents we found in the safe. We'll also need to speak to Mrs. McCormack again. I have a feeling that she's not told us anywhere near what she knows. So, for most of you today it will be about knocking on doors in Preston to see what Jackie Connerty's neighbours can tell us about him and then following up on any leads. We'll hold another briefing when and if we get anything new. Keep in contact Mac.'

Mac assured him that he would.

He sat there deep in thought for a while until he suddenly realised that it had now gone nine thirty and that breakfast finished at ten. He put his jacket on and went downstairs.

After an excellent breakfast he got a taxi to the town centre and decided that he'd have a little look around before going to the Bridge Bar. He asked the driver to drop him off at the top of Main Street so that he could walk down the hill towards the river. It wasn't very far to walk and he'd take his time. Anyway, it was easier walking downhill.

He remembered this street as always being thronged with shoppers when he'd been young but today it was almost devoid of people. He passed by a brightly coloured shop that had its door open only to find that it was a bookie's. He could see a large red shop on the left situated halfway down the hill, it was one that Mac remembered his mother dragging him into when he was young. His view of the emptiness inside was only obscured by a large 'To Let' sign propped up against the window. Looking at the layer of dust on the sign Mac surmised that it had been there for some time. He stood outside and looked in at the empty space.

He remembered that a bell had jingled every time the door opened. He remembered the smell of a freshly made bed as he walked inside and the shelves that ran right up to the ceiling that were tightly stuffed with linens and fabrics. This was where his mother went about the serious business of buying sets of Irish linen sheets as presents for any upcoming weddings back in England. His mother always used to take her time doing this and seemed to want to see every sheet they had in the place before she could even start narrowing it down a bit. The assistant had a ladder that moved on wheels from left to right that she used to reach the highest shelves. He enjoyed watching her scurry up the ladder to the top but even that palled eventually. It all seemed to take forever to a young boy who just wanted to get back to playing with his cousins.

He stood there and looked inside at the emptiness as the memories washed over him. He felt sad for what he had lost but also for what the town seemed to have lost.

He carried on down the hill past the bank where he found that a few shops were still open and actually sold things: a butcher's, a takeaway food shop and a pharmacy. He stood outside the pharmacy and looked at it. It didn't seem to have changed at all. It had the same Victorian style lettering above the long glass window, the same three large glass bottles on a shelf containing brightly coloured liquids above a display of various medicinal products. He guessed that the products might have changed somewhat from those of more than forty years ago but the general idea was still the same.

He remembered his father going there early one morning. Mac had insisted on going with him. Any time that he could have his father to himself was good. His father hadn't spoken much though and he'd walked a little too quickly for Mac's little legs. Mac had begun to wish that he hadn't come as his father was quiet and looked worried all the way there. When they got to the pharmacy his father spoke to the pharmacist in a low voice so that Mac couldn't hear. The pharmacist, looking very doctorly in a long white gown, slowly nodded and whispered something back to his father. His father exchanged some money for a bottle in a white paper bag. They went back as fast as they could.

Mac remembered that his mother had a bump at the time and, looking back, he guessed that she must have been at least six months pregnant with his youngest sister. Looking at the pharmacy now he wondered if that was the reason that his father had looked so worried.

He carried on further down the hill and stopped outside the town's one and only department store. He'd thought that it was huge when he'd been a child but it just looked like another shop to him now. His mother had always passed this store by and said that she would never set foot in it. He'd always wondered why. He was tempted to go inside and have a look around but he found that his feet wouldn't cross the threshold.

Just past the store he came across the bus station. It was nothing grand just somewhere to get out of the rain and buy a ticket from an automated machine. There was a bench outside and Mac decided to make use of it. As he sat there, he remembered the old single decker buses as they pulled up in in front of the station after the long trip from Dublin. They had no amenities onboard in those days so there would always be a mad dash to get to the toilets before everyone else. It wasn't too bad for the men and boys who could squeeze up but Mac well remembered his sisters doing the 'wet dance' as they waited in a long queue outside the door mysteriously marked 'Mna'.

Then they'd all be happy and excited thinking of the long summer and all the adventures that lay ahead of them. The school holiday had seemed like a veritable eternity stretching out before them. But it always ended eventually and going back they would all be miserable. For the children it was the end of freedom as the iron constraints of a new school term loomed ever closer. Their mother and father weren't happy about it either. It would be another long year before they'd be able to go back and see their relatives and friends. They were all too aware that some of the older ones might not be there the next time they came. The long miserable trip back to Birmingham had seemed to take forever.

The memories had flooded back with some force, grabbing him by the scruff of the neck and dragging him back to a time that he'd all but forgotten. He hadn't been expecting that. It was like going up into an attic for the first time in years and finding all those things that had once been so important to you but were now lying dusty and discarded. He felt sad. Sad for the town and how it had diminished in so many ways and sad that he'd neglected this part of his life for so long.

He needed a pint.

He crossed over the bridge and across the River Erne. He saw the aptly signed 'Bridge Bar' right in front of him. It was a small building painted dark green and sandwiched between a hairdresser's and a newspaper shop. He stopped for a moment and looked at the newspaper shop as memories of cold white ice cream wafers being eaten on hot summer days came into his head. He went into the pub.

It was twelve thirty and there was only the barman, a balding old man dressed in a white shirt with the sleeves rolled up, and three workmen in stained overalls who were obviously having a liquid lunch. He ordered a pint and asked about Johnnyboy McGloin.

'Oh, it's Johnnyboy you're after then,' the barman said as the Guinness was given time to settle in the glass. 'He's always here around one o'clock so you won't have too long to wait.'

He thanked the barman and took his pint to a corner table where he sat down to wait for Johnnyboy's arrival. He noticed that the barman and the workmen spoke to each other in low tones and looked over at him once or twice. At ten to one the workmen went, leaving just Mac and the barman in the pub. An uncomfortable silence followed but it didn't last long.

Silences in Irish pubs are generally frowned upon unless there is only the one person in the room and sometimes not even then.

'So, you're over from England then?' the barman asked as he wiped the bar with a cloth.

Mac nodded.

'Over here on holiday, are you?' he persevered.

Mac knew that a conversation was going to be had whether he liked it or not. He stood up and took his drink over to the bar.

'No, I came over for a funeral. Well, that was the idea anyway,' Mac replied.

'A funeral?' the barman stopped wiping and thought for a while. 'The last funeral would have been...yes of course, Annie Sweeney.'

'Did you know Annie?' Mac asked out of curiosity.

'No, no, I made it my business not to know Annie if you know what I mean. She was a strange woman and as likely to turn on you as not.' The barman had a thought and stopped. 'Oh, I'm so sorry. I take it that you're a relative?'

'I'm her nephew but please don't be sorry. That was pretty much what everyone thought about her as far as I can gather.' Mac leant over the bar and said in a low conspiratorial voice. 'I have to admit that I didn't like her much either.'

This got a real laugh from the barman. They both turned as the door opened and a wrinkled old man in a well-worn grey suit and matching flat cap came in. He had a walking stick in one hand and the Donegal Democrat newspaper in the other. Johnnyboy McGloin!

'A pint please, Donal,' he said.

He cast a keen eye over Mac as he waited. At first, he looked a little puzzled but, a few seconds later, a smile came over his face and he nodded to himself. Mac realised that in that brief time he'd figured out who he was. Johnnyboy took his pint to the very table that Mac had been sitting at. Mac followed him.

'Mr. McGloin, would you mind if I join you?' he asked.

'Not at all Mr. Maguire or do you still use the honorary title of Detective Chief Constable?' Johnnyboy said with a twinkle in his eye.

Mac smiled and sat down.

'It's just plain Mr. Maguire these days. How did you know who I was?' he asked.

'Ah, that was easy. I heard that Dessie Maguire's boy was in town for a funeral and then that he was helping young Aiden Maguire who was looking into the strange death of Jackie Connerty over in England. I might have recognised you anyway as you're very like your father. A bit shorter perhaps, but otherwise very like him.'

'Really?' Mac asked. 'You knew my father?'

'I wouldn't say that I knew him well but I've had a few pints with him in my time. I used to go and watch him and your uncle when they both played for the Ballydove hurling team. Your father was a real trier and strong as a bull but Rory, now there was a player. He could have been a really great hurler if he had stayed in Ballydove instead of skedaddling off to England.'

Mac had a sudden memory of his Uncle Rory. When he'd been young his father had taken him quite a few times to watch Rory play Sunday football for his works team. He was a winger and he was both fast and skilful with the ball. His father used to say that it was a pity that Rory hadn't come to England sooner as he might have gotten into a professional side and he could even have become a star like Peter McParland.

'Rory played football in England. He was really good at it too,' Mac said.

Unfortunately, his uncle had died well before his time. He'd had an accident at the factory he'd worked at and afterwards an infection had set in. It took him some weeks to die. Mac remembered how it had broken his father's heart. He never did get over it.

'Yes, it was shame him dying when he did,' Johnnyboy said. 'Anyway, I dare say that you're not here to talk over the old times, are you? I take it that you're here about an event that has happened much more recently.'

Mac smiled. He was well aware that he'd more than met his match in the old man sitting opposite him.

'Yes, I'm helping the police in England with the murder of Jackie Connerty. I've often found that knowing as much as you can about a murder victim can be very useful and I was told that, if anyone can tell me about Jackie's past, then that person is you.'

The old man nodded at the compliment.

'Well, I think I can help you there alright. Just give me a minute or two to have a think.'

'Shall I get us a couple of pints in while you're doing that?' Mac suggested.

Johnnyboy smiled as he said, 'Now, that would be an excellent idea. I've always found that thinking works better with a little lubrication.'

As he stood up, he noticed that Donal the barman had been listening avidly to their conversation and had already started pouring the pints as he walked towards the bar.

'Would you mind if I join you?' Donal asked as he handed Mac the dark beers.

Mac didn't. Donal poured himself a pint and took his and Johnnyboy's to the table.

'Thank you kindly. Now, as to your request I'll start with two stories about Jackie that I think you might find interesting,' Johnnyboy said.

He sat still and closed his eyes for a moment. Then he opened them and started telling his story. Mac knew from his tone of voice and his skill in speaking that Johnnyboy was, in actual fact, a shanachie, a traditional Irish storyteller. He smiled, sat back, made himself comfortable and listened...

'Some thirty years or so ago there was a fine strong young lad called Pedar Moohan who lived just outside the town. Like many of the men in the area his father had gone to England for work but, after a year or so, he'd stopped writing and not long after that he stopped sending money home too. In fact, he was never seen again in Ballydove. So, it fell to young Pedar at the age of fourteen to become the family's breadwinner. Even at that age he was sought after by most of the local farmers as they all knew that he was a good worker and that he was someone who took every job he did very seriously.

However, for all his physical prowess, he might be described today as having mild learning difficulties. He never learnt to write more than his name and every book was closed to him as he never learnt to read. Still, he could earn more than enough by the strength of his muscles to put food on the table for his mother, his younger sister and brother. When he was just twenty years old, he went with a friend of his to the hiring fair in Donegal Town and there he met a girl. Her name was MaryAnn Kilbriggan and she was to be the ruin of his life.'

At this point Johnnyboy stopped and took a sip from his drink. Mac noticed that another customer had come in but, rather than interrupt the story, he'd positioned himself quietly behind Donal and was listening as intently as they were.

'Now, Pedar had never walked out with a woman before, had never even kissed one, and MaryAnn was far from being ugly. She saw that Pedar was a fine strong good-looking man and I'd like to think that she fell for him too but, as the story will show, she may just have seen him as being a stepping stone on her way upwards in the world.

So, they got married and Pedar worked twice as hard to keep up with the daily demands from his new wife for the latest clothes and perfumes. She flaunted herself around the town as if she were one of the quality but, in truth, she was just an orphanage girl who never even knew who her mother and father were.

Only a few short months after they were married Pedar found himself deeply in debt. He'd borrowed money on the promise of work to pay his wife's bills but the work had fallen through. Now, you might think that a man in that position would tell his wife that her extravagant spending would have to stop but not Pedar. He was totally besotted by her. She kept telling him that buying her nice things was a way of showing how much he loved her and he was so stupid in love with her that he believed the nonsense she told him. It was MaryAnn who suggested that he should start working for Jackie Connerty. It was easy money or so she told him. Now, Jackie was looking for a man to drive a van across the border that was full of smuggled goods and he was paying good money as it was such a risky job. This was the time of the Troubles after all and the border was crawling with policemen and soldiers on both sides.

At first Pedar, who was generally a law-abiding man, was dead set against the idea but MaryAnn whispered and whispered in his ear and eventually she wore him down. And so, he went to work for Jackie. Everything went well for nearly six months or so and MaryAnn was seen around the town in even finer clothes but everyone could see that his new line of work didn't sit well with her husband. Pedar was now doing two or three runs a week at night down the little country lanes with no bother so far from the police or anyone else. From his work on the local farms, he knew lots of tracks that a van could drive down that weren't on any map. Then one night his luck ran out. He had to cross a main road every now and then but he was always careful and watched out for any traffic. However, this time Pedar didn't see the police car as it was hidden in the bushes. It had broken down and the two officers had pushed it off the road and were waiting for someone to come and tow them back to the station. Pedar had his lights off but it was a full moon that night and so the policemen could see the van clearly. They called it in and Pedar was intercepted at the end of the track by two police cars.

Big as he was, he gave himself up without a struggle and the policemen, recognising him, were as gentle with him as they could be. They took him back and questioned him but he wouldn't say anything until he'd spoken to MaryAnn. If he'd have had any sense he'd have called for his mother and gotten some proper advice but, as I said, he was mad in love with his wife. Now, Pedar might have gotten off with a light sentence, as it was a first offence, and if he had given Jackie up to the police as being the owner of the goods being smuggled. Any sane man would have done exactly that but unfortunately not Pedar. MaryAnn had gotten to him first and had somehow persuaded him to take the blame for everything.

So, he stood up in court and told the judge that the smuggling was all his idea and that everything in the van belonged to him. The judge, who I heard had a massive barney with his wife on the morning of the trial and so was in a foul mood anyway, threw the book at him and gave him seven years. Everyone was shocked and saddened by this except, of course, MaryAnn who disappeared from the town as soon as Pedar had been sentenced. The rumours were that Jackie had paid her a good sum of money to persuade Pedar to take all the blame thus leaving Jackie in the clear. She'd always talked of going to Dublin and that's where most people reckoned that she'd headed.

So, poor Pedar had seven long years of confinement to face up to. He was used to being outdoors and under God's skies and he suffered in prison ten times more than you or I might have. Not only that but, while his mother visited him regularly in jail, he kept asking for his wife and he wondered why she hadn't come to see him. His mother made excuses at first but she had to eventually own up to the truth. His wife had left him. She said after that she could see the life gradually going out of his eyes and they were more or less dead the last time she saw him. Two days later she got the call, Pedar had killed himself.

Her fine strong boy had been the apple of her eye and the light of her life but she carried on as best she could, poor woman. Then her daughter, Imelda, went to work as a nurse in Dublin and a little later her brother Anthony followed her to go to university there. So, once her remaining children had left Ballydove, the poor woman didn't seem to want any more of life and her heart stopped beating. Pedar's sister and brother came back for their mother's funeral but never came again after that. We also never saw hair nor hide of MaryAnn Kilbriggan about the town again which most people took as a blessing.'

As sad a tale as it was Mac almost felt like applauding at the end.

'Oh, that was a great story, sad but great nevertheless,' Donal said. He turned to face the man standing behind him. 'Will you go and get us all a drink, Jamie? It'll be on me.'

Johnnyboy sat there with a smile on his face as he waited for the refreshments to arrive and for everyone to be comfortably seated. Then he started again.

'Now this all happened around twelve years or so ago and tells the story of how a hundred-euro bet can lead to the ruin of a man's life.

During his time in England Jackie had taken up golf in a fairly serious way. He'd only started playing as he'd found that a golf course was a good place to not just meet businessmen but to do business too. He was over on one of his rare visits and had taken to going to the club just down the road to play a round or two. One day in the club's nineteenth hole he met a man from Belleek, which as you know is just over the border there, and it was clear from the start that he and Jackie would not get on. This man, let's call him John, disliked Jackie on sight and Jackie disliked him back. They were like two dogs meeting for the first time who just didn't like the smell of each other.

So, Jackie does what he always does and tries to get one over on John and make him look small. He went right through his repertory of bar tricks but John seemed to know the answer to them all. Jackie lost quite a few euros that night as well as some face. In exasperation, he challenged John to a round of golf the day after next and a hundred euros would ride on the result. He also insisted that the money be immediately placed with the club steward saying that, if one of the players didn't turn up, then the money would go to the one who did. Jackie, however, didn't like the fact that John had accepted the bet so quickly and that he had smiled when he did it.

The next day Jackie had a chat with the club steward and discovered that John had a handicap that was way better than Jackie's and so he would be certain to win the bet. Now, most men with anything about them would play the game, lose and pay up or, if they were of a more cowardly persuasion, just not turn up and lose the bet anyway. But not Jackie. He knew that a great number of people from Ballydove and the surrounding area would be turning up to watch the match in the hope that he would at last get his long-awaited come-uppance. He was not about to give them that pleasure at any cost. So, Jackie cooked up a plan.

Now he and the club steward knew each other well and had done so for some years. He was a long-established customer of Jackie's as most of the drinks and cigarettes which he sold in the club bar at full price were either stolen or smuggled giving the steward a nice profit on the side. Jackie was going to use that as a lever to get the steward to do him a favour. He knew that John was playing a round with a friend the next day and so he hid himself and took as many photos of him as he could. He took the camera to a young man who was skilful in the ways of...er...photo-shopping I believe it's called. Anyway, this skilful young man produced a photo of John seeming to fondle a girl of a tender age, a very tender age if you know what I mean.

So, Jackie passes this on to the club steward who passes it on to the Club Captain saying that an anonymous member found it on a website and gave it to him. Now, you might well ask what this member was doing on such a site but no-one did. I'll speak more of this later. Anyway, upon getting the fake photo of John, the Club Captain, who was a Papal Knight and a pillar of the community, immediately blew his top and ordered the security guards to be on alert so as to ensure that John never polluted the club grounds with his presence in the future. So, on the appointed day, half of Ballydove trekked to the golf course to see Jackie get his come-uppance but they all went home again sorely disappointed. Jackie even gave his opponent an extra fifteen minutes to turn up but, of course, he knew he wouldn't as John was in the process of being frog-marched from the club grounds between two burly security men.

And that's how Jackie won the bet.'

Johnnyboy stopped and took a thoughtful sip from his drink.

'Well, Jackie may have thought that he had the last laugh but unfortunately it didn't stop there for John. The Club Captain, being a Papal Knight and pillar of the community and all that, felt it was his solemn duty to let John's employer know about the photo. They had played golf together quite a few times so John's employer took the Captain's word as gospel and sacked John the next day. He didn't say why to John's face, of course, but word soon got around. John suddenly found that just about all his friends and colleagues had turned against him, even his own wife in the end. I find it amazing that people, when hearing about such a serious allegation, don't ask for at least a smidgeon of proof but, as they say, if you throw a certain brown substance hard enough some of it will stick.

So, John, having no other option, ended up leaving Ireland altogether. He went to work in Scotland and was never heard of again. The Captain of the golf club, however, was heard of again. He was arrested by the police some time afterwards for having several thousand images of child pornography on his computer. They went back years it was said in court. I've often found it to be the case in life that those that accuse others the most vehemently of a sin or a crime sometimes do so because they too are guilty of the same sin or crime.'

Once again Mac felt the urge to applaud.

'Now, Donal and Jamie, if you would be so good, I'd like a private word with Mr. Maguire for a minute or two,' Johnnyboy asked.

They both reluctantly made their way back to the bar leaving Mac and Johnnyboy to themselves.

'There's a third story that I'd like to tell you and you'll understand why I wanted to keep this just between ourselves when I tell it. Unlike the previous

215

stories this one happened a little more recently and it might have a little more bearing on your case.'

Mac settled back and listened.

'There was this young lad who lived in Bundoran and he was a veritable wizard on the computer. There wasn't much he couldn't do if he put his mind to it. This was the same young man who had photoshopped the damning photo of John for Jackie in order that he could win his bet. Jackie had told him it was for a joke that he was playing on an old friend. For years afterwards this young man, whose name was Joe, would have nothing to do with Jackie after he learnt to what use the photo had been put to. That was until one day when Jackie found that he once more had a use for him.

After playing a round at the local golf club here in Ballydove he noticed a very unusual trophy in the clubhouse commemorating a hole-in-one. It was shaped exactly like a golf ball, but a bit larger, and seemed to be made from gold. Inside the trophy was the very golf ball that had rattled into the hole in just one stroke. It had the person's name, the hole and the date on the outside but, instead of being engraved, the lettering was raised.

Jackie was very taken with it and asked who had made it. He wasn't too surprised when it turned out to be none other than young Joe who had now gone into 3D printing for a living. He could produce pretty much anything with it and he even made some tractor parts for Willie McCafferty's old Massey Ferguson. Now, Willie is well over forty but that tractor is even older so getting parts for it is no easy thing. I saw it at the Agricultural Show last year and it is a lovely thing indeed. Anyway, I digress.

So, Jackie started a charm offensive on young Joe and ordered a similar trophy from him for a business-man friend of his who he said had recently made a hole-in-one at a golf course in England. It was of course a lie and, Jackie being Jackie, he had something else in mind than just ordering a golf trophy.

He watched closely while Joe showed him how he'd coded the trophy, it wasn't anywhere near as simple a process as it might seem, and the material that would be used to print the trophy. Jackie took a close note of everything he saw. Then Joe made the mistake of leaving Jackie alone with his laptop for a few minutes while he attended to a problem with the printer and afterwards found that Jackie had quickly cooled on the idea. Jackie left saying that he'd be in touch.

Of course, the only person Jackie got in touch with was with the manager of a golf accessory company in England. He sold him the idea for the trophy and the code he'd stolen from the laptop for well over fifty thousand pounds. Nice payment for what was essentially a few hours work.

Joe only became aware of Jackie's betrayal when, some months later, someone asked him how he'd managed to get his trophy into a prestigious English golf catalogue. Joe had a look and found that the trophy shown was exactly the same as his right down to the small hidden upside down 'J' that he used as a trademark. To say that he was incandescent would be putting it mildly. He cornered Jackie one night in a pub and confronted him. He was so mad with rage that he threatened to kill him. Jackie just laughed at him and called him a 'lightweight' which didn't help matters much. Young Joe had to be escorted from the pub. As they dragged him out, he shouted that he'd get his revenge on Jackie if it killed him. Everyone in the pub heard these words.

'That's it, I'm afraid. There's no end to this story...or perhaps there is,' Johnnyboy said as he gave Mac a meaningful look.

Johnnyboy's story was very interesting. In fact, it was interesting enough that Mac was going to follow up on it.

'Can you tell me the real names of those involved in the stories?' he asked.

'Of course, the names in the first story were all real, it being so long ago I felt it couldn't hurt. The real name of the man in the second story was Paul Dudgeon but I'm afraid that it will do you little good as I heard that he took to the bottle in a serious way when he was over the water and that he died a few years ago from liver failure.'

Mac wrote the name down anyway. Perhaps someone connected to him might have sought revenge.

'Now young Joe's surname is Devlin and, as I said, he's from Bundoran. The last I heard he was still there trying to make a go of the 3D printing.'

'How did you hear about him threatening Jackie?'

'It all took place in the back room of Magee's bar. It was Wee Tim Mullins who escorted him from the pub and who told me all about it.'

Mac would get Aiden to confirm that with Tim when he got back from Dublin.

'Now, Mr. Maguire, it's time that you paid the piper,' Johnnyboy said with a mischievous smile.

'Pay?'

'Tell me all about you and your sisters in England and what you're all doing over there. If anyone asks me whatever happened to Dessie McGuire, and they will, I'll have all the answers for them.'

Mac smiled. He realised that Johnnyboy was, in fact, a sort of local information exchange and that knowledge was worth more than money to him. Mac spent a few minutes telling him all about himself and his sisters, what they all worked at and the names of their husbands and children. Johnnyboy sat back with his eyes half-closed and looked half-asleep but Mac was sure that he could ask Johnnyboy to repeat what he'd said in a week or a month or even a year and he would be able to recite it word for word.

He had one more question for Johnnyboy before he left.

'I was walking by the department store earlier on and I remembered that my mother would never set foot inside the place but she'd never say why. Have you any idea why?'

'Now your mother was a Mulreany from Dungloe, if I remember right.'

Mac nodded.

'Well now, Dungloe is a fair stretch of the legs from here but I did hear something from your relatives here in Ballydove that might be of interest. Your grandmother, Mary Mulreany, was born a Roarty and she had a younger sister called Grace, an apt name as it turned out as she was full of airs and graces. Their mother died young of the tuberculosis and so it was Mary who brought up her younger sister. It seems that she made many sacrifices for Grace but got little thanks for it as we'll see.

Now, when Mary was eighteen, she married a local farmer called Dan Glackin and was happy to do so but her younger sister wanted something better. She was supposed to have been a fine-looking woman and she had great ambitions too. And so, Grace moved to Ballydove in search of a husband. She used to go to the department store here regularly as it was the most fashionable place to shop for miles around and it was there that she spotted John Loughlin, the son of the man who owned the store. He wasn't much to look at, that's for sure, but Grace didn't care about that. He was rich and that was all that mattered to her. So, it didn't take her long to get her hooks into him and eventually they were married.

A few years after that Dan Glackin died. His young widow was left penniless as she now she had no-one to work the farm. She had a young son, your Uncle Bryan, to look after and she now had no resources. In desperation she wrote a letter to Grace asking her for help but, when she got no reply, she wrote again thinking it must have gotten lost in the post. Once again though she got no answer. At the third time of writing, she did at last receive a reply but it was not the reply she'd been expecting. In a very cold letter Grace informed her that she no longer wanted to have any contact with her older sister, or anyone else that she knew in Dungloe come to that. She said that she now moved in 'different circles' and that any further 'begging letters' would be ignored.

Well, Grace got her wish as Mary never said another word to her for the rest of her life or even admitted that she existed. She worked the land as best she could and she had some help in that from a young man who lived on the next farm along. That young man's name was James Mulreany and so you can guess that all that working side by side must have brought them closer together. So, they got married and a little while after that your Aunt Rose was born then your mother and finally your Aunt Annie. After all her hardships Mary and her husband were blessed with a long and good life together from what I've heard.

As for Grace her husband also died quite young not long after his father went. He always was somewhat sickly but it seems that his death was no great burden to his wife as she now had total control over the store which she ruled with a rod of iron. She never remarried or had any children and I often wondered if, on her death bed, she ever regretted the decisions she'd made in life. The store she'd worked so hard to build up eventually went to a relative that she absolutely despised so one might well wonder what the point of it all had been. Anyway, that's why your mother would never set foot inside the department store.'

'Thanks, that's a part of my family history I knew absolutely nothing about. Would you mind if I look you up again before I go back to England?' Mac asked.

'Of course, I'm here most days and a quiet pint or two with you would be no hardship at all,' Johnnyboy replied with a warm smile.

Mac thought about Johnnyboy's stories as the taxi took him back to the hotel. As they passed the department store, he thought about his mother and he could still see the angry look on her face as she dragged him past its doors. At least now he knew why. He wondered how two sisters brought up in the same environment could turn out to be so different. He'd come across this himself in a case not so long ago so he thought it probably wasn't such a rare occurrence.

As soon as he got back to the hotel, he called Martin and asked him to check something for him. He then had a nap and rested his back for a while before getting a bite to eat. The bar was quiet for which Mac was grateful. He sat there nursing a pint and thinking about Johnnyboy's stories, especially the one about Joe Devlin. He finally remembered to check his emails and found that he had one from Martin. He read it avidly and learnt something of immense interest about Mr. Devlin.

It looked as if they might have a suspect at last!

Chapter Nineteen

It was Tuesday morning and the weather was officially 'soft' according to the nice young lady on reception. Mac glanced outside. It was raining but the raindrops were so light that they seemed to hover in the air like a mist. He stood in the doorway, hesitating as to what to do next.

'So, how are you today, Mr. Maguire?' the receptionist asked brightly.

'Oh, I'm fine, thanks,' he replied. 'I'm just waiting for someone to pick me up.'

'Well, I wouldn't wait outside if I were you,' the young lady advised him. 'The rain doesn't look that bad from here but, believe me, you'd be drenched in just a few minutes.'

Mac decided to follow her advice and stayed inside the lobby while he waited for Aiden to arrive. Even with the rain it was quite bright outside but Mac was all too aware of how deceiving the weather can be in this part of the world. He thought once again of Granny Mulreany and how she had spent most of her waking moments watching the weather coming in from the west. The only times she'd allow herself to be driven indoors were if the rain was either 'lashing' down or if it was deemed to be 'too soft'.

He smiled. Today was a 'too soft' day for sure.

Aiden's car pulled up outside and Mac waved to him before making a dash for it through the rain. He had his fedora hat and a waterproof jacket on but, after only a few seconds in the rain, the water was dripping down from his jacket and making a little puddle on the floor. He glanced over at the driver.

'I don't think we've met before, my name's Mac Maguire,' Mac said with as serious an expression as he could muster.

'Ah, get away with you!' Aiden said as his face started reddening.

'I must admit that you look quite a lot like that young Aiden Maguire but you can't be. He was such a sad and serious man and he was never one for smiling much.'

Mac was, of course, joking but there was something in what he said. Aiden did indeed look like a different person, a small smile now played around his face and the tenseness that Mac had always felt in his presence was no longer there. Indeed, he looked relaxed and happy.

'Thanks Mac,' Aiden said a serious expression briefly showing on his face. 'Following your advice was the best thing I've ever done.'

'I take it that it went okay with Caitlin then?'

'Better than okay, much better than okay actually. I did as you suggested and waited on her doorstep. She was surprised to see me sitting there but she was kind enough to let me in and we talked. I told her everything, as you suggested, and I half expected her to show me the door afterwards but she didn't. She held me and told me that she cared and that she understood. She knew everything yet she still wanted me, Mac. It was the best night of my life. We just talked and planned but the best thing of all was just being with her. I'd missed her so much. Anyway, with all that talking we soon agreed as to what we should do next.

On Monday I went and saw my old boss and told him everything as well. He was understanding too. He asked if I wanted my job back and I said yes. In truth, I'd loved working in that team. He then told me that he'd heard that a police investigation was underway and they were looking into Bishop Crotty's past. He gave me the number of the lead investigator in the case. It turned out that I was the fourth person to make a formal statement and the investigator told me that there were many more in the pipeline. For some reason I'd always thought that it might just have been me. God knows that I wouldn't have wished it on anyone else but it did make me feel a lot better knowing that there were others out there who could back my story up. Then, on Monday afternoon, Caitlin and I went out and bought an engagement ring.'

'You proposed to her?' Mac asked in wonder.

'Well, we were getting on so well that I thought why not? I've wasted far too much time Mac, I just didn't want to waste any more,' Aiden said. 'She's coming down on Friday morning and we're going to tell her parents everything. Everything, no more lies or evasions. I can't tell you what a weight off me it is.'

'What about your father?'

'I've already told him. We sat down last night and talked. He blamed himself at first but I convinced him eventually that it wasn't his fault, or even my mother's, it was all Bishop Crotty's. However, his time to suffer is coming. I've been told that they'll be making an arrest later this week. Anyway, enough about me, you said that you had a lead?'

Mac told Aiden the story just as he'd gotten from Johnnyboy.

'So, it looks like we've found someone with a motive but what about the opportunity?' Aiden asked.

'It seems that a passenger called Joseph Devlin was in the airport on the morning that Jackie Connerty was killed. Indeed, he was on the same flight over that I took. Not only that but he checked in early, almost twenty minutes before Jackie was killed.'

'And, if anyone would know how to make a 3D plastic knife, it would be him,' Aiden said. 'Good work, Mac.'

He phoned the station and got Joe Devlin's business address and a minute later they were on the road to Bundoran. They went south, cutting across land, and Mac didn't see the sea again until they'd gone through the town centre. Here the street was lined with pubs, restaurants, bookmaker's shops and amusement arcades. In all respects it was a typical seaside resort. They passed by one amusement arcade that stood on a corner. It looked incredibly familiar to Mac but he couldn't quite remember why.

A few seconds later the buildings disappeared and there was a panoramic view over the beach to the soft grey-blue sea beyond. Although the beach wasn't anywhere near as impressive as the one at Rossnowlagh, it had sand and it had the sea and, when he'd been young, they were all the ingredients that were needed for a great day out. Again, a vague memory of the amusement arcade came back to him but he still couldn't quite pin it down.

They turned left and drove away from the sea and passed by an assortment of bungalows and houses. Mac noticed that they got more modern the further down the street they drove. Aiden pulled up outside a small building that had a large sign saying that it was a 'Surf School'.

Aiden got out and Mac followed him. He noticed a small sign pointing to the right that said 'JayDee 3D Printing' and guessed that was where they were heading.

'Do they really do much surfing here?' Mac asked.

'Oh, God yes. I've been told that the waves are really good around Bundoran and quite reliable too. They even held the European Championships here some years ago,' Aiden replied.

Mac was impressed. Unlike poor Ballydove, it seemed that Bundoran was moving with the times.

They walked around the corner and Aiden tried the door. It was locked. There was a bell next to it and Aiden pressed it. When there was no answer, he pressed it again. The door opened a split second later.

'Sorry but I was doing something,' a somewhat flustered young man said.

'Joe Devlin?' Aiden asked showing his warrant card.

'That's me,' the young man said trying to look calm but failing. 'I've been expecting you. Come in.'

He led them into a room that contained two large machines each of which had a massive grey metal box next to them. Mac guessed that these were the printers. One of them was working and making a whirring sound as the printing head moved backwards and forwards and there was a sort of electric smell in the air.

'So, how can I help the Gardai?' Joe asked.

He was dressed in a black T shirt, ripped jeans and scuffed trainers and he looked younger than Mac had expected. He was clean shaven, slim and, at the moment anyway, unable to keep still. He picked up what looked like a golf tee and turned it end over end with his fingers.

Mac could see that Joe Devlin was very nervous. Whether this was due to his inexperience with police interviews or guilt was something that Mac hoped they'd soon establish.

'I believe that you knew Jackie Connerty?' Aiden asked.

Joe's shoulders slumped and he put the golf tee down and crossed his arms. It was clear that he was hoping that the interview might have been about something else.

'Yes, unfortunately I did,' he replied in a quiet voice.

'I take it that you've heard about his murder?'

Joe nodded his head as an answer.

'I believe that you had something of a grudge against Jackie. Is that true?' Aiden asked.

'It wasn't me!' Joe almost shouted. 'I didn't kill him. I knew you'd come around here accusing me...'

'Joe, calm down, we're not accusing anyone...yet,' Aiden said in a placating tone. 'We just want you to tell us the truth. Did you have a grudge against Jackie?'

'Yes, I suppose so,' he eventually admitted. 'I was angry at him for a time and I had every right to be. He stole my idea.'

'When you confronted Jackie in Magee's pub did you say that you'd get your revenge on Jackie if it killed you?'

Joe thought about this for a while.

'Yes, but, as I said, I was angry at the time. When I eventually calmed down, I realised that Jackie might have actually done me a favour.'

'How?' Aiden asked.

'Well, when someone told me that he'd gotten fifty thousand for my hole-in-one trophy design, I totally lost it but when I thought about it later it gave me an idea. I'd never realised that there was so much money in golf accessories and so I started doing some research. That led me to a small company in North London that looked interesting. They were selling golf gift sets and the owners were quite young and willing to listen to me. My idea was that some items from each set might be customisable so that it could have someone's name on it and a date perhaps. They could be also made from different materials depending on what people wanted. Here I'll show you.'

He took a box down from a shelf and opened it. Inside lying on black velvet were three golf balls, six gold-coloured tees, a tool for removing tees that was also gold and a small version of the claret jug trophy that's awarded to the winner of the British Open every year. Mac picked up a tee and found it was heavier than he'd expected. He looked at it closely. The name 'Joseph Devlin' was clearly visible in raised lettering. He rotated it and read 'Your event' and then 'Your date'.

'This was the first one I did. I took it over to England as a sample and they liked it,' Joe said.

'What's this made of?' Mac asked.

'Gold, fourteen carats,' Joe replied.

That would explain its heaviness. Mac was impressed.

'It's selling really well, especially in America, so I should thank Jackie if anything. I'd have never thought of it otherwise,' Joe said.

Mac and Aiden looked at each other. It seemed that Joe might have a good point.

'Why did you turn up so early at the airport?' Aiden asked.

'I couldn't sleep. We'd had a glitch with printing off a new product. That's why I'd flown over in the first place. I sorted most of the problems out but there was still something not quite right with the code. I planned on sorting it out when I got back here but it was bothering me and I found that I couldn't sleep. So, I went to the airport early, checked in, found a comfortable seat in a coffee shop and went to work.'

Mac thought about the layout of the departure area. The restaurants and bars were in an area that you had to walk through before you got to the Accessibility Area.

'And you stayed there for how long?' Mac asked.

'Until a half an hour or so before the flight.'

'Did you notice anything as you walked towards your gate?'

'Yes, there were a lot of policemen in an area to my right not too far from the coffee shop. I didn't think much about it at the time but I guess that was about Jackie, wasn't it?' Joe said.

'Yes, it was,' Mac said. 'Would you mind if I took your photograph?'

'No, I suppose not,' Joe said hesitantly.

Mac took his phone out and clicked the camera button. He then turned and pointed towards the door with eyes. Aiden got the message.

'Thanks, Mr. Devlin. That will be all for the moment,' Aiden said.

'Is that it?' Joe said looking both puzzled and relieved.

'For now,' Aiden said.

As soon as they got outside Mac took his phone out and sent a copy of Joe's photograph to Martin Selby. He then rang him and asked him to check Joe's movements in the airport via the CCTV images.

'Martin should be able to confirm if young Joe was where he said he was fairly quickly,' Mac explained.

'I thought we might have been onto something but it's my guess that he's telling the truth,' Aiden said.

'Yes, I think you might be right there. So, what's next?'

'I don't know,' Aiden said with a shrug of the shoulders. 'I suppose we should go and make sure that Tim Mullins can confirm what Johnnyboy told you about the death threat. I know it's probably a waste of time but, if I'm honest, I can't think of anything else to do right now.'

The problem was neither could Mac.

As they drove back, they passed by the amusement arcade again and a picture came into his mind. Auntie Rose.

The thing Mac always remembered first about Rose was her smile. She was a large, good-natured woman and Mac had always been happy to see her. Especially as it usually meant that Fiona and Thomas would be there too. Unlike Declan, these cousins were fun to be with, especially Fiona, who was great at making up games to play. The memory of a day from long ago came into his head.

The day had been sunny and so Aunt Rose and his mother had decided to take themselves and their children off to Bundoran for an outing. After spending hours on the beach, they were sitting outside on a wall eating fish and chips. Mac noticed Rose sneaking off around the corner. He saw his mother smile and then heard her say something about Rose having her 'mad moment'. He was intrigued and sneaked off after her.

He followed her into the amusement arcade and saw her pull a carrier bag from her voluminous handbag. It was only then that she spotted Mac. She gestured to him to come over. At first Mac thought he'd be in for a telling off, not that he could ever remember Rose telling him off before, but her smile assured him that this wouldn't be the case. It was the smile of a very naughty schoolgirl.

'Here,' she said as she opened the bag.

It was full of big brown pennies!

'I've been saving these up all year so I could have a little flutter,' she said excitedly. 'This is going to be the year I win big. I just know it.'

She counted out eighteen pennies and put them in his hand. She then put a finger to her lips, winked at him and sat down at the nearest one-armed bandit and started feeding it with coins.

Mac worked out how many bags of sweets or ice creams eighteen coins might buy but the flashing lights and the sound of coins rattling into the machines hypnotised him. He saw a game where you could bet on a horse race and he tried a penny. He lost by a whisker so he had another go. In less than five minutes the eighteen pennies had gone as had all his dreams of sweets and ice creams. He felt foolish and sad. He never had any liking for gambling after that.

He went back to his aunt and watched her empty the last pennies from her bag into the machine. When the very last one had disappeared into the slot she turned and gave Mac a sad look. However, she could never stay sad for very long.

'Oh well, maybe next year,' she said with a big smile as she took his hand and led him back.

They were nearly back in Ballydove by the time Mac became conscious of his surroundings. Since he'd come back to Ireland the memories of his past had come thick and fast, both good and bad. This last memory had been a good one. He'd forgotten how much he'd liked his aunt.

Tim, who for all his size looked more like a boy who'd just had his favourite toy snatched from him, confirmed every word of Johnnyboy's story.

'I'm in court with those pair at two thirty,' Aiden said as he looked at his watch. It was nearly twelve. 'Fancy a coffee?'

They sat in silence at Aiden's desk for a while sipping at their coffee. The silence was broken by Mac's phone. Aiden could only hear Mac say 'Okay' a couple of times and a 'Thanks' at the end.

'That was Martin. He said it was an easy job to pinpoint Joe Devlin's path through the airport using face recognition and the CCTV footage. He picked him up sitting outside one of the coffee shops and then traced his steps both backwards and forwards from that point. Using the time stamps he's certain that Joe was sitting outside a coffee shop working on his laptop at the time that Jackie Connerty was murdered. Indeed, he didn't go anywhere near the area that Jackie was sitting in until well after the police had arrived. Martin could see Joe Devlin glancing over at my boss Dan Carter as he passed by on his way to the departure gate.'

'So, another dead end then,' Aiden said. 'Any ideas?'

'Well, we could always speak to Maggie Connerty again,' Mac suggested. 'She was still upset the last time we spoke to her and she might have remembered something since then. I was also wondering if it might be worth telling her about Jackie's second wife and seeing how she reacts. It's a long shot but you never know. She might have found out somehow herself and it's a pretty good motive for murder.'

'Okay, that's worth trying. Fancy something to eat first?' Aiden said. 'I could drop you back to your hotel afterwards and then pick you up after the court hearing.'

Mac thought that this sounded like a plan. He suddenly felt very tired and he knew that lying down for an hour or two wouldn't do him, or his back, any harm. Back at the hotel exhaustion overcame him and he fell asleep as soon as his head hit the pillow.

The explosion woke him from his nap. He felt his bed move with the force of the blast. It was dark and he could smell smoke and hear shouting coming from the corridor. Then he saw the flames. He knew that he had to get out of the room quickly or he'd be burnt alive and so he opened the door and ran out into the hallway. He turned and watched the door close behind him in slow motion ending with a soft click.

That was when he woke up.

There was no fire alarm, no smoke and no shouting. He felt disoriented and confused. He'd thought that it was night but he could clearly see daylight coming in through the window at the bottom of the hallway. He tried to open the door to his room but it was locked. He went to look in his pockets for the key and to his horror found that he didn't have any pockets. He was standing in the hallway in a T shirt and a pair of boxer shorts.

Memories of the day came back to him, Aiden's good news and Joe Devlin and his printing machines. He remembered that he'd gone for a nap and realised that it must have been a bad dream that he'd had. He'd had plenty of lucid dreams before now due to his pain medication but none quite like that. He'd really believed that there had been an explosion.

He began to feel worried as to what was happening to him until he realised that he had a far more pressing problem to deal with. How to get back into his room.

He stood there for a while trying to think what he should do next. He certainly couldn't go down to reception dressed in just his underwear. He heard someone coming along the corridor and looked around for something to hide behind. There was nothing. He'd just have to brave it out.

Luckily it was the woman who cleaned the rooms who appeared from around the corner. She had a bottle of spray cleaner in one hand and some cleaning cloths in the other. She stopped in surprise when she saw Mac.

'I've somehow managed to lock myself out,' Mac said the wheels spinning madly in his head as he tried to come up with a good reason for his predicament. 'Someone knocked the door but when I came out to look there was no-one there and the door closed behind me.'

It was a bit on the weak side but at least it was some sort of explanation as to why he was standing in the hallway in his underwear.

'Sure, that's no problem. Here I can let you back in,' she said with a smile as she pulled a key card from her pocket.

And she did.

Mac went in sat on the edge of the bed. He didn't need to hold his hands out to see that they were shaking.

Chapter Twenty

The case was going nowhere and Dan Carter was getting grumpier by the hour. His sergeant, DS Adil Thakkar, had worked with him for some years now and he knew the warning signs. Life might soon be getting a little more difficult for him if something didn't break on the case soon.

Dan was sensing that their options for moving the case forward were closing down and he desperately wanted to find whoever killed Jackie Connerty and, by extension, all those people who had died in the fire and from the toxic white puddings. He was trying to think of something that they hadn't already tried and he wasn't having much luck.

They were still in the process of interviewing Jackie's friends and neighbours in Preston but nothing had come from it so far. They'd also interviewed Jackie's wife again but she'd pleaded her innocence in having anything to do with her husband's death. She'd also denied knowing anything at all about his business dealings. He still wasn't sure if he believed her but he was glad that he'd made her surrender her passport. Frustratingly, he was still waiting for the report on Jackie's house as the forensics teams had their hands more than full. They'd had three more deaths reported and each crime scene had to be processed as a priority and the deadly white pudding carefully removed.

That made sixteen dead in all, Dan thought, besides the casualties from the fireworks explosion. If only they'd known about the white puddings earlier. Even a few hours more warning might have saved some of those lives. The picture of the dead woman with the baked beans on her cheek flashed into his mind. It didn't help his mood any.

'So, what's next then?' Adil asked hoping that Dan had thought of something.

Dan shrugged. In truth he had no ideas at all and he was glad when he saw Martin walking towards his office. Perhaps he'd thought of something. Martin poked his head around the door.

'Those files have come in from the airport at last. I've had a quick look at them but nothing's leapt out at me.'

Dan sighed. He knew that Martin's 'quick look' was better than most people's detailed examination.

'Send them around to the rest of the team anyway, just in case,' Dan said. 'You never know.'

'What files are those?' Adil asked.

'They gave us most of the employee details fairly quickly but there were other people working in the airport at the time, contractors and the like. Apparently, they keep their details on a separate system and it's not linked to the main computer for some reason. I wouldn't hold your breath though, if Martin can't find anything that's probably because there's nothing to find.'

Even Dan's silences had become grumpy, Adil thought, and he was relieved when it was broken by the phone ringing.

Dan listened for a while then said, 'Okay we'll be right down' and then put the phone down. 'There's a man in reception who says that he has some information for us,' he said eagerly as he stood up.

Thank God, Adil said to himself and said a little prayer that it might be something worth listening to.

The man proved to be middle-aged, grey-haired, well-dressed and obviously embarrassed. It was clear that he would sooner have been anywhere else than where he was at that minute.

Dan asked if it was okay if they recorded the interview and then got him to state his name and address.

'So, Mr. Hartley. I believe that you might have some information relevant to our inquiries into the murder of Mr. Connerty,' Dan said.

Mr. Hartley looked mystified so Dan showed him a photo.

'Yes, that's him, although I knew him as McCormack.'

'How did you know him?'

Mr. Hartley looked up to the ceiling before saying, 'I gave him twenty thousand pounds.'

'Tell me about it,' Dan said suddenly looking interested.

'I heard about it from a friend of mine. It was chance to buy a share in a real racehorse, something I'd dreamed about for years. I looked on the web site and it all looked professional enough. No money was asked for up front and so I registered an interest. I was invited to a day out at a racing stable near Newmarket to view the horse for myself and so I went along. I must admit that I was impressed with the stables and the horse and so I coughed up five thousand pounds for a share in the horse.'

'How did you pay?' Dan asked.

'Via my credit card on the day. They gave us a few glasses of wine and Mr. McCormack was very persuasive so I thought, why not? I worried about it afterwards but then the horse won its first race and I got a cheque for a hundred and twenty pounds so I thought that it must be for real. A few weeks later I got another cheque for two hundred pounds and I was made up.'

Dan knew the script for this type of con; get some money from the punters and then give him some of it back as profits to get their confidence and after that comes the sting.

'Go on,' Dan prompted.

'Mr. McCormack then invited a 'select group' of twenty of us, as he called it, to the stables. He then told us that a lot of the original investors didn't have enough faith in the horse and were willing to be bought out and, if we invested more, then we could multiply our profits enormously. He said that he himself was putting sixty thousand pounds in but he needed our support. He was very persuasive and I think that all of us, bar one, coughed up the extra money.'

'Let me guess. The horse got injured and had to be shot,' Dan said wanting to cut to the chase.

'How on earth did you know that?' Mr. Hartley said giving Dan another mystified look.

'It was a scam, Mr. Hartley, and one as old as they come. Is that why you came here, to get your money back?'

'Well, no but...was it really a scam? I thought it was just bad luck that the horse got injured.'

Dan thought that some people shouldn't be allowed out by themselves. He asked for the name of the horse and the stables he'd visited. He ended the interview and left Adil to get Mr. Hartley's details. He headed straight for Martin.

'How are you getting on with Jackie Connerty's laptop?'

'Slowly,' Martin replied glumly. 'The trouble is that I don't know the context to anything on there so it's difficult to know what it means. He seems to have used a sort of shorthand a lot.'

'Well, try this,' Dan said.

He gave Martin the name of the horse and the stables and explained what they meant.

'Okay, let's have a look then,' Martin said looking a little more cheerful at having something a little more concrete to work on.

Dan left him to it.

The team dribbled in for an informal debrief. After half an hour they all concluded that they were no further along than they were the day before. Dan had started telling them about Mr. Hartley and the race-horse scam when Martin joined the group. He was smiling.

He's found something! Dan thought.

'I used the horse's name you gave me as a search term and I found some files that were buried down on level seven or so. The files were password protected but stupidly they'd used the same password as the one to open the laptop. It was a list of names, addresses and numbers. Here I've printed some copies off,' Martin said as he handed them around.

'Wow, if the '20k' on the right means twenty thousand then there's a lot more than twenty investors here, isn't there?' Dan said.

'That's right, it looks as if he sold the horse at least ten times over,' Martin confirmed.

'Then it gets injured and has to be put down and so no-one asks for their money back. That's clever,' Adil said.

'I think you might be especially interested in the name and address that's near the bottom of the page, second column from the right,' Martin said.

'My God!' Dan said with surprise. 'Martin, I think that you might just have cracked the case!'

An hour or so later the man whose name had been on the list was sitting in an interview room. He'd been picked up by a police car and brought to the police station with no explanation. Yet, both Dan and Adil were puzzled in that he didn't look the slightest bit perturbed about this. Dan noticed the pungent smell of cigarette smoke that hung around him and saw the brown stains that he had on the fingers of his right hand.

Dan explained that the interview would be recorded and then turned on the recorder.

'Can you please state your name and address for the record?' he asked.

'Er...Ken Barrington,' he said and gave the same address that had been on the sheet of horse investors.

'I'd just like to confirm that you do not wish to have any legal representation at this time,' Dan said.

'Er...yes...I think,' he said uncertainly.

'Can you please answer yes or no,' Dan insisted.

'No...er...sorry yes,' he said again.

Dan carried on.

'Where do you work, Mr. Barrington?'

'Well, you already know that. You've seen me there,' he replied.

Dan pointed with his eyes to the recorder but he didn't get the message.

'Mr. Barrington I need you to tell me where you work and what you do there for the recording.'

Adil could see that Dan was already getting a little exasperated.

'Oh, oh I see,' he said seeming to notice the recorder for the first time. 'Okay then, I work at the airport in the accessibility area helping people with disabilities catch their flights and I arrange the lifts that take them to their departure gates and sometimes it's a wheelchair and sometimes it's a...'

'Thank you for that,' Dan interrupted feeling that he might get a reply on the scale of War and Peace if he'd let him go on. 'I'm going to show you a photo and I want you to tell me who it is.'

Dan turned the photo over and pushed it towards Mr. Barrington.

'That's Mr. McCormack,' he confirmed.

'How do you know him?' Dan asked.

'I once invested some money with him,' he replied cheerfully.

'In a horse?'

'Yes, that's right. How on earth did you know that?'

'How much did you invest with Mr. McCormack?' Dan asked ignoring his question.

'Well, five thousand at first and then another fifteen thousand. It was my redundancy money.'

'What happened to your twenty thousand?'

'I lost it all when the horse died.'

'And how did you feel about that?'

'What do you mean?' Mr. Barrington asked with a puzzled look.

'Were you happy or sad about it?'

'Well, sad of course. It was a lovely looking horse.'

Dan wasn't quite sure whether his interviewee was playing games with him or whether he was just a bit strange.

'How did you feel about losing twenty thousand pounds?' Dan persisted.

'Well, not good, if that's what you're trying to find out, but it couldn't be helped, I suppose,' he replied with a shrug of the shoulders.

'How much of your redundancy money did you have left after you lost the twenty thousand?'

'About five hundred pounds, I think,' he said with a little smile.

Dan was now certain that he was playing games with him.

'And you didn't feel angry about it?'

'What was the point? It was a punt and the horse died. What could I do about that?'

'Mr. Barrington, it was a scam. The man you knew as Jackie McCormack sold that horse several times over. We're not even sure that it really died,' Dan said with some feeling.

As he watched the realisation very slowly dawning on his face, Dan changed his mind. Mr. Barrington was definitely strange.

'So, it was all a con then? Well, I am feeling a bit angry now. Someone should arrest him then,' Mr. Barrington said pointing at the photo.

'What?' Dan was getting confused now. 'We can't arrest him, he's dead.'

'He is? Well, it serves him right then.'

'But you know he's dead. He's the man who was found dead in the accessibility area at the airport.'

Again, Dan could see the wheels moving very slowly in Mr. Barrington's mind.

'But his name was Connerty, wasn't it?'

'Yes, that was his real name but he also used the name of McCormack too,' Dan explained. 'It was an alias. You didn't recognise him?'

'No, well I thought he looked a bit like him, I suppose, but the name was different so I didn't give it any more thought. So, to sum it up you're saying that the man who was killed in the airport was the same man who diddled me out of my redundancy money. Is that right?'

Dan confirmed Mr. Barrington's suspicions. Adil could hear the exasperation in his voice as he did so.

'You know, if I'd have known that then I might very well have killed him myself. Yes, I very well might have,' Mr. Barrington said with utter certitude.

Dan quickly ended the interview and thanked Mr. Barrington.

As they went back to the team's room Dan said, 'Well, he's either innocent or the greatest liar that I've ever interviewed. If I'm honest, I'm still not totally sure which it is. Was he for real do you think?'

'Unfortunately for us and the investigation, yes,' Adil replied. 'I honestly don't think he'd made the connection between the man who was dead in the airport and the man who'd scammed him out of twenty thousand pounds until just now. In fact, I don't think he even realised he'd been scammed until just now.'

Dan looked at his watch. It had gone six o'clock.

241

'Let's call it a day, shall we? We'll try again tomorrow,' Dan said grumpily.

'Well, you never know, Mac might come up with something. He usually does,' Adil said trying to cheer his boss up.

'Let's hope so,' Dan said attempting a smile. 'Come on, I'll buy you a pint.'

Chapter Twenty-One

The first thing Mac did was to call Aiden. He pleaded back pain and asked him if they could postpone seeing Maggie Connerty until tomorrow morning. Aiden was happy to oblige as he had a mountain of paperwork to plough through before he left to go back to his old job in Dublin. This made Mac feel marginally better. The second thing he did, after getting dressed, was to go down to reception. He was hoping that the nice young lady he'd seen before would still be on duty and, luckily, she was.

'I think that I might need the number for a doctor,' Mac said.

'Are you not feeling well then?' she asked with some concern.

Indeed, Mac didn't. He felt slightly nauseous and as tight as a coiled spring.

'Something like that. Is there a local doctor that I could see?'

'I take it that you're normally resident in the UK?' she asked.

'Yes, yes I am,' Mac replied.

'So, your best bet is to drive up to Beleek just across the border and see the doctor there. Believe me, it'll be a lot simpler doing it that way,' she said.

She offered to call the doctor's surgery for him which was just fine by Mac. She did that.

'They said that if you go there now you should be able to get seen by the doctor,' she said. 'They also said that you might have to wait a while though.'

That was fine by him. She gave him the address and he found that he couldn't thank her enough.

It took him just ten minutes to drive to the UK border and five minutes more to find the doctor's surgery which was tucked away by the side of the pharmacy. Inside, there was just an old man and a young woman with a baby in the waiting area. Mac was thankful that it didn't look too busy. He explained his situation to the middle-aged lady behind the counter who said that she should be able to get him in to see Dr. O'Connor in twenty minutes or so.

It was more like forty by the time she finally called his name but Mac truly didn't mind. He was just glad to be seeing someone. If he was being honest the dream, or whatever it was, had really shaken him. He needed to know what was happening to him.

Dr. O'Connor was probably in his sixties and, although his hair was iron grey, unlike Mac he had plenty of it. He had the same long face as Aiden's and when he spoke his accent was as soft as the morning rain had been.

'How can I help you, Mr. Maguire?'

Mac told him about his shaking hands, his dreams and the way he'd been feeling lately.

'Has anything happened to you that might have set off these feelings?' the doctor asked.

Mac told him all about the firework explosions in Derry and why he had been there. The doctor thought it over before asking his next question.

'When the explosions started what were you thinking about?'

Mac had to give this some real thought before he remembered.

'I did think of something but it was just before the explosions started. It was the smell, I remembered it from before. I shouted at everyone to run which was just as well as the garage door blew off a few seconds later.'

'What had happened to you before?' the doctor gently asked.

'I was working on a case in Paris with two of my colleagues. We'd found a small factory unit that belonged to someone who'd been murdered but the gate had been left open and we thought that this looked more than a bit suspicious. We called it in and we were walking away when a bomb went off. I looked around as soon as I got my senses back and one of my colleagues was lying on the floor. She didn't move and I thought she was dead. Luckily, it turned out that she just had concussion.'

'And the other colleague who was there?'

'Well, it was the opposite with him, I suppose. We thought that he was okay but it turned out that he'd been hit by a piece of shrapnel that had lodged near an artery. It nearly killed him.'

While he was talking a feeling of fear and intense sadness nearly overwhelmed him. He found that he had to fight back the tears.

This didn't go unnoticed by the doctor.

'Traumas like that don't just go away, Mr. Maguire, they're always there somewhere at the back of our minds. The brain processes traumatic incidences somewhat differently to other memories. They don't have time stamps as other memories do, as far as your brain's concerned, the traumatic memory is fresh in your mind and might have only happened yesterday. That's to ensure that you can react immediately if the same danger threatens again. From what you've said it worked too. If you hadn't reacted to the smell of the fireworks so quickly then you and the other policemen there might well have been hurt.'

This hadn't occurred to Mac before although it was patently obvious thinking about it now.

'So, when you experienced another explosion, it just brought all those feelings back,' the doctor continued.

'I dare say that the loss of life associated with the Derry explosions might have only magnified your feelings.'

'It's PTSD, isn't it?' Mac said feeling more than a little stupid.

It was so obvious that he wondered why he hadn't thought of it before. Then again, perhaps he knew but just didn't want to admit it to himself.

'Yes, I think it's highly likely that you're suffering from Post-Traumatic Stress Disorder and I'd find it somewhat surprising if you'd never experienced it before. From what you've said, you've been a policeman for quite a long time and you must have seen some distressing things.'

Mac thought for quite some time.

'Yes,' he said softly, 'a long time ago. I'd forgotten all about it until you asked the question. I always try to treat every case as a puzzle in order to stop myself from getting too personally involved, kind of keeping the horror of it all at arm's length if you like. That's generally worked for me but there was one occasion when I couldn't help myself and a case got right under my skin.'

Mac told the doctor the story. He'd been a Detective Inspector at the time and he'd been working on the abduction and murder of a young girl in Walthamstow, North London. The girl had been playing outside her house, a quiet residential side street, when she had disappeared. She'd been found the day afterwards by a dog walker on some rough ground near Epping Forest. To say that she'd been brutally murdered would be to put it mildly. She'd been raped and cruelly tortured before she died.

'She was only seven,' Mac said.

Mac paused and the doctor gave him space to process his thoughts.

'She was the same age as my own daughter at the time. I was okay during the investigation itself, it kept me busy, I suppose. I was so desperate to catch the man who did it that I couldn't think of anything else. However, once we caught him, I sort of fell apart.'

'How did the PTSD show itself?'

'I started hearing voices, well, one voice. Hers. It didn't matter where I was, I'd hear this little voice from right behind me pleading, 'Help me, please help me.' I'd never heard the girl speak or heard any recordings of her voice but I knew it was her. It was so real that I reacted to it every time. I think people thought that I was going mad. I suppose I was really. Then I started seeing her, mostly in my dreams but sometimes when I was awake too. Once or twice, I saw her when I was looking at my own daughter. That was absolutely terrifying.'

'Did you see someone about it?' the doctor asked.

'Yes, I went to the police doctor. She listened to me and she was very nice. She said that it should eventually go away by itself and, thankfully, she was right.'

'That was good advice. Being where we are, I've had to deal with quite a lot of cases that are very similar to yours. The first thing we usually advise is something called 'watchful waiting' which is a nice way of saying that we'll do nothing at all for at least four weeks. If the symptoms persist after that time, then you must go and see your doctor at once. I'll be sending your doctor's surgery a letter telling them what we've discussed. I suggest that you make an appointment with them as soon as you get back anyway just to make sure that they're fully aware of the situation.'

Mac promised that he would.

'I wouldn't worry too much, Mr. Maguire,' the doctor said. 'In most cases it does fade away quite quickly and telling someone else about it can really help too.'

'So, I was right to come and see you then? To be honest, I was wondering if I was just being a bit silly,' Mac said with a shrug.

'You did exactly the right thing. In fact, I just wish that everyone was so sensible. I believe that you also suffer from chronic back pain. Have you got anything that you take to help you to sleep?'

Mac told him about his little blue knock-out pills.

'Good, if the feelings get too bad don't be afraid to take them. I've found that sleep can really help too.'

'Thank you so much, doctor,' Mac said with real gratitude.

As he drove back to Ballydove, he did indeed feel relieved. He made a detour and drove back via the main street and pulled up outside a small florist's shop he remembered seeing there. He caught a young woman who was in the act of closing up but she was more than happy to serve one last customer.

He rang the hotel and, thankfully, the young lady he'd spoken to earlier didn't answer as she'd just gone off duty. He asked the man who answered the phone what the young receptionist's name was and also the name of the lady who serviced his room. The young lady's name turned out to be Kaylin and the older lady was called Bridget. He was told that they would both be back on duty in the morning.

Armed with this information he then ordered the two biggest bouquets they had and threw in a box of Belgian chocolates as well. He asked for them to be delivered to the hotel with a message that read – *'Thanks for your kindness from a very grateful Mr. Maguire'*. He watched as the young florist wrote the first message. She spelt 'Kaylin' as 'Caoilfhoinn'.

'Is that really how you spell it?' Mac asked giving her a puzzled look.

The young florist assured him that it was and she told him that she could be so certain as she'd gone to school with Caoilfhoinn's older sister. Mac was forgetting for a moment how small a place Ballydove really was. Bridget, however, was spelt just as he'd thought it would be.

While a simple bunch of flowers could never repay the two women's kindness to him, it did indeed make him feel a little better. He drove back to the hotel in a good frame of mind.

He had a bite to eat and then went to his room. He rang Aiden and asked him if he could pick him up tomorrow at ten. That was fine by him. He then set his alarm for eight thirty the next morning. It wasn't even seven o'clock when he took the two little blue pills and lay back. With some luck he shouldn't be too groggy in the morning.

He fell almost immediately into a deep sleep and slept until the alarm woke him the next morning.

Chapter Twenty-Two

He was back in Paris leaning against the wall and, as he turned around, he heard a noise so loud that it was almost silent. Kate was lying motionless on the ground. Then huge fireworks screamed out of the gate hitting Kate and going into a nearby crowd that seemed to have come from nowhere. He heard the fire engines coming but they were taking too long. The sirens got louder and closer and...

Mac woke up and realised that the sound he was hearing was not fire engines but his alarm going off. He turned it off and sat up. The anxiety he'd felt in his dream still gripped his chest and his hand was shaking again.

He reminded himself that the doctor had told him that it might take up to four weeks before it went away. It couldn't happen soon enough as far as he was concerned.

Once showered, shaved and dressed he felt a little better and was more than ready for his Full Irish breakfast. Once again, there was a little more white pudding than usual on his plate which cheered him up. He'd calmed down a little by now and, once he'd had the first forkful, he found that he was ravenously hungry. He enjoyed everything he ate and mopped the plate clean with an extra slice of toast.

Caoilfhoinn was once again on reception and she greeted him with her usual brightness. There was no sign of any flowers yet but it was still early in the day.

'You definitely look a little happier today, Mr. Maguire,' she said with a smile.

'Do I? Well, yes, I suppose I am really,' he replied. 'It's a lovely morning so I think that I'll wait outside. I'll see you later.'

'Have a nice day now,' she said as if she meant it.

It was a lovely morning indeed. Although the air was still crispy cold the sun was shining and the sky was at its bluest blue. Mac sat down and waited for Aiden. He realised that the anxiety and the bad feelings that the dream had generated had evaporated in the face of a good breakfast and the bright sunshine.

Yes, he did indeed feel better. He checked his phone and discovered that he had an email from Martin. He opened it in the hope that it might be a new lead but found that it was just some files detailing the airport contractors who were on shift at the time of the murder. Mac knew that Martin would have already gone over the list with a fine-toothed comb so he doubted that he'd glean anything of value from it. He'd have a look at it later when he had some time.

He sat there bathing in the sunshine and trying to think of nothing when his reverie was interrupted by Aiden's car pulling up.

'Good morning, Mac. Thankfully you don't look as bad as I thought you'd be,' Aiden said.

'No, a good night's rest seems to have done the trick,' Mac replied.

As they pulled off, he wondered why he just didn't tell Aiden what had really happened. After all, Aiden had told him everything about himself. Did he really think it was an admission of weakness or something? Nonetheless, he knew that he wouldn't tell Aiden unless he had to.

'How did the hearing go?' Mac asked.

'Well enough. The judge agreed with me about bail and the lads are now kicking their heels in Loughan House Prison just down the road. The trial's been set for four weeks from now so they'll have a bit of a wait.

By the way, after the hearing yesterday I popped back down to Bundoran and I let Joe Devlin know that he was off the hook,' Aiden said.

'I'll bet that he was relieved about that. To be honest I'd nearly forgotten about him,' Mac admitted.

'Ah well, I just thought that he might have been worrying. So, what do we tell Maggie Connerty then?'

'Just about everything, I should think. It's all going to come out sooner or later anyway. If I'm being honest, I think that it's a million to one shot that she's anything to do with her husband's death but you never know.'

'How are the team in the UK doing?' Aiden asked.

'Scraping the barrel just like we are, as far as I know,' Mac said. 'I'm rapidly coming to the conclusion that it must have been a professional hit after all. It doesn't take much to upset some of these drugs gangs and Jackie might have rode his luck once too often. If that is the case then we've got very little chance of finding out who did it and why.'

Once more they waited for a couple of minutes before getting out of their car. They didn't need to knock on the door. Theresa was there holding it open for them.

'How's she doing?' Aiden asked.

Theresa shrugged. It wasn't a positive shrug either.

The crowd had gone and it was just Maggie sitting by herself on the sofa. She still looked lost and the redness around her eyes attested that the tears had not yet stopped.

'We've got some news for you, Maggie,' Aiden said.

'You've caught the man who took my Jackie away from me?' she asked in hope.

'I'm sorry but we're still working on that,' Aiden said as he glanced over at Mac. 'No, it's about Jackie and his life in England.'

She looked puzzled.

'What about his life in England then? All he ever did was work from what he told me.'

'Well, I'm afraid that what he told you wasn't quite the truth. He had another wife there, Maggie,' Aiden said.

There was a look of incomprehension on her face and the words wouldn't come out for a while.

'Another wife? I don't understand.'

'He married another woman in Luton, bigamously of course, and they set up house there together. They've been living together for nearly thirty years.'

'Thirty years? Another wife?' she said as though she didn't understand what the words meant. After quite a long silence she looked at Aiden and asked softly, 'Did they have children?'

'Yes, they had two girls. They're both at university.'

There was another but much longer silence.

'Fuck him!' she said loudly with real anger. 'The bastard always told me he didn't want children and then he goes and has two with some whore in England. I've wasted my life on that man.'

She got up and marched into the bedroom.

Aiden, Mac and Theresa watched Maggie as she stormed out of the room and then looked at each other. The three of them were absolutely speechless. Maggie's sudden outburst had taken them all by surprise. A few minutes later she appeared at the door fully dressed and with her coat on.

'Aiden, can you do me a favour and drop me down to Magee's Bar? I'm badly in need of a drink,' she said. 'Several drinks actually.'

Aiden did as he was told and drove Maggie and Theresa to Magee's Bar.

As she got out, she said to Aiden, 'Oh and tell Jackie's whore that she can bury him the bastard and tell her not to invite me to the funeral either.'

They watched her as she linked arms with Theresa before they both disappeared inside the pub.

'Well, now that was some transformation!' Aiden exclaimed.

'It was mentioning the children that did it. She must have desperately wanted some herself,' Mac said.

'She was always good with kids. She'd have made a great mother.'

In the end Maggie had just been another of Jackie's victims. He stolen money from most of them but, with Maggie, he'd stolen her life.

'Fancy a coffee?' Aiden asked.

Mac couldn't think of anything better to do.

Mac gazed out of the window of the coffee shop while Aiden went to get their drinks. The street had been empty when he'd first sat down but it was now full of small groups of school children in light blue uniforms who had obviously been let out for lunch. He'd noticed that there were lots of children and lots of middle-aged and elderly people in Ballydove but he realised that he saw very few people of either sex in their twenties or thirties. He assumed with some sadness that that slice of the demographic was away working in Dublin or England or America. Aiden would be joining them soon.

'We've pretty much come to the end of the road with this case, haven't we?' Aiden said as he handed Mac a coffee.

'Yes, that's just about all we can do, for now at least,' Mac replied. 'Let's not totally give up on the case though. If you don't get the answer right away it can sometimes come with time. So, what about you?'

'Me? Paperwork and more paperwork,' Aiden said. 'I've had my start date confirmed for my new job or perhaps I should say my old job. Anyway, I'll be working in Dublin in just over four weeks and I can't wait. It'll mean that Caitlin and I will be together again.

We've agreed that I should move in with her. What are you going to do?'

'I'll have another review of the evidence and see if anything leaps out at me. It sometimes works. You can leave me here if you like. I'll get a taxi back to the hotel later. Oh, and I'm not forgetting that I've got a horse race to go to on Saturday. I'm really looking forward to that. I'll probably fly back home on Monday.'

'Right then,' Aiden said as he stood up, 'I'll see you on Saturday at Ballintra if I don't see you before. Take care of yourself, Mac.'

He held out his hand and gave Mac a robust handshake.

Mac sat there for a while longer thinking about Maggie Connerty, Aiden and life in general. He looked at his watch. It was nearly one o'clock. He decided that it was time for a pint and a few more of Johnnyboy's stories.

Mac almost fell asleep as the taxi took him back to the hotel afterwards. He needed a nap. He was a satisfied man though and it was no wonder if he felt a little drowsy after several pints and several hours of the best storytelling Mac had ever heard. Johnnyboy's stories weren't about Jackie Connerty this time but about battles and giants and heroes and swans and magic. His tales of Ireland's mythical past cast a spell over everyone in the pub including Mac.

As he walked into the lobby Caoilfhoinn caught him by surprise when she came around the counter and gave him a peck on the cheek. He could feel his cheeks start to redden.

'They're lovely, Mr. Maguire,' she said as her eyes pointed towards the biggest bunch of flowers that Mac had ever seen. 'It's really nice you know that you're appreciated. Oh, and Bridget says thanks too. She was really touched that you'd think of her.'

'It's little enough, believe me. You've both been so good in helping me when I really needed it,' Mac said with total sincerity.

He set his alarm for seven o'clock which would give him just over two hours in bed. He was still smiling as he closed his eyes. However, his mood darkened and he felt some trepidation when he thought about waking up. He definitely didn't want to end up in the hallway again.

He needn't have worried. There were no fires and no explosions just the sound of his alarm going off. He turned it off and sat for a while on the edge of the bed thinking about what he should do now the case had ended. He decided that he'd have a few quiet days to himself. He'd stay at the hotel tonight and perhaps start going through the case file again. Then tomorrow he thought that he might go out for a drive and see a bit more of the country. He also reminded himself that he needed to go and see Declan at some point before he went home. As much as he didn't want to, he knew that he owed him a visit.

They had corned beef as a special on the menu that evening and that cheered him up even more. Comfortably full, he took himself and a coffee over to a quiet corner of the bar and got out his tablet. He scanned the case files, stopping from time to time to examine a document or a photo that caught his fancy and, by the time he'd finished, he found that it was nearly ten o'clock. He was about to shut his tablet down when he remembered Martin's email. For completeness he thought that he might as well go through those documents too. He ordered another coffee.

They were basically a read out from an electronic clocking-in system for the contractors who serviced the airport. He was scanning the second page of a long list of names when something caught his eye. He had to look again quite carefully before he spotted exactly what it was.

So that's how it happened! he thought as he leaned back in his chair and smiled.

Some investigations are like onions and it takes lots and lots of successive layers of evidence to gradually build a case and to finally come to some sort of conclusion. Then there are other, rarer cases, where just one piece of information comes to light and everything falls into place. This was such a case.

He rang Dan to let him know. It was late but he knew that he wouldn't mind hearing this piece of news.

He was right too.

Chapter Twenty-Three

It was Dan Carter's second interview of the day and his sergeant, Adil Thakkar, could tell that he was really looking forward to this one. All his grumpiness had disappeared and it was replaced by a grim smile and a glint in his eye. They were both already sitting behind a table when they walked into the interview room.

Dan turned the recorder on and then said, 'Can you please state your name and address for the record?'

'Mrs. Diane McCormack,' she snapped making her annoyance very clear. 'I'd like to know why I was dragged here today. They wouldn't even let me take a shower first.'

'We've got some news for you, we've caught the man who murdered your husband, the man who you knew as Jackie McCormack,' Dan said.

'You've caught Jackie's murderer?' she asked with an uncertain smile. 'I'm sorry, I thought this might have been about something else.'

'I'll be covering a few other things as well but I thought you might like to hear the good news first,' Dan said.

He watched her closely as it dawned on her that this might mean that there would be some bad news to follow. She looked nervous to say the least.

'Who was it?' she asked.

'It was a man who knew Jackie some thirty years ago in Ballydove, Donegal. His name is Anthony Moohan, a name that I think you know well.'

'No, no I don't think that I've heard that name before, I...'

258

'Please don't waste my time. You know that name very well. After all, it is your surname, isn't it, MaryAnn Moohan?' Dan said.

She flinched on hearing the name.

'I've never heard...I don't know what you're talking about,' she said getting more agitated.

She turned and looked at her solicitor, a middle-aged grey man in a black suit. He shrugged his shoulders by way of an answer.

'I asked you not to waste my time!' Dan said forcefully. 'Do you deny being Mrs. MaryAnn Moohan, nee Kilbriggan, who was married to Pedar Moohan in Donegal some thirty years ago?'

'No, you've made a mistake. My name was Diane Smith before I got married. I've got a passport...' she protested.

Dan impatiently interrupted her again.

'Yes, you have,' he said pulling a passport out of an evidence bag and sliding it towards her. She made no move to pick it up. 'It's false though, isn't it? Before you say anything, while the passport's real enough, the information you supplied in your application wasn't, was it?'

She didn't answer and looked at her solicitor again but he was studiously looking at the wall opposite.

'I've got something else here that might interest you,' Dan said.

He took a piece of paper and slid that towards her too. She looked at it and then shrank away as though it might have been radioactive.

'You're not curious? Well, I'll tell you what it is then. This is the death certificate for a Diane Smith who died in Dunstable at the age of six months. You used the birth certificate belonging to a dead baby to apply for your passport, didn't you?'

'No, no it wasn't me,' she protested.

'Don't try blaming Jackie because it's your signature on the original application and on all the renewal documents since.'

'Is that why you asked me to come here then? A false passport?' she asked hopefully.

'Oh, there's more Mrs. Moohan, much more,' Dan said.

'Don't call me by that name,' she shrieked. 'It's hateful to me.'

'But I have to Mrs. Moohan because that's your legal name. I can't call you Mrs. McCormack because the John McCormack whose birth certificate was used to fraudulently obtain a passport for Jackie Connerty died at birth too,' Dan said pointedly. 'You were also still married to Pedar when you married Jackie, weren't you, Mrs. Moohan? Your husband didn't commit suicide until two weeks after you had your sham marriage to Jackie. So, we can now throw bigamy into the mix as well.'

She turned and almost shook her solicitor. He decided that he might as well say something.

'Is that it, Detective Superintendent Carter? Neither of these charges are that major...'

'No, that isn't it. I'm only getting started,' Dan said with a smile on his face.

She gave her solicitor a worried glance and then stared down at the table. She knew what was coming.

'You've said on several occasions that you knew nothing at all about your husband's business dealings. Is that correct?' Dan asked.

She gave it some thought before saying in a near whisper, 'No, I never...he never told me anything.'

'Can you please speak up, Mrs. Moohan. I can't hear you,' Dan said.

'NO, NO, NO!' she shouted. 'Now can you hear me!'

'I can,' Dan said with a smile as he sat back in his chair.

A picture of a cat playing with a mouse jumped into Adil's head. Dan was enjoying himself.

'Well, that's very strange then,' Dan said as he opened a thick file and spent some time leafing through it before continuing. 'We've had an expert looking at a laptop that we found in the office you have in your house. Someone has been using that laptop to contact some very unsavoury people via an encrypted app. Do you know anything about that?'

'No, why should I? That was Jackie's laptop, I've never touched it,' she replied.

'That's strange as it has your fingerprints all over the keys. It was also logged into several times when Jackie was out of the country and, before you say anything about Jackie taking it with him, we know he didn't. Like most computers nowadays it knows its location and we've found that it hasn't left your house since the day it was purchased. The last time a message was sent via the app, Jackie was already dead so it could only have been you that sent it.'

She looked away and sullenly stared at the wall.

'We know that you tried to clean up when you heard that Jackie had been killed. We found no mobile phones in the house and we couldn't help noticing that someone had been burning papers in the back garden.'

'My phone packed up on me when I was in town shopping,' she said without turning her head. 'It had been playing me up for weeks and I'd had enough of it so I just threw it in a bin. As for the papers I always burn anything with my name on. I don't trust shredders.'

'You were in a hurry though, weren't you? If you'd have checked you then you might have noticed that some of the papers at the bottom had been so compacted that they didn't completely burn up. We've learnt a lot from them. Then there was the money and those documents in the safe. They also had your fingerprints all over them and this puzzled us for a while. So, why hadn't you burnt those documents too and made off with all that money? It was then that we realised that your loving husband didn't trust you, did he? He allowed you to help him in his nefarious little schemes but he didn't trust you with the password to the safe containing all that money, did he? I'd also bet that he told you all about the security features on the safe as well just in case you wanted to have a go.'

Dan could see from her face that he'd hit the bullseye. She turned in her seat so that she was side on to Dan and stared straight ahead at the wall.

'Mrs. Moohan, we're still digging but believe me when I say that we've already got more than enough to prove that you were a willing helper in Jackie's criminal activities.'

She didn't answer. She raised a hand to her mouth and started biting her nails.

'We still haven't got to the worst of it yet though. Isn't that right, Mrs. Moohan?' Dan said.

He waited for an answer. She eventually swivelled in her seat and faced him.

'I've no idea what you mean,' she said glaring defiantly at him.

'Oh, I think you do,' Dan said with certainty. 'When you heard about Jackie's murder you thought only of yourself. You knew that those white puddings were deadly and you knew exactly where they were going. You also knew about the fireworks and where they were stored. You said nothing though, you just scurried around trying to cover up in the hope that you'd get away with it.'

Dan looked at her with an intensity that made her sit back.

'Over thirty people are dead and you could have helped us to save them. If, instead of trying to save your own skin, you'd come straight to us, many of those people might be alive today. If you'd have done

262

that then you'd be facing a much lighter sentence that the one you're going to face now. When I testify in court against you, I am going to make absolutely sure that each and every member of that jury knows that you could have saved those people but you chose not to.'

She turned away and started biting her nails again.

'Have you anything to say?' Dan asked.

She didn't move.

'Very well. You'll be detained pending charges. I'll let you have a word with your solicitor. This interview is ended,' Dan said as he turned off the recorder.

Dan and Adil got up and headed for the door. Just before he left the room Dan turned.

'Oh, I nearly forgot. In case you're thinking that at least you'll have your nice house to go back to when you finally get out of jail, I'm afraid that won't be happening. Everything you own was bought with dirty money and, under the Proceeds of Crime Act, we'll be confiscating the lot. The house, the cars, all those lovely paintings plus anything else you have in your name. I just thought I'd let you know that before I left,' Dan said with a bright smile.

Out in the hallway a beaming Dan turned to Adil and said, 'I thought that went well.'

Adil could only shake his head and laugh.

Chapter Twenty-Four

Mac had been on tenterhooks since he'd made the call to Dan. He didn't sleep well but, for once, this wasn't anything to do with his pain or the PTSD. He was up early in the morning and went down for breakfast as soon as it opened. He knew that he probably wouldn't hear anything until later in the day but that didn't stop him looking at his phone every two minutes. After breakfast he went back to his room, sat on the side of his bed and wondered what to do next.

Of course, the thing he was least looking forward to doing was visiting Declan so he decided that this should be one of the first things he did. He waved to Caoilfhoinn who was on the phone as he walked by and she gave him a cheery wave back. Outside the air was once again crisp and the sky was once again blue. He stopped for a moment and closed his eyes as the sunlight warmed his face. It was such a nice day that he decided to go for a drive first.

He told himself that it was probably a bit early to go calling on Declan anyway which he knew wasn't quite true.

He drove down a road he hadn't gone down before and found himself heading east. He drove past the concrete eyesore that was the dam and the hydro-electric works. He wondered once again how, in years past, people could so easily let go of their heritage in the name of modernity and progress. He'd heard that they'd bulldozed many historic country houses as well as destroying the picturesque water fall in building the dam. He drove between two ugly steel towers that carried the electricity away from the site. He was glad to leave it behind him.

He drove past some quite stylish bungalows and then the land on his right disappeared and was replaced by the lake. Again, he saw that surreally huge sky as he looked over the steel grey water to the green fields on the other side and the blue mountains in the far distance. It was more than beautiful. He pulled over and got out of the car. He stood there for quite some time just looking out over the water and absorbing the exquisiteness of the scenery and the peacefulness that surrounded him.

He drove slowly on down the narrow lane. There was no traffic and he was in no rush to get anywhere. The sun was still shining although he could see some dark clouds gathering over the mountains. He watched and wondered if they might be heading his way. He knew that the weather in Donegal can change by the minute.

The lake accompanied him for many miles. At times it would disappear from view only to reappear around a bend in the road looking even more lovely. He passed by a stylish modern bungalow painted white with black gingerbread trimming under the roof and the gable ends. Just a few yards away from it there was an incredibly small stone cottage. It had a tiny door, painted red, and a single window. He knew that a whole family might have lived in that once.

The lake disappeared as he drove through a small forest. Around the corner it once again reappeared but this time on both sides of the road and he felt as if he was driving along a very low bridge. That was to be the last that he saw of the lake but he had to admit that it had gone with a flourish. He carried on through some attractive countryside, lush green fields dotted with clumps of trees. He came to a fork in the road and decided to turn right on a whim. More lovely country-side greeted him and he drove on in perfect peace. Eventually he noticed that it was starting to get a little more built up. Then he saw the road sign. It had the figure '30' inside a red circle.

He was back in the UK. He hadn't even known that he'd crossed the border. He wondered where he was. He passed by some houses and bungalows that were exactly the same as the ones he'd seen on the other side of the border and turned left into the town's main street. A sign above a shop said 'Beleek Motor Supplies'. He was back in Beleek then. He'd only had a glimpse of the town while visiting the doctor so he thought that he'd take a closer look.

He parked up and had a little walk around the town. Unlike Ballydove, it looked like a fine, solid and prosperous little town and it certainly had no lack of pubs. He entered one and ordered a coffee. It was quiet inside and that suited him perfectly. He knew that he'd be going home soon and he was trying to figure out what he'd learnt so far on his trip to Ireland.

He thought of the three towns that he'd spent time in: Ballydove, Beleek and Derry. One not doing so well perhaps unlike its mirror image over the border and another split in two by more than a river. Derry had depressed him a little but, on reflection, he wasn't sure if he was right to feel like that. As Aiden had said, it had certainly come a long way from the violence filled days of the Troubles. While he remembered the flags, he also remembered the many other areas of the city that had no flags flying and could only hope that time was slowly shrinking the cancer of sectarianism in the city.

The thought of a driving holiday around the area came back to him. He'd ask his best friend Tim about it when he got back. It would give him the chance of another look at Derry and, if nothing else, he knew that they'd both love the pubs.

He walked back to the car thinking these thoughts. He looked at his phone again before he started the drive back to Ballydove and his cousin Declan. There were no calls and no messages. He started to feel uneasy and wondered if something had gone wrong.

He pulled up outside his Aunt Annie's house and felt even more uneasy. He had never liked visiting this house. It always seemed grey and musty inside while the world outside its windows looked fresh and colourful. This fact was highlighted for Mac as the house on either side had been freshly painted, one sky blue and the other lavender. The drab rendering of Annie's house seemed even greyer and shabbier by comparison.

He rang the bell and felt a surge of hope when no-one came to answer the door. He was almost about to go when the door opened and Declan's sad face appeared. It looked as grey as the rendering.

'Oh, it's you Dennis. Will you not come in?' Declan said in a quiet voice.

Mac followed him inside through a parlour that hadn't changed since Mac had been a boy and into the kitchen. Declan looked lost and confused. Mac supposed that, for him, the natural order of the world had changed when his mother had died.

'How have you been keeping, Declan?' Mac asked.

'Oh, I don't know if I'm honest. Would you like a cup of tea?' Mac was about to say yes when Declan carried on. 'Only I have no milk, I'm afraid, or tea bags come to that.'

Mac looked in the kitchen cupboards. He didn't seem to have much of anything.

'Come on, I've got the car outside. Let's go and do some shopping,' Mac said.

In the supermarket Declan started putting things automatically into the trolley. When he put a packet of Rich Tea biscuits in Mac felt he had to ask the question.

'Declan, do you really like Rich Tea biscuits?'

Declan gave this question some deep thought.

'No, not really but mother always used to get them...' he replied his voice trailing off.

267

Mac put the biscuits back on the shelf.

'Declan, there's just you in the house now so you can buy anything you want,' Mac said. 'Anything.'

'Anything?' Declan replied uncertainly.

'We're in a supermarket crammed full of stuff. Just get whatever you like.'

This new perspective on life took a little while to take root in Declan's head but, once he got the idea, he seemed to enjoy shopping. When he got back to the biscuit shelf, he picked up a pack of chocolate covered tea cakes and didn't even glance at the Rich Tea.

Looking at the well-stocked cupboards in Declan's kitchen Mac felt glad that he'd visited after all. He looked at his watch. It had gone one o'clock and he was about to start saying his goodbyes when he turned and looked at Declan. It was obvious that he was lonely.

'Would you like a cup of tea now that we've got some?' Declan asked as he roused himself and stood up.

'I was just thinking that we can do a bit better than tea. Do you fancy a pint?' Mac asked.

'A pint?'

Mac realised that the whole concept of going for a drink must seem alien to Declan, let alone doing it in the middle of the day. His mother had been a lifelong Pioneer and frowned on all alcoholic drink and even more so on the people who drank it. That being the case he was surprised at Declan's answer.

'Do you know what Dennis? I think I'd love a pint,' he said with an actual smile.

'Good for you, Declan!' Mac exclaimed. 'Now tell me, do you like stories?'

To make a good day even better, Mac finally got the message from Dan as they were about to enter the Bridge Bar for a session with Johnnyboy McGloin.

The text message said – '*Anthony Moohan confessed all. Good work Mac! Mrs. Moohan on her way in. Looking forward to it. Dan*'

Knowing Dan, Mac would bet that he was. From the short conversations he'd had with him he knew that the recent deaths had really affected him.

He opened the door of the pub and there was Donal behind the bar. Jamie was leaning on the bar with another man that Mac hadn't seen before and, best of all, Johnnyboy was sitting in his corner. Mac went straight to Donal and pulled out his wallet.

'Do you have a card machine in here?' Mac asked.

'Yes of course, you can pay for your drinks by card if you like,' Donal said as he pointed to the card reader behind him.

Mac gave him his credit card.

'Keep that behind the bar. I'll be paying for everyone's drinks until I leave the pub,' Mac said with a wide smile.

'And here was me thinking it was going to be a slow day. Are we on for some more stories then?' Donal said excitedly as he started assembling two pints of Guinness.

'I certainly hope so but I'll be telling the first story,' Mac said. 'It's all about how a storyteller helped to solve a really puzzling murder.'

Chapter Twenty-Five

Mac woke up smelling smoke. He heard voices shouting and the crackle of flames. He knew it was a dream though and it quickly faded from his consciousness as he woke up. The emotions that had accompanied his previous dreams, the fear and anxiety, weren't there this time. It was just a dream after all.

He hadn't set an alarm and so he wasn't surprised when he picked up his phone to find that it had gone ten o'clock.

Too late for breakfast, Mac thought.

He didn't mind though. The day before had been an exceptionally good day. The drinks had flowed in the Bridge Bar and Johnnyboy had been on top form. Even Declan, once he'd had a few, turned out to be good company. This got him thinking as to how Declan's life might have been changed if he'd only managed to escape his mother's clutches a little earlier. He also thought of Maggie Connerty who had wasted a lifetime being married to a lie.

Even though he was late, they were good enough to make him a coffee and a white pudding sandwich which Mac wolfed down. He then stood outside and wondered what to do next. It was Friday and he had nothing to do and he was glad of the fact. A lot had happened since he'd come 'home' and he felt that he needed a space of time to digest it all. Tomorrow he'd be going to the Ballintra races and then on Sunday, Maureen had once again invited him to lunch. He was really looking forward to his weekend.

He then remembered that today was the day that Aiden and Caitlin were going to tell Mick and Maureen the truth about what had been going on between them. He said a little prayer for the two of them.

He looked up at the sky. It was cold and sunny but he could see rain clouds in the distance.

A changeable day then, he thought. Not exactly a rarity in this part of the world.

He got into his car and drove. He found himself once more going east and driving alongside the lakeside. He found a place to pull over that had a lovely view over the water, the fields and the mountains beyond. He thought of everything that had happened since he'd come back to Donegal and was amazed that he'd been able to fit all that into less than two weeks. He thought back to finding Jackie's body and the flight over. It now seemed an eternity ago.

Paddy and Tim in the pub, Maggie's tears, the drive across the border, the wide river splitting Derry, Cally's death, the dread realisation of the deadly white puddings, the firework explosions, the woman crying as she watched her house burn down, the sergeants' taunts of 'taig', the divisive flags and the stark murals, Aiden's dark confession, Maureen's roast beef dinner Johnnyboy's stories, Joe Devlin...

The memories swirled around Mac's head as he sat on the bonnet of his car watching the dark clouds slowly advancing towards him.

He'd sure have some stories to tell his friend Tim when he saw him on Monday evening in the Magnets, he thought.

He sat as if in a trance only awakening when the first fat drops of rain hit his face. He woke up, realised that he was about to get soaked and scurried into the car. He sat there for a while longer listening to the rat-a-tat of the heavy rain drops battering his windscreen.

He knew that it would take quite a while before he sorted out exactly what he thought about everything and he was willing to let it go at that. His phone pinged. He had an email.

It was from Dan. Reading between the lines it seemed that the interview with MaryAnn Moohan had gone well too. He'd said that if he was interested Martin could send him the audio of the Anthony Moohan interview.

Mac was interested, in fact very much so. Although he was fairly certain of the 'why' he was more than curious to know exactly how it was done. By the time he got back to the hotel the audio file had arrived.

He took a cup of coffee up to his room, lay back on the bed and played back the recording. It started out with Dan asking for confirmation of Anthony Moohan's name and address. He gave an address in St. Albans.

'Anthony, do you know why we've brought you here today?' Dan asked.

This was followed by a short silence.

'For the record, Mr. Moohan has just nodded. Anthony, please give a verbal answer for the recording if you can. Tell me why you think you're here,' Dan said.

Anthony's voice was light and his accent seemingly unchanged by his long stay in England.

'I'm here for the murder of Jackie Connerty,' he answered simply.

'Did you kill Jackie Connerty?'

There was another short silence.

'Yes, yes I killed Jackie and I have no regrets about it.'

'Anthony, why did you kill Jackie?' Dan asked in a soft voice.

'I hadn't thought about him for years, decades really and then I saw him in the shopping centre in Welwyn. He was coming out of Marks and Spencer's and he had a woman on his arm. I'd have known her anywhere. It was MaryAnn Kilbriggan, the bitch that my brother had been fool enough to marry. I followed them back

272

to their house and then started making some discreet enquiries about the pair of them. I found that they were living as man and wife under the name of McCormack.

I'm not normally an emotional man but I felt such anger towards them both that I couldn't rest or think about much else for days afterwards. Pedar had been a good brother to me. He was bit slow but he was the kindest of men and I loved him. He always thought the best of people and that, I suppose, was his downfall. He believed his wife when she persuaded him to plead guilty and let Jackie off the hook. Between the two of them, they'd killed him.

It was clear that she hadn't gone to Dublin after selling out her own husband as we'd all thought. Instead, she'd sneaked off to join Jackie in England. From what I could see of the house and the cars parked outside it appeared that they'd done well. Indeed, they looked the perfect couple. This only made me madder and I mean mad. I think the intensity of the anger I felt drove me temporarily insane. Looking back on what I did it all seems unreal, as though I'd read it in a book somewhere or seen it on TV.

I thought about reporting them to the police but I wasn't sure if they could be charged with anything. Anyway, I knew I had to do it myself, whatever it was. It would be the only way that I could rid myself of the burning anger that was eating me up inside. So, I thought and I thought and finally a plan emerged.

I work at three airports in the area maintaining the navigational beacons and checking the data and so I'm often on site. I made sure that I bumped into Jackie at his local pub one night and we got talking. He became very interested when I told him that I worked as a contractor at the airport and even more so when I admitted to being up to my eyes in debt because of my gambling addiction. I must have been quite convincing because he fell for it, fell enough at least to agree to a meeting. He said that he was flying out to Ireland in a week or so and, if I worked at the airport as I said, I could meet him in the departure lounge before his flight. I agreed.

It wasn't quite what I'd hoped for, somewhere remote and dark would have been better, but it was what it was. So, I had a week to come up with something. I do 3D printing as a hobby. I've always been interested in coding and building physical objects straight from code is something that I've always thought as being quite magical. The idea of using a plastic knife came to me as I lay awake in bed one night and I knew instantly that it would work. It took me four days to get it right though. It was triangular for strength and it was narrow so it could be easily hidden away. It was more like a stiletto than a normal knife, I suppose. It only had one job and that was to pierce Jackie Connerty's cold heart. I tested it on some joints of meat I'd bought and I found that it worked really well.

I'd printed the knife so it would be the right size to be inserted into an electronic machine that I use for recording data. It had a large stylus attached to it and I simply replaced this with the knife. I always work alone and I plan much of my work to suit myself so no-one was surprised when I arrived early that morning. I'd managed to get my hands on a cleaner's uniform and a broom a couple of days before and I'd hidden them away. I'd made some enquiries and I knew that the man who would be on shift in the accessibility area was a smoker and so he could be relied on to disappear from time to time. I also knew that the first accessibility request was for a six thirty flight so it was unlikely that there would be any witnesses around. It was all falling into place and I almost felt as if God was on my side.

I dressed in the cleaner's uniform, put on some latex gloves and hid in the toilet with the broom while I waited for the accessibility assistant to go out for a cigarette. He did so five minutes or so before the planned meeting time. I pulled the peak of the baseball cap I was wearing down so my face couldn't be seen and made my way towards where Jackie was waiting. I could see him sitting just where I'd told him to. I put my head down and I started sweeping the floor. He looked like he was half asleep as I came closer. He briefly looked up at me and then closed his eyes again. I was just a cleaner and so could be safely dismissed from his thoughts. It made me feel good as I came towards him, knowing that I would be the last thing that he'd ever see.

I'd practised what to do and I'd gone over it again and again in my mind. I felt strange and detached from it all, as if I wasn't really there but just observing everything from a distance. I was on autopilot I suppose and I didn't think at all, I just let things happen. I came behind Jackie and pulled the knife from my pocket. He was fast asleep when I pushed him down and then I stabbed him in the back as hard as I could. Three times I stabbed him and I have to admit that it felt good. It only took a few seconds and then I sat him back up and held him there while the last of his life drained out of him.

I felt for a pulse. There was none. Jackie Connerty was dead and I was happy. As I closed his eyes, I noticed that he had his boarding pass tucked into his top jacket pocket. I took it out and put it beside him hoping that it would buy me some time. I quickly made my way back to the toilet and waited for the accessibility assistant to come back. Unfortunately, he decided he needed to go to the toilet first and so he came in and used the urinal. He then washed his hands but thankfully he never looked at the cubicle where I was sitting on the toilet with my feet in the air.

I made my way back and carried on with my work. The interruption was no more than ten minutes and, if anyone had asked, it could easily be accounted for by a toilet break. Once I got back home, I melted the plastic knife and made it into some new filament for the 3D printer. I then used the material to make a fridge magnet that said, 'Revenge is a dish best eaten cold'. It seemed apt somehow.'

'Thank you, Mr. Moohan,' Dan said. 'Is there anything else you want to add?'

'Not really, only that I'm glad Jackie's dead.'

There was a short silence.

'I'm afraid that there were some consequences to Jackie's death,' Dan said.

'Consequences?'

'Did you hear about the deaths caused by the drug contaminated white puddings and the fireworks disaster in Londonderry?'

'Sure, they were both on the news. Are you telling me that they were connected to Jackie Connerty somehow?'

'More than connected, they happened because Jackie died. If he'd have been alive more than thirty people would have been saved from being either burned to death or dying after ingesting fentanyl.'

There was a much longer silence.

'Christ...Christ!' Anthony said. 'I didn't know. I honestly wouldn't have done it if I'd known.'

'I believe you, Anthony,' Dan said, 'and I can understand why you wanted Jackie dead. However, in giving in to your anger, you signed the death warrants of a lot more people than just Jackie.'

'I'm sorry, I'm so sorry...'

The interview ended there. Like Dan he could really sympathise with Anthony Moohan but, when you murder someone, you send out a ripple that can change the course of other people's lives forever as well. Jackie himself had thrown the dice far too often and thought that he would always win. As a gambler, even he must have known that snake eyes must come up eventually and that he would lose.

As it was, he was gambling with other people's lives as well, not that Jackie would ever lose any sleep over that. A charmer and a chancer he may have been but, as far as Mac was concerned, there had been no humanity in him whatsoever.

He went down for some dinner and then sat in the lounge to drink his coffee. The news was on a big TV screen and the lead story was the news of the arrest of Bishop Crotty for multiple counts of child sexual assault and rape. He looked a worried man as he was filmed being dragged into a police car and Mac thought that he had every right to be. With any luck he'd spend the rest of his life in jail.

He felt as if he needed something positive to think about and remembered that the Ballintra races were taking place tomorrow. He was looking forward to it. He then had a sudden thought. He rang Declan and asked him if he'd like to go with him. Declan's diary was apparently empty and he said that he'd be more than happy to go to the races with Mac.

'To tell the truth I haven't been to a horse race since I was in my twenties,' Declan admitted. 'From what I can remember, I think that I enjoyed it too.'

Chapter Twenty-Six

There was a queue to get into the temporary parking area, a field, and then a short walk to get to the racecourse itself, which was yet another field. A temporary fence marked out the course itself and the spectators stood inside a large oval where there were fast food vans, cake stalls, competitions in progress and, of course, lots of bookies shouting the odds. There were six races in all and Mac hurried to get a bet on the first one. He picked a name at random and was surprised to find that Declan was right behind him in the queue at the bookies clutching a ten euro note in his hand. He had an excited glint in his eye.

Mac kept his eyes peeled and eventually saw Mick and Maureen coming towards him. Seamus, Siobhan and the two children followed and, after them, came Aiden and Caitlin. They looked every inch the happy couple as they ambled towards him hand in hand. Caitlin spotted him and ran ahead of the rest. She almost jumped at him as she gave him a big hug. The last time he'd seen her she'd been a teenager. She was all grown up now.

'Thanks, Uncle Denny,' she said. 'Thanks for sending Aiden back to me.'

'Oh, it was nothing really. He wanted to go. I just gave him a little push that's all. How did it go with your parents?'

'Fantastic, they were really great and more than happy to have Aiden in the family. Did you see the news?' she asked.

'I did and I think it might just be the closure that your husband-to-be needs.'

The rest of the family caught up with Caitlin and Mac glanced over at Aiden. He gave Mac a nod back and the huge smile on his face said everything.

'You'll be coming to lunch tomorrow I hope, Denny,' Maureen asked. 'There'll be quiet a crowd by the look of it.'

'I wouldn't miss your roast beef for the world,' Mac replied.

'What about you, Declan. Would you like to come for lunch too?'

Maureen had been surprised to see Declan there and it was clear that she was surprised even further when he took up her offer with alacrity.

Then the bell went. The first race was starting!

Mac of course lost the bet, and the four after it, but he didn't care. The races were exhilarating. Being so close to the horses meant that you could feel the ground shake as they got closer and the speed of them was unbelievable. Even more unbelievable was the fact that children as young as thirteen were riding these monsters of horses at breakneck speed. In the last race Mac put down his final bet and was more than surprised when it came in first. They said their goodbyes to Mick and Maureen and the rest and promised that they'd both be at Three Brothers Farm tomorrow afternoon at one thirty on the dot or preferably even earlier.

A happy Caitlin gave him another hug and Aiden shook his hand.

'Thanks again, Mac,' he said. He was about to walk away when he turned back. 'You know Mac, for the first time in my life, I'm actually looking forward to the future and it feels strange.'

'Don't be afraid to be happy, Aiden. Don't be afraid.'

'I won't.'

And he was gone. Mac watched him as he ran to catch up with Caitlin. He whispered something in her

279

ear and she stopped and kissed him. He suddenly missed his Nora with a pain that pierced his heart.

'Don't be afraid,' he mouthed silently.

Declan caught up with him.

'So, how did you do?' he asked as they joined the queue at the bookies.

'I won on the last race but I'm still forty euros down on the day,' Mac replied. 'Still, I don't care, that was the best day out I've had in ages. How about you?'

'Oh, I'm up a little,' Declan said with a mischievous look. 'Only the odd hundred and twenty euros mind you.'

'A hundred and twenty? Well done, Declan!'

'So, fancy a pint or two on me afterwards?' Declan asked with a wide smile.

'That I do,' Mac said as sincerely as he'd ever said anything in his life. 'That I do.'

The End

I hope you've enjoyed this story. If you have please leave a review and let me know what you think. *PCW*

Also in the Mac Maguire detective series
The Body in the Boot

The Dead Squirrel

The Weeping Women

The Blackness

23 Cold Cases

Two Dogs

The Match of the Day Murders

The Tiger's Back

The Eight Bench Walk

A Concrete Case of Murder

The Blood Moon Murders

https://patrickcwalshauthor.wordpress.com/

Made in the USA
Las Vegas, NV
07 March 2022

45197024R00166